# Frontier Legends Book One: Through the Door.

Joshua Lartman

JOSHUA LARTMAN

Copyright © 2018 Joshua Lartman

ISBN:
ISBN-13:

# DEDICATION

I would like to dedicate this book to every single black and brown boy and girl in the world who has never had the best representation in everyday media. For those kids who watched Saturday morning cartoons and never saw a person who looked like them or who never saw enough of themselves. For those who looked at comics and animation and felt left out. Black and brown children can be in action, fantasy, sci-fi, adventure, and mystery and not be a side character, stereotype, or a token. Black and brown kids can be in a galaxy far away or in a magical world.

JOSHUA LARTMAN

# ACKNOWLEDGMENTS

I would like to acknowledge all the people who helped and believed in me. My dad, mom, sister, and brother for the constant words of support. My friends and family for the kind words. And a special thanks to Mr. and Mrs. Hodge for the walkthrough they gave me, so I could become self-published, start my dream, and tell a story.

JOSHUA LARTMAN

# Book One
# Chapter One
# Through the Door

The story begins on the side of a mountain where a man and his nineteen-year-old son are walking to the guest house. The father Ishtarel is a towering man with wooly black and grayish hair that comes down to his shoulder, his eyes are brown, and he has dark skin. His son is a tall lean muscular eighteen-year-old with the same skin tone as his dad and his hair has kinky spikes.

"I need you and your brother to clean up the guest house we're having company over. And, where is he?" Said Ishtarel.

"Kirby! Where are you?" Jabari shouted but there was no response.

"Kirby!" Yelled Ishtarel.

"I'm already here." Kirby yelled as he walked out of the guest house. He is a twelve-year-old boy with dark brown skin like his dad, a puffy afro hair, with light brown eyes he got from his mother who he never got the chance to meet. They walk through the door to a room filled with boxes.

"So, you both know we are having company over, your Aunts and Uncles are coming." Ishtarel reminded them.

Jabari uttered "I know. We'll do it."

" I need to go make a call." Said Ishtarel. He leaves his sons to clean up the guest house.

"Okay, Kirby let's get work." Jabari's sentence stops short because Kirby has disappeared, he decided to play a game of hide and go seek at Jabari's expense.

"Kirby come on this is no time to play games I want to get this done. I am meeting my Kelvin, Tiff, and Charlie tonight. Kirby!" He spoke into the room but no response, but snickering can be heard throughout the first floor. "Fine then but when I find you, I'm throwing your toys in trash" He threatened but still there was no response. But a shuffle of boxes in the corner draws his attention.

"Now I got you," Jabari said with a grin on his face "Got you!" He said thinking he got his brother but ended up grabbing their dog, Pitou. A small pitch-black dog with a mane surrounding his neck, he had bright red eyes, he let out a small bark. "Sorry little guy, I was looking for Kirby. Do you see him hiding anywhere?" Pitou again lets out a bark, then jumps out Jabari's hands and walks away and as he does once more snickering can be heard from behind a big brown box. He then turns his head to see the top of Kirby's hair, he creeps up from the side and gets behind and grabs. He picks him up and laughs while saying "Stop playing around. We need to finish this.".

"Noooo! I want to play hide and seek". Kirby whined.

"You hid. I found you. We played. Now start sweeping and going to start upstairs." He replied to his little brother.

"Nooooo" Kirby exhaled.

Jabari then gives him an offer. "I'll buy you a cinnamon roll."

"Fine but if I find something cool or a toy, I'm playing with it. Okay, what to do first? What do you think I should do first?" Kirby asks as he looks towards the dog for a response.

But Pitou just let out a bark. Kirby starts to move the boxes around and finds a loose floorboard. He moves it out the way and finds a curved sword that is like a Khopesh and a wide oval shaped shield. Pitou jumps up and runs to the main house.

"Oh, man this is so cool. Pitou, do you see? Hey, where did he go? Jabari!" Kirby yelled with excitement.

"What?!" Jabari yelled.

"COME HERE. I FOUND SOMETHING. I'm going to ask dad where he got this from." Kirby said with such excitement.

"Kirby! Put that down right now!" His dad yelled with a stern voice as he walked over and took both the sword and shield from his hand.

"What's going on?" The older brother said in all the confusion.

"What do you think you're doing? These are not toys! You don't play with these!" He yelled with a stern voice.

Kirby responded with a small timid voice " I was just holding it."

"I don't want you to touch any of these things Kirby. You could hurt yourself, that's why they were hidden." He said in a calmer voice.

"Sorry", Kirby said with a cracking voice and teary eyes.

"I didn't mean to yell but I don't want you just touching anything that could hurt you sweetheart. These are dangerous, that is why they were under the floor. I'm sorry so, don't cry, look after you two are done I'll give you a treat, sounds good?"

"Okay." Kirby said wiping his eyes and sniffling,

"Why do you even have these? Where did you get these from? Why were they on the floorboards?" Jabari rapidly fired all his questions.

"Ishtarel that's not important right now, the point is I don't want Kirby to hold these things. Including you." Ishtarel replied.

"So, why did you ask us to clean the guest house if you didn't want anybody to find it?" He said with a sarcastic remark.

"Don't get smart with me boy. Take these, put these things up and get to cleaning." He said with an irritated voice.

Ishtarel then gives the weapons to Jabari to go put up and walks out to the house to call Uncle Tazama. Jabari walks upstairs with them leaving Kirby to clean the downstairs but before he does, he tells Kirby not to feel too bad because his dad was looking out for him. As he goes up stairs Kirby tears fade away and he begins to move the boxes then a flash of light engulfs the room and from the outside Pitou notices and runs to the room. As the flash fades away Kirby begins to open his eyes dazed and confused, he sees that a door has appeared out of nowhere. Ishtarel while on the phone with his brother feels an ominous presence.

"Tazama, I need to check something. What the ...? I can't move, it's so cold. What is this?"

Ishtarel unable to move due to an unknown force meanwhile Kirby will see an unexpected visitor.

"Woah! What was that? Where did this door come from?" Kirby said as he opened it but led nowhere but the wall.

"What? What kind of door is this? It doesn't go anywhere but the wall!" He shouted in confusion. Then Jabari shouted from upstairs.

"Kirby, who are you talking to? Are you even cleaning?" Jabari said as he questioned his little brother. "Come down here and look at this. Jabari! Pitou, you see the door too right, it's not just me?"

He then runs out the room through to see where the door leads to. The door is on a wall, but Kirby comes to find that the door is not appearing on the outside of the house, looking even more confused he runs back in and tries to open the door again.

"This is so weird, JABARI came down here! You need to see this!"

"I'M COMING." He said as he ran downstairs, with the sword and shield in his hand because he didn't have the time to put it up. "What's going on? What is it? Why were you screaming?"

11

"That door right there came out of nowhere." Kirby said as he stood next to him pointing at the door. Pitou walks to the door and sniffs it and immediately runs back to where the boys are growling at the door.

"Get behind me. Where does it go?"

"I don't know."

"Stay here, I'm going to open it".

But before he could even touch the door handle, a thin veil of blue light started to shine through the door. As this happens an eerie presence fills the room. Ishtarel breaks through whatever was holding him back and jets to the guest house. This presence bothers Ishtarel and he runs to see what's going on. But a blue force field surrounds the guest house preventing him from getting through. The next thing they know, the entire room gets cold, the door slowly opens, then a tall, menacing looking blue shadow figure. Towering at 7ft tall. long arms, big hands with claws 1ft long, skinny legs that bend backwards, oval shaped head with a row of fangs in his mouth, crooked horns sticking out from both sides of his head, and light blue diamond shaped eyes. And if that wasn't scary enough the creature says the younger brother's name in the most frightening way.

"Kirby." The monster said as he turned its head 480 degrees clockwise.

"DAAAAAAD." Kirby shrieked in fear.

"KIRBY!" His father yelled as he banged on the force field.

The blue shadow figure gets on its hind legs as he gets up, his knees bend backwards and the cracking of them echo through the room and it lifts its foot and begins to walk towards the brothers. With every footstep, his long claws on his feet tap and scrape up against the floor, the monster opens their mouth and smiles showing his row razor teeth. Jabari puts Kirby behind him.

"Stay behind me! Whatever you do, don't leave my side." Jabari said as he takes the sword and tries to remove it from his sheath, but it won't budge. "Dammit, it won't come out."

"Jabari! Look out!" Kirby warned his brother as the monster lunged at him with full force.

Jabari grabs Kirby and jumps out of the way of the incoming beast the monster flies through the wall and lands outside where Ishtarel looks in shock and horror as he is wondering why this thing is here and attacking his kids. On the inside Jabari picks up Kirby and runs up the stairs, he hides Kirby behind the shield in one hand and with the sword. The monster comes back in the house and sees them running as it begins to chase after them Pitou comes and jumps on the monster's face and starts to scratch at its eyes. The monster then swats at Pitou but ends up hitting its own face as Pitou jumps and runs upstairs with the boys. They run into the last room on the right side of the hallway and barricade themselves. Jabari moves all the furniture in front of the door to hold off the monster.

"What are we going to do?" Kirby asked with fear in his voice.

"Shhhs. Not so loud." He whispered.

The silence was so eerie all you could hear was the breathing and the sound of the monster footsteps getting closer and closer until it stopped. All is quiet, the door to the room next door can be heard opening, then the room is silent but breathing of an otherworldly beast can be heard from the wall, the monster smashes his head through the wall and lets out a horrific wave. Jabari takes the sword and bashes the monster on its forehead, this causes the monster to get mad and breaks through the wall, the constant wrecking causes the floor to cave in and they all fall through and land in the room with the door the creature came through. The boy's father can be heard telling them to hold on. Then Ishtarel closes his eyes and when they open, they glow like gold. He then punches the force field with all his might when the punch lands it literally rocks the entire mountain, but it has no effect. Back in the house Jabari tries to get up and panics when he can't find Kirby, but muffled screams can be heard from behind him. He turns around to see the monster holding Kirby and covering his mouth, the monster then tries to go back through the door. But Jabari is not done; he takes the sword and with all his might tries to pull it out of the sheath.

"Come on! Why won't you come out? Come on, damn it!" He says as he tries to unsheathe it with all his might and can pull it out an inch and a golden light comes from the sword this light shines on the monster and it causes it to drop Kirby. The monster starts to wild out and the door starts to close and pulls the monster back in. As that happens Kirby runs away from it, but the monster grabs him by his leg.

"Let me go! Jabari!" Screams Kirby for his brother.

Jabari runs to grab his brother and tries to pull him back, then Pitou tries to help by biting Jabari pants legs and tries to pull back. As this is going on the force field outside starts to fade and this allows Ishtarel to get through, he runs to the house. It feels as if time slows down, he runs as fast as he can but as he runs through the doorway the monster pulls both his sons through the door along with the dog and the door shuts in front of his face. He gets there and opens it, and the door leads nowhere and with a pained look on his face, he says.

"No."

# Book One
## Chapter Two
## The Brand-New World

The brothers, Pitou and the monster are pulled through the door, they fall through a tunnel of light and as they do Jabari takes the slightly unsheathed sword and jabs it in the monster's eye. This causes it to let go of Kirby but as they reach the end of the tunnel it spits them out in midair and both brothers file off in different directions.

They both land in different parts of a forest, Jabari, and Pitou land on one side while Kirby lands somewhere by himself. In the distance on opposite sides, two men can see the brothers flying apart and both go to check on them. Kirby lands on a branch that flips him from one to another until he lands on the ground.

"Ow. That hurt! Where am I? Jabari! What kind of a door leads to a forest?"

"Sounds like a good question, let me know when you get an answer." A mystery voice said.

"Who said that?" Kirby quickly responded.

"Look behind you kid."

When he does Kirby sees a small brown, rabbit looking creature standing on its two back legs. He has two big floppy ears that reach past his body and fall right on the ground. And the rabbit then causally asks Kirby...

"So, why are you falling from the sky kid, walking so boring for you?" Said the little rabbit.

"Ahhhhhhh. You're a talking rabbit!"

"Yes. Yes, I am a talking rabbit. And you are a talking boy. Now that we pointed out the obvious. Who are you?"

" Kirby. Hey, how can you talk like me?"

" 'Like you?' Not only is that rude, but you also didn't even answer my question or ask who I was in return for me asking you. Rude."

"Sorry. What's your name rabbit?"

"My name is Terri. Thank you for asking."

"Do you know where I am Terri?'

"Of course, I do, you sir are in a forest."

"Yeah, I kind of got what I mean, where is this forest?"

"I don't know but you might want to move if that shield is about to fall."

As he said that the shield that was used by Jabari falls from the trees and almost hits Kirby but thanks to Terri's warning misses.

"This could come in handy if I see that monster." He said as he reached to pick it up and his eyes began to glow a light began to shine the same light that shined when Jabari touched the sword. Kirby's eyes start to glow, and he sees a house like his but larger it is in the woods in a valley. He sees another building on the north end of the valley. Also, in that valley he sees golden roses blooming across the land. The vision fades and he sees one last one, a port with ships.

"Hey, that monster you mention was 7ft tall. long arms, big hands with claws 1ft long, skinny legs that bend backwards, oval shaped head with a row of fangs in his mouth, crooked horns sticking out from both sides of his head, and light blue diamond shaped eyes." Asked Terri who gave an exact description.

"Yeah, how did you know?" Kirby asked.

"It's coming this way."

Kirby turns around to see the monster running on all fours to get to him."

"No. No. No. Run!" He said as he grabbed Terri and ran.

"Hey, what are you doing? Why did you grab me when it wanted you? Now it's going to think I'm with you."

"I don't know. I just did."

"What kind of reasoning is that? He is catching up. (as the creature, close in on them) Hell no I'm not going out like this."

Terri spreads his ears like wings and grabs Kirby and flies them high in the sky above the trees.

"You can fly?"

"Yeah, faster than running."

As they are floating, two strangers from different spots below see them and so does Jabari.

"Is that Kirby? Why is he flying? Come on Pitou." Jabari said with hastes towards Kirby as well as the two strangers.

"Hey, how long can you keep this up?"

"Depends on what I'm carrying, you're not that heavy."

"Can you fly faster?"

"Why?"

"Because that thing can fly too!"

They both scream as the creature flies to them. One of the two strangers sees Kirby and Terri in danger. The nearest leaps threw the trees and stabbed the beast with a spear. As Kirby and Terri watch they see a young man around Jabari size with light brown hair and teal eyes. He has brown skin with green armor covering his upper torso and shoulders. With brown combat pants and boots. He grabs Kirby and Terri pulls them to his chest and then the man strikes the monster in the head with his spear killing the monster. The man lands on the ground with Kirby and asks.

"Are you ok?" said the mystery man.

"Yes, thanks for telling me and Terri."

"Yeah, thanks and it'sTerri and I' Kirby." Terri corrected Kirby. Then the man replied

"No thanks are needed. I was glad to be helpful to anyone or rabbit in need.

The mystery man smiles letting them know they are safe then from a distance Kirby hears a familiar voice.

"Kirby!" Jabari yelled through the trees for his little brother.

"Jabari!" Kirby yelled back.

"Who's Jabari?" Terri asked.

"My Brother!" Kirby told him.

"Hey, you never mention a brother." Terri told him.

"Maybe because we were being chased. Thanks for the help, mister , but I need to catch up with my brother. See you later." Kirby said at a fast pace and ran off.

"Hey, I helped save your life so you know he didn't do it all on his own. Hey where are you going?" Terri ranted to the boy then asked the mystery man.

"To make sure he gets to his brother safely." Mystery man

"Hey, wait, don't leave me alone here. What if there are more of those things?" Terri asked in a terrified voice.

"Then I guess you better not run into one." The man said jokingly.

"Kirby!" Jabari yelled.

"Jabari!" Kirby Replied.

"That's his voice, it's coming from over there. It's Kirby!" Jabari said as he ran in the direction.

Jabari runs and bumps into the second stranger. A black male the same size as Jabari with reddish orange hair like fire. He is wearing armor covering up his torso and shoulder armor with grey pants and combat boots. Also, he has fingerless gloves.

"Watch where you're going." Mystery man #2 shouted at Jabari.

"You watch it pal! You ran into me!" Jabari replied to the man.

"No, I didn't." Mystery man #2 replied.

"Yes, you did. I don't have time to go back and forth with you." Jabari said growing impatience with the young man.

"You know what your right words aren't going to settle this. Draw your weapon." Mystery man #2 said as he drew his blade.

"What are you crazy about? I am not a swordsman!" Jabari said loudly and irritated, stepping back from the blade.

"Then why are you carrying a sword?" Mystery man #2

"Long story and don't have time to explain. I need to find my... Kirby" He said as he saw his brother running towards him with the first mystery man behind him along with the rabbit.

"Kirby, you're ok?" Jabari said.

Both brothers hug each other with relief.

"Kirby I'm glad I found you. Are you ok?" His brother asked with concern in his voice.

"Yeah, and hey Pitou. But you'll never believe what happened when I landed." Kirby said.

"Kirby right now I'll believe anything" His big brother replied.

Then Terri chimes in.

"So, you, this big brother I heard so much about. Why are you letting your little brother fall out of the sky?" Terri asked.

"Kirby, why is there a talking rabbit with you?" The older brother asked.

"He helped save me. A talking rabbit saved me. Can you believe it? And a Mystery man."

"Who?" Jabari asked.

"He means me. My name is Elon." Mystery man #1 said finally revealing his name.

"You saved my brother's life? Thank you, I really appreciate it." He said, shaking the man's hand.

"No thanks, I'm just doing what anyone would have done at that moment." Elon said with a smile on his face.

"Hey! I helped too." Terri.

"And you too Terri. I really appreciate it." Jabari said while chuckling.

"Now that you both have been reunited. Who are you two? Because I know that I have never seen anyone with clothes like that before. And after you answer that I have another question. What are you doing falling out of the sky?" Terri questions both foreign brothers.

"Terri, I answered the last one we were being chased by." Kirby replied.

"But that still doesn't answer the first one who you guys are. That rabbit's asking some good questions because you two don't look like you belong here, and your clothing is just odd looking." Mystery man #2 added in.

"Now you know you look strange if a guy with sleeveless armor and red hair says you don't belong." Terri said with a smart tone.

"I have a name for you , little rodent. My name is Blaine. And I am the greatest flame swordsman in the world. A true legend in the making." Blaine exclaimed.

"Wow." Kirby said with his face full of excitement at the thought of a flame swordsman.

"Um but you do know most legends are people who are dead, right?" Jabari said, confused.

"Flame Swordsman? You wouldn't happen to be from the Vermillion Nation, would you?" Elon asked.

"Yeah. And judging by your emblem you're from the Celadon Nation, right?" Blaine detected as he looked at Elon.

"Vermillion? Celadon? What kind of places are those?" Jabari questioned both men.

"This is the Evergreen forest, in the Kingdom of Hue, in the Hue nation." Elon kept giving Jabari information little by little.

"Question. The Hue Nation is located where?"

"Palette" both Blaine and Elon said at the same time as it was obvious to Jabari.

"What?! We're not on Earth?" Jabari said first with a shout and then a worried voice.

"Of course, we're on earth, we're standing on it right now. See? The dirt and ground underneath us." Blaine said as he tried to reassure Jabari.

"Earth? You know the name of this planet where humans live." Kirby chimed in.

"That's not it, the name of this world it's called Palette. We have humans and a whole variety of other creatures," Elon explained to the brothers.

"No, listen, my brother and I are from earth."

"Do you mean you are from the earth as in the ground?" Both men question.

"My world, his world, our world! Let me explain."

Jabari explains everything that has happened up until now. Blaine and Elon look with confusion.

"So, you, him and this dog are from another world and that thing pulled you both here." Terri goes over.

"Yeah, that's what happened."

"Well, if that thing pulled you from a door in your guest home where the door is, why did it appear out of nowhere?" Terri asked.

"We don't know. I was downstairs cleaning and then in a flash of light it appeared." Kirby said as he acted out how the events unfolded.

"Hey Elon, was it? You believe them?" Blaine asked with uncertainty in his voice.

"They don't look like they have a reason to lie, especially to people they have never met before in their lives and a talking rabbit who walks on its legs." Elon concluded.

"Then let me be the first to welcome you to Palette! That's the name of our world." Terri exclaimed in a Jubilee.

As Terri welcomes the brothers to the new world of Palette, Kirby gasps with excitement to tell his brother what occurred in the forest when the monster approaches him.

"Hey, Jabari! I meant to tell you I saw our house, but it wasn't our house. But I saw something that looked like our house."

"What are you talking about Kirby?"

"When that thing chased after me, I used the shield, I had a vision of our home, my eyes started to glow, and I saw a house like ours, but it was way bigger than it is in the woods in a valley. I saw another building on the north end of the Valley. Also, in that Valley, I saw golden roses blooming across the ground. Then it faded away, and I saw that thing where boats stop when they're not sailing."

"A dock?" Said Terri thinking to himself there is no dock anywhere near here.

"A port?" Blaine said.

"Golden roses? I heard of those flowers so rare, so beautiful that they were thought to be a plant of fiction. But I heard those only grow in Zanatar's Valley, a place lost to time." Elon told the group.

"Zanatar? That's my last name but I never heard of this place." Jabari replied with a shocked look on his face. You know a lot about these flowers, have you been there before?" Asked Jabari.

"No, but I heard a woman who was compared to an angel lived there many years ago. But legend has it that the valley shields itself to stay hidden." Said Elon.

"But wait, isn't that a children's story? Do you really believe that and do you two live there?" Blaine asks them.

"No, but if Kirby saw it when he touched the shield it must mean something. Like when I pulled the sword even just a little a light scared off the monster" Jabari told them.

"So, if Kirby saw this when he touched the shield it must mean something. Like maybe, it's trying to tell you to go there. Like it might be the way home for you guys. So, go." Terri said to them.

"Easier said than done, we don't know how to get there." Jabari said as he banged his head against a tree in frustration.

"Well, I think I know what your problem is, you're not very optimistic." Terri deduces.

"My optimism has nothing to do with this!" he replied to the rabbit.

"Let's go Jabari, maybe it will be the way home. All we need is a map." Kirby shouted with enthusiasm.

"Your brother is right. I'm sure if we get an atlas it would help. There should be one in the next town over, I think it's called Drawlins." Elon said with reassurance.

"We? You're going to help us? But you don't even know us."

"True I don't know much about you but what I do know is you and your brother need help and I don't mind helping you get home."

"Count me in." yelled Blaine.

"Really! Yay!" Kirby said.

"Wait, why?" Jabari questioned.

"Travelers from a world called Earth. Otherworldly swordsman. This will be an epic tale people will tell of me when

I'm a legend. And I want to help two stranded people get home." Blaine said, trying to assure them he wants to help.

"For a second I thought it was all for you for a moment. You ain't fooling nobody." Terri said.

"Thanks, I really appreciate it we both do."

"Come on Pitou." Kirby said as he grabbed the dog and threw him on his shoulders.

"Hey, wait, I'm coming too."

"Why rabbit?"

"Because I said so."

The brothers are off to Drawlins to find an atlas, joined by their three new allies they set off to find a way home but up in the trees a mysterious blue looking shadow crow watches them as they make their way through the woods, it has the same eyes as the monster. Diamond eyes.

"Ok so when we get there we'll go to the market and find a map, will look and see where ports are located and decide which one to head to." Blaine explained.

"Drawlins is just a small town nothing much happens there from what I heard so, it should be easy just to get in and get out." Elon added.

As the group makes their way through the forest, they come upon the small bustling town of Drawlins. They ask around for a map. And citizens point toward the town market from where they can get one. They all go in and try to find a map.

"Kirby stays right here next to me and moves when I move. Ok? Be my second shadow."

"Ok, Jabari." He assured his big brother.

As Jabari, Blaine, and Elon look for a map, Kirby, Pitou and Terri are right behind them until Kirby notices a strange looking creature.

"Wow look at Pitou and Terri. (Points at a mysterious creature pulling a vegetable cart) it's like weird panda mixed with a dog."

"What's a panda Kirby?" Terri asked.

"It's a bear with black and white fur. And they're found in this place called China."

"I have never heard of it nor have I heard of this 'China' you speak of."

"They call it Wilva. But you're right it does look like a panda mixed with a dog, I thought I was the only one who thought that." Said a mystery man. Who appeared behind them and Terri let out a yelping sound?

"Who are you mister?" Kirby said causally.

"Seriously kid, you don't know this guy. Don't talk to strangers." Terri said.

"Right. My name is Kirby." The little boy said with innocence and a big smile on his face.

"My name is Yamato. Excuse me, I didn't mean to startle you."

Yamato is a man standing at the same height as Jabari. A black man wearing a Japanese style Gi and a straw hat. He has long black hair tied back in a ponytail. He also has two swords, one is a katana and the other a long Japanese sword with strange looking markings on them.

"I was just passing through to the next city Shaden and your clothes caught my attention. You wouldn't happen to be from out of town, would you?" The man asked Kirby.

"You could say something like that." Kirby replied.

"Hey, should you be really talking to strangers? I mean I know he introduced himself and technically he's not a stranger per say but still, I think your brother or your parents should have told you this." Terri said as he grabbed Kirby and pulled him in.

"He seems like a nice guy. Hey mister…(Gasp) where did he go?" Kirby asked when he turned his head and Yamato had disappeared.

"He disappeared!" Terri screamed in shock.

"Nope I'm behind you. I went over here to look at this poster, but I should be on my way. What was your name again little boy?"

"Kirby. Kirby Zanatar and it's nice to meet you."

"Well then Kirby you have a nice day, it's been nice meeting you and I wonder if our paths will cross again." Yamato said walking away.

"See you later. I wonder what poster he was talking about. He must mean that one right there. (points up at the highest on the billboard.) I can't reach it."

"I got it." Terri flies up and gets the poster.

"Thanks. Wow, Pitou, Terri, come look at this."

"What is it? 'A tournament only for those brave enough to even dare participate'? Like fighting? Says it is in Tone Town."

While Kirby, Pitou, and Terri look at the poster, the same crow from before watches from the trees. Meanwhile, Jabari, Elon, and Blaine are trying to search for money to pay for an atlas.

"Where do we start looking?" Jabari asked both men.

"We need an atlas, so let's try to find someone selling books or something." Suggested Blaine.

"Atlas," you say. I have atlas of this place, that place, and the other place. I have many atlases for you to choose from" said the overweight merchant man with a dirty brown mustache, beer belly and a bald spot on his head.

An old overweight white man calls their attention in a thick Russian like accent.

"Really? Mind if we look at them?" Jabari asked cheerfully.

"Hold on you can't just trust anybody at these things we need to make sure this is legit." Elon chimed in.

"How dare you question my product's authenticity?! I'm hurt. That will be 30 Hueleons."

"30 Hueleon? I'm going to assume that Hueleon is money. Where will this go?" (Jabari hands her a twenty-dollar bill)

"What kind of money is this? I had never seen it before. Where are you from? Is it worthless? Are you trying to cheat me?" Overweight Merchant berated the money.

"It's money from a faraway place." Jabari tried to pass it off as valuable.

"Will I ever visit this faraway place?"

"Maybe not." Jabari replied.

"Okay, then I don't want it. No sale!" Overweight Merchant said as he handed the money back.

"Come on old man. Why won't you take it?" Blaine asked the man, sounding annoyed.

"You say this money comes from faraway places but you won't tell me what place so that means you are trying to play me. Away with you." Overweight Merchant rants as he explains why he won't take the money.

"You're berating his money but most of these maps are just stains on paper." Blaine responded.

"How dare you? Shoo! Go away. And I am not old. I am 27 years old." Yelled the overweight man.

"So, what you're saying is time just wasn't your best friend, neither was bathing or brushing your teeth apparently." Jabari scolded the man.

"Go away!" He said as he turned away in frustration.

"Sorry, we don't have money to help you?" Elon apologized to Jabari.

"It's fine."

"Hey, you're looking for a map, right? I got a map right here." Said a woman with silky smooth looking dark skin, hair long, puffy, and out, and hazel eyes. She has a slim thin build, wears glasses, she's worn a long graduation looking robe with a teal and light blue color, and has a book strapped to her back.

"Yeah, but we don't have and Hueleon."

"That's fine that money from faraway I'll take that."

"Really? That's it?"

"Yes, that is all I want, I have never seen it before."

"Great here."

Jabari smiles as he trades with the woman thinking "Finally someone who wants to help them."

"Are you sure it's real?" Blaine as with concern.

"Everything seems to match up." Elon said, analyzing it.

"Bye thanks. I can't wait to examine this." The female Merchant said with glee.

"Thank you so much um..."

"My Name is Elamilia. Bye."

She said as she got her book from behind her back and opened it. Her book begins to glow, and she levitates and flies off.

"Cool." Blaine said.

"Hey Kirby, come on we got the map but there are several ports so think about your vision. What else can you remember that will give us an idea of where we need to go?" Jabari asks.

"I saw a sign that said 'Run something in the city." Kirby said.

"It could be Rangi City." Blaine said.

"Worth a shot. There is not much else we can go on." Elon said.

Jabari and the others look at the map to see what to do now. They plan where to go, and which would be the quickest way to get to Rangi city.

"We got the map and from what it says we must go down this road to Shaden City, then east to the capital Hue City then east again Tint Town either go across this huge lake or go around it. Going across the lake would take hours on a ferry but going through the woods would take a whole day. Following that is Tone Town, Dye Town, Wawa Town, and then after that the port in Rangi city then from there we can make our way to Zanatar's Valley." Elon explained to the group what they would do.

"Well let's get going." Jabari said.

As our heroes make their way towards Shaden town Kirby has remembered something interesting to tell Jabari.

Book One
Chapter Three
On the Road

"Hey Jabari, we met someone today named Yamato. And you never guess what will happen. Guess."

Kirby , what did dad and I tell you about talking to strangers?

"You are not that good at guessing." Terri told him with seriousness.

"I just told you his name is Yamato. We also saw some dog looking panda thing today and Yamato knew what a panda was! And…"

"Kirby I'm sure everyone knows what a panda is."

"What's a panda?" Both Blaine and Elon asked Jabari.

"You guys don't have pandas in this world?"

"No. What are they?" Elon asked again.

"Their bears."

"What kind of bear?" Blaine asked.

"It's a bear. What? You guys don't have bears here?"

"We have cat-bears, dog-bears and gorilla bears but I never heard of a panda bear." Blaine told him.

"Well, pandas are just black and white that's just it."

"That's it? The world you two must come from is very strange." Elon told him.

"That's what I was saying, no one here has heard of a panda bear. They don't have any in this world. But there was this guy Yamato knew what one was and said that the Wilva the thing I saw looked like a panda and a dog mixed together."

"But how did Yamato know what a panda is and not anyone else?" Jabari asked his little brother.

"I don't know."

As they are walking, they can hear rustling coming from the bushes.

"Hey look there is something in the bush moving." Terri pointed out as two bushes rustled.

"Kirby got behind me."

"And all of you stay in front of me." Terri said.

They all prepare for the worst but out pops a small red creature with a flame on its head.

"What is that thing?" Kirby asks.

"That is a fire spirit called a Flamey. A small fire creature who shoots little ember attacks." Blaine tells him.

"Kirby be careful I don't want you to get too close to that thing. And don't try and touch it!" Jabari said as Kirby got closer to it.

"Can I hold him please?" Kirby asked his brother.

"No!" He replied.

"But why not have all my tetanus shots?"

"That's not the point! It shoots fire!" He told his little brother.

"Your brother's right kid. You need to be more careful. Those things may be small, but they burn like a volcano pit. (Touches one by accident) Ah crap, that burns, aw damn it." Blaine screams as he accidentally touches one of the little fire spirits.

"Let me see I have something in my bag that can help. Here, let 's rub something on there, try this Aloe Vera. Is that better?" Elon told him to apply the Aloe.

"Yeah, much better. Thanks." Blaine replied.

"Do you carry medical supplies with you?" Jabari said surprised.

"Just some antidotes, potions, and other necessities. Back in my home country, my dad is a well-known doctor. So, I take after him when it comes to these things."

"You're an emergency medical doctor on the move. It's like that TV show in our world called 'Mobile ER'. We don't take you to the Doctor! We will take the doctor to you!' That's their Catchphrase." Kirby told them comparing the show with Elon.

"What's a TV Show?" Terri asked.

"It's something people use to keep them entertained and it's very fun and other times it's trash." Kirby said to the rabbit.

"Hmm, I must meet this so-called TV. It's hard for me to entertain myself sometimes, you know being in the forest all the time. Usually I pick a fight with other forest creatures that are smaller than me." Terri bragged about the last part.

"Ok enough let's keep moving." Jabari told them.

The crew continues down the road towards Shaden then Blaine strikes a good question at Jabari.

"Hey Jabari, let me ask you something you say you're not a swordsman, but you carry that nice-looking sword, why?" Blaine asks.

"It's my dad's. I just picked it up to help Kirby when that thing snatched him. The strangest thing happened when I picked it up, it started to glow bright and the thing fled." Jabari told him.

"Cool, do you know how to sword fight?" Blaine asks.

"Probably not like you but I did take fencing in middle school."

"Middle school?" Blaine said, confused.

"It's nothing." Jabari told him.

As they keep on their way Elon notices the presence of something in the trees.

"You okay?" Terri asks.

"There is someone following us."

"Who? Where?" Blaine asks as he darts his head left and right looking for something.

"Hey, look at the town!" Kirby said.

Before Elon could say anything, Kirby jets off with Pitou because he sees the sign that says Shaden City.

"Kirby Hold up!" Elon yelled.

Out of nowhere these hooded looking shadow figures appear and attack Kirby but before any of them could hurt him Elon swoops in and pulls Kirby out of the way. The monster resembles the beast from before that pulled them to this world.

"It kind of looks like that thing from the forest but it doesn't look that strong." Jabari said.

Both Blaine and Elon attack from both sides but are both knock backed. Jabari then draws his sword and at that moment his eyes and sword start to glow red and green. He swings his sword at them creating a slash of red and green energy that resembles a fury of razor leaves on fire decimating both monsters.

"Nice but I thought you said you didn't know how to sword fight that well. How did you pull off that attack?" Blaine asks Jabari.

"I don't know. I felt like something inside me just exploded and it told me to swing."

"Are you okay Pitou?" Kirby asked Pitou.

"Kirby why did you just run off like that!? We are in unfamiliar territory; you have no idea what's around the corner and you go running off and almost get yourself killed! You need to stay by my side always, do you understand you don't run off like that?!" Jabari yelled as he scolded his brother.

"I'm sorry." Kirby said with a breaking voice.

"Kirby come on don't. I didn't mean to yell but you need to stay by my side."

Kirby starts to cry and runs off.

"Come on, don't cry, come back.'

"Didn't have to yell at him like that geez. Come back Kirby." Terri said as he chased after the crying kid.

"I didn't mean to make him cry. You guys understand, right?"

"I mean I've never had a little brother before but he's just a kid and you're trying to look out for him. He might not get it." Blaine gave his opinion.

"I can talk to him if you want, I have experience with these types of things." Elon said as he chased after Kirby.

"Hey wait Kirby. He didn't mean to yell at you like he was just looking out for you. Hold on. How can you run so fast?" Terri said flying after him.

Kirby runs and bumps into a man and drops Pitou in the process. The man with silver hair but not nearly old enough to be an elderly man. Wearing a sky blue shirt that drops down to his feet with the sides missing from the knee down. Wearing black pants, an orange cape, with glasses and brown boots. He grabs Kirby's arm and questions him.

"Excuse me little boy, watch where you're going! Why are you running with your head down? Why are you crying?" Said the man with a demanding voice and a stern face.

"There you are Kirby. You shouldn't run off like that. I'm sorry if he bumped into you." Elon apologized to the man.

"I'm sorry I didn't mean to cause trouble for you guys. I can't do anything right."

"You didn't cause any trouble for anyone."

"But Jabari said…"

"He said what he said because he cares about you and worries for your safety. He loves you and wants to protect you and you must realize that. Come on, let's go back and find the others." Elon said, calming down Kirby.

"Yeah, what he said." Added Terri out of breath when he catches up.

"Bark." Pitou barks as he jumps next to Kirby."

"Okay." He said with a sniffle.

"Hey, there you guys are. Told you they would bring him back." Blaine said to Jabari.

"Hey, are you mad at me?" He asks his little brother.

"No." He told them.

"Can I get a hug?" He asks his little brother.

"Yeah."

"I'm sorry I yelled at you."

"It's ok. Elon told me why you yelled, it's because you care."

"What did you tell him?" Blaine asked Elon.

"What he needed to hear." He replied.

"Hey if I didn't know better, I thought you had a little brother of your own." Blaine

"No, I'm an only child. But I was kind of like a big brother figure in my town."

"We should get ready to check in before the night." Blaine said.

"Yes, well let's find a place to eat while we're here." Elon added.

"But none of us have any money." Jabari reminds them.

"Any idea on how to make some money?" Terri asked.

"I ran past that post board and saw a paper that said reward" Elon said.

"'Wanted dead. A monster down in the Pokadua Valley causing havoc. Three people have already died from this beast. Please kill it.' Here's a picture of it. And it looks like that thing from before we came into town and the monster in the forest." Jabari reads from the poster then tells them.

"Did that poster say it killed three people? Whatever these things are, they are causing a lot of problems." Terri said terrified.

"Look at how much money they're offering. 50,000 Hueleon!" Elon added.

"That's more than enough." Blaine said.

"So, let's go beat this thing then." Kirby said with pep.

"Not you. You can come but stay where you won't get hurt." Jabari told him.

"The directions say the valley is east of here that's half a mile from the village. Let's go." Blaine said.

# Book One
## Chapter Four
## Enter the Lightning Bounty Hunter

As they make their way to the Pokadua Valley they can hear a male voice in the distance making grunting noise.

"Who or what do you think is making that noise? I don't want to be that rabbit but look at the entrance to the valley there's a danger warning sign." Terri said, shaking.

"Well, if this thing had killed three people, they would have put up these signs. Kirby stays here with Terri and Pitou. You two watch him. Blaine, Elon and I will go and kill the monster." Jabari told both Pitou and Terri.

"Don't worry we will be back with that monster's head and we'll be eating like pigs." Blaine fantasized.

As Kirby stays behind with Terri and Pitou the others make their way into the valley to find the monster.

"So, Kirby why do you think these things are appearing?" Terri asked.

"I couldn't tell you. But this monster here makes four we see and... Do you hear that? Hey, that's the same noise we heard coming up here."

"Yeah." Terri answered.

"There is that same noise." Jabari noticed.

"Someone is up ahead." Said Elon.

As they push forward, they can hear a man screaming and see him flying above them and back to where they left Kirby.

"Now that noise is getting louder and louder. Now it's starting to get dark." Kirby pointed out.

The screaming gets louder and the area around Kirby gets darker and Terri screams.

"Look Out!" Terri screamed as Pitou bit Kirby's shirt and pulled him out the way. Out of the sky, a man crashes to the ground.

"Watch where you're landing buddy you almost hit us." Terri yelled at the man.

A black man with long blond wooly hair, bright yellow eyes wearing black pants and a black shirt, with a grey belt and a silver belt buckle with a lightning symbol on it and some grey bands on his wrists and a black headband and silver colored boots gets up and groans. He tries to get up and dust himself off.

"Are you on mister?" Kirby asked worried about the man.

"I'm fine, why do you ask?" The man asks.

"Because you fell from the sky and hit the ground that made this huge crater." Kirby tells him.

"Don't worry it takes a lot more than a little fall to stop Galvan." Said the man who we assume to be Galvan.

"So, I'm guessing his name is Galvan." Kirby assumed.

"Wow, how did you figure it out?" Terri said with a sarcastic tone.

"Hey, is that a talking rabbit?" Galvan asked.

"Yes. Yes, he is." Kirby said.

"Does the dog talk too?"

"No. No, he does not." Kirby answered.

"What is a little kid like you doing here? It's too dangerous. Oh, I see you came to watch me in action as I take down this monster am I right?" The man asks.

"No. Not really." The boy told him.

"Are you sure about that?"

"Yeah. I'm pretty sure."

"Damn! I thought I was inspiring kids!"

"To what? fall from the sky?!" Said Terri.

"And you're sure aren't trying to be just like me." The man asks.

"No thanks, falling from the sky to the ground is not in his future. It's in his past." Terri added.

"But seriously kid, leave before you get hurt. Kind of wished I would have warned those other guys but if me flying through the air and falling out the sky isn't warning enough, I don't know what is."

"Wait, you saw my brother and the others?"

"Your brother?" Galvan said.

"My brother and our new friends are going to take down the monster."

"Well sorry to break it to you, if I can't beat that thing your brother doesn't stand a chance." Galvan said, shocking Kirby.

"Just because you lost doesn't mean they will. Don't listen to this guy Kirby, he fell from the sky and his sword looks weird that's probably why he lost. Terri said.

"My sword! This is of the strongest blades there are and if this couldn't beat that beast then nothing could."

"Shut up! Kirby didn't listen to this guy. He fell from the sky and landed on his head. He is delusional." Terri said, trying to reassure Kirby.

"What do you call me rabbit? Seriously, what did you call me? I don't know what delusional means." Galvan said.

"I got to go help him come on." Kirby said, jetting off into the valley. Kirby starts running in the direction of his brother as fast as he can to see if he can help. Pitou follows right after him.

"Wait he said stay right here! Why don't you listen? You stress me out more than I should be. Look at what you do to me!" Terri said to Kirby.

"Hey, wait kid, don't be foolish!" Galvan tells him.

"This coming from the man that fell from the sky!" Terri said.

Meanwhile with the others.

"Do you guys think that thing sent that guy flying?" Jabari asked Elon and Blaine.

"Look out!" Blaine shouted.

A large tentacle swings their way and Jabari dodges the attack while Blaine pushes Elon out the way. They look to see a shadow figure with a tall humanoid like figure but with a long serpent head and multiple tentacles. The monster lets out a screech like a roar.

"Any ideas?" Elon asked.

"Take out his arms then his head." Jabari directed the two without hesitation.

Blaine leaps into the air and swings his flaming sword down on the monster's left arm and Elon takes his spear and cuts through the other arm. Then Jabari takes his Khopesh and cuts the head off.

Wow, that was easy. Why have they been having a hard time?

"Hey behind you!" Elon said.

As Jabari turns, he sees that the monster is up and well and has regenerated his limbs and head as if they were new.

"Now we see why they could beat this thing." An annoyed Elon said.

"Damn! How can we kill this thing when it can just grow back its head and limbs?" Jabari thought to himself in frustration.

Meanwhile, Kirby, Pitou, Terri, and Galvan are trying to catch up to the others.

"Galvan, where did the monster flung you from?" Kirby asked him with worry in his voice.

"I wasn't flung!"

"Fine then where was the monster before he tossed your ass like a rag doll?" Terri asked, scolding.

"Who do you think you're talking to like that rabbit? Do you know who I am?" Galvan asks.

"The blond moron who fell from the clear blue sky left a human shaped in the ground and almost hit us." Terri said, taking shots at him.

"Hey look, it's them! Jabari." Kirby pointed towards them fighting the monster.

They arrive at the scene to see that the others are having a difficult time fighting this monster.

"What? Kirby? I thought I told you to stay back!"

"Don't worry kid, I'll save them." Galvan said as he jumped into the fight without one thought.

"Save them? You could barely save yourself!" Kirby said.

When Galvan jumps into the fray Kirby notices something in the beast. It goes by so fast that he must try to watch.

"Hey, guys look. Every time they attack the monster it regenerates. And every time it does, I can see a blue ball, but it moves to a different area every time I see it.

Kirby observation is right there being a palm size light blue orb in the beast that does move.

"Terri, you got to go tell them." Kirby tells him.

"What why me?"

"Because I was told to stay away." Kirby tells him.

"Now you listen?! Ok, I'll fly over there and tell them. Hey Jabari! Guys!" Terri said, trying to get their attention.

"Terri, what is it?" Said Jabari while holding the monster back.

"Aim for the blue orb, watch for it."

"What blue orb?" Jabari asks.

"I see it. Jabari the lower back." Elon pointed out.

"I got it." He replied.

Jabari runs from the side dodging every single strike from the beast. The monster runs him up against the side of the cliff. Jabari leaps off the cliff and then tries to strike him on the orb but the monster moves back. Blaine and Elon come from the sides, but the monster moves its orbs again. But in the moment Galvan tries to attack and hit the beast exposing the orb then Jabari strikes the blue orb. This destabilizes the monster, and the monster disintegrates leaving the head behind.

"How did you know to do that Terri?"

"I didn't. He saw the blue marble."

"Kirby you saw that. Nice job kid." Blaine congratulated Kirby by patting his head.

"Insightful as ever, following my footsteps." Said Galvan.

"Who is this guy?" Blaine asks.

"This is Galvan he fell from the sky." Kirby told them.

"But not like you guys, he got his ass smacked across the sky by that thing." Terri added.

"Quiet rabbit!" Snapped Galvan.

"Um that's a great story and all but why the hell are you here?" Blaine said.

"I am Galvan, one of the most feared bounty hunters from Acacia."

"Then how come I've never heard of you before?" Blaine said with an unimpressed tone.

"Maybe you heard of another name, the Lightning Slayer of Acacia."

"What?!"

"Have you heard of him before Blaine?" Elon asks.

"I heard of a story, but the man was a moron who couldn't control the power of his weapon and the sword was far beyond his abilities to control it. He blew up a harbor and called himself a lightning slayer." Blaine told them.

"Well, that story sounds more accurate." Terri said.

"What's going on? I'm completely lost" Jabari asked Elon and Blaine in confusion.

"He is a Lightning mancer from the Acacia Republic." Elon told them.

"What is Acacia?" Kirby asks.

"One of 10 elemental continents and Acacia Republic is one of its states in this world. Like Vermillion and Celadon. Acacia is known for its fierce fighters and soldiers in their battalion." Elon informs them.

"That's right. But none of them compare to that of me. I once took on an entire lightning falcon, a notorious gang on my own." Galvan said.

"That's great and all but why are you here in the first place? You're in Hue." Blaine asks.

"Just making some extra money taking on jobs. So, if you don't mind, I'll take that head as proof."

"Hell no! We killed this thing, so we got the money all you did was get flung across the sky." Blaine snapped at him.

"You didn't do anything either, your leader did all the work and killed the beast. All you did was stand there looking helpless." Galvan replied.

"Say that again to my face you moron." Blaine told him as both bucked up to each other.

"Call me a moron, just know that this moron is also the greatest swordsman in the entire Acacia Republic."

"I doubt that to be true but if you want let's test that out" Blaine said drawing his sword.

"Fine let's. Just to let you know my sword was forged from the scale of a thunder behemoth."

"That's cute now let me let you know that my sword was made from fire dragon scales."

"Fire Dragon!" Elon said with shock.

"Is that bad?" Kirby asks.

"Fire dragons and Thunder behemoths are rare creatures, and those two monsters are natural enemies. If they clash with their weapons, who knows what will happen." Elon warned.

"If anything is more dangerous than a moron with a sword it is two of them who don't know what they're doing." Terri said, trembling behind Pitou.

"Hey both, you calm down." Jabari told them.

"Don't worry this will be over quickly." Blaine told him.

"You're right so after I'm done with you, I'll take that monster's head." Galvan taunted him.

Right before they clash a fiery crimson aura surrounds Blaine and an electric yellow aura around Galvan as they swing their swords. Elon steps in and stops both their attacks with his spear.

"Hey Elon, what's the big idea?" Blaine asked.

"Yeah, why'd you jump in?" Galvan added.

"Because the clash between both of your weapons would have leveled this whole area and the proof that we killed the monster."

"What?!" Jabari, Kirby, and Terri said frantically.

"Both of those monsters are S-rank level monsters, both of their scales have magical properties even when they are not attached to them, both of you are probably good swordsmen but if those two weapons collide, kiss the head, the money, and this whole valley goodbye." Elon tells them.

"Whoops sorry." Both said.

"Besides, the person who really deserves the reward is Kirby. Without his keen eye, we would have never stopped this monster." Elon said.

"Really?" He said with big wide eyes and a smile.

"Yeah, without you we probably would have never seen it so congrats." Jabari said.

"Jabari can Galvan join us for dinner when we get back?" He asked his brother.

"Sure, I don't see why not." He tells his brother.

"Great, now we have a blond idiot along with a redhead idiot." Terri said.

As they return to the town, they show the head of the beast and receive their reward. They buy themselves a room for the night then head on over to the mess hall to get something to eat.

"I don't think we really had the chance to introduce ourselves. My name is Jabari, and this is my little brother Kirby."

"My name is Elon and this is Blaine. I'm from the Celadon Nation and Blaine is from the Vermillion Nation."

"So, what brings you two all the way over here if you're from Celadon and Vermillion?" Galvan asked both men.

Elon looks hesitant to answer the question.

"I was going to train with someone, but something came up and they couldn't make it. Then that's when I ran into Jabari." Blaine told him.

Elon is still looking a little hesitant and Kirby notices, but Elon gives a response.

"I was just visiting a friend. But that person wasn't there. And that's when I saw Kirby falling from the sky, I went to go check on him."

"So, Jabari, where are you and your brother from?"

"Uh well you see my brother and I are from Zanatar's Valley?"

"Wait Zanatar's Valley? I thought that place was made up like in a fairy tale." Galvan said while laughing and falling out of the chair.

"No, it's not! I saw it myself in a vision! When I grabbed my shield when I was attacked by the monster that pulled me here." Kirby told him.

Jabari tells Galvan about everything that has happened until now and Galvan responds with a shocked look.

"Uh yes. We're leaving in the morning we're heading to Hue City. It's on our way to Rangi City". Jabari told him.

"Woah. Hey, let me ask you a question Kirby. The monster that attacked you, what did it look like and how strong was it?" Galvan asked the boy and he responded.

"It looked like the monster that brought me here but the one in the valley was kind of stronger?"

"Why are you asking?" Blaine asks him quickly.

"Because I've never fought something like that before and it gave me a real challenge it made me think differently on how I would fight." Galvan said.

"But yet all you did the second time was swing your sword around and followed the advice of a kid." Terri said with a smart mouth.

"Mind if I join you guys? I have a feeling if I stick with you guys, I'd fight tougher opponents and I'll get stronger. So, can I?"

"I don't see why not." Jabari responded as his little brother cheered.

"It will be good to have strength in numbers if we keep running into these monsters and they keep getting stronger." Elon added.

Unnoticed by the group they were being watched by a female figure who was cloaked in a grey hood. In the morning they get their stuff together and head out on the road to Hue City, the vacation hot spot in Hue Kingdom. They head towards the city limits and pass the city borders.ghtrt

"How long will it take to get there?" Galvan asked.

"Judging by the map it will take a couple of hours by cart but by walking it would be more like 18 hours." Elon told the group.

"And this is the only route and I doubt we have enough money to buy horses for all of us to ride on." Blaine told them counting the reward money they have left.

"Maybe if we buy a cart and two horses." Jabari suggested.

"That would be the equivalent of four horses still."

"If I could suggest something?" Said an unfamiliar voice.

"Who said that? Who's there? Show yourself!" They all shouted.

"Down here, gentlemen." Everyone looks down to see that the voice is coming from Pitou. "Hello".

"Whaaat!?" Everyone yelled at the sight of Pitou talking.

"Since when can you talk?" Jabari said in disbelief.

"I've always been able to talk." Pitou.

"Then why have you kept quiet for this long?" Jabari asks.

"I was just waiting for the right moment, you know with the whole, both of you being dragged into an entirely different world."

"What? The whole time we spoke to you in our world but all you said was bark." Kirby said.

"Like I said I was waiting for the right time so, your dad wanted you guys to live a normal life. So, I went on being a "normal" dog. But there were times I've slipped up around Kirby, but he thought it was all in his head."

"Ok, how can you help us?" Blaine asks.

Pitou's body starts to glow and here grows into a large hound like beast standing at 6 ft. tall on all fours, with vast black fur and a vanilla white mane, sharp pointed ears, sabretooth fangs, with yellow eyes and red pupils.

"What? How? When?" Jabari asked.

"He had a growth spurt Jabari." Kirby said.

"I'll explain everything when we get back to our world but right now let's focus on just getting home. Go buy a cart and I will pull us there." Pitou said.

"Ok Blaine, Galvan, and I will go buy the cart that's big enough for all of us, Elon and Kirby go buy some supplies." Jabari ordered them, and they replied with yes sir.

Elon takes the money and buys the biggest car from the shop in the Shaden City cart shop. Elon and Kirby go buy supplies for the group and the others get the cart. While all of this is going on the same woman from the inn is watching them. They get everything together by attaching Pitou to the cart and pulling them and setting out on the road.

"Alright, Pitou let's go." Jabari said.

"Got it."

"So, Pitou, what do you call that transformation?" Kirby asks.

"I just call this my wild fang form."

As the group rides along the countryside, they go to Hue City and they pass the time with conversation.

"Wow, riding along the countryside is amazing, just look at it all." Galvan said.

"Yeah, usually all I ever see is forest, but this is really nice." Terri added.

Blaine notices Elon isn't that impressed.

"What's wrong, Elon doesn't seem so impressed with the countryside." Blaine says.

"It's nice but I'm used to it in the Celadon Nation. Do you like the view Kirby?"

"Yeah, I've never seen something like this near our home. We live on a mountain side estate with trees but it's near the city. I wonder if our dad is okay."

"I'll tell you this to you Kirby, you and your brother will get home." Elon reassured him.

"Elon, can you tell me more about the continents in this world?" Jabari asked, curious.

"Sure." Elon responded.

"The first thing you need to know is that 10 continents specialize in a different element of the world. Fire, Flora, Lightning, Water, Light, Dark, Earth, Air, Steel, and Ice. See this map in the atlas. I'll start with Vermillion as the fire nation, Celadon as the Flora nation, Acacia as the Lightning nation and Cerulean as the water nation. Then there is Ebony the dark nation and Ivory the light nation. The last four are Acajou the earth nation, Cyan the air nation, Pewter the steel nation, and then finally of the ten element nations is Frost as the ice nation."

"The power of these ten nations came into these powers eons ago when all ten were at war with each for a long time. There was so much death, the fighting continued until the gods stepped in and broke it up. So, the gods that stepped in used his powers to make sure there were checks and balances between each nation, so no other nation was more powerful than the other. They gave each one of the nation's powers to them so one was powerful than another but also weaker against another nation."

"It goes like this fire is stronger than flora, then flora is stronger than lightning, then lightning is stronger than water and water is stronger than fire, it was a cycle. The dark and light balanced each other. Then the next cycle was earth stronger than air, air was stronger than steel, steel stronger than ice, and then ice stronger than earth. So, then the gods told them they are balanced, and they could not break into another war and if so, the other nation needs to step in. Now each nation has people who can control the elements."

"The majority could use it but there is the one percent who couldn't. Like me, I'm a Floramancer which means I control flora. Blaine is a pyromancer he controls fire, Galvan lightning mancer he controls lightning. Then there are other nations that remained neutral during the war which were Hue, Teku, Ryeanne, and Hyeanna. These four use different types of magic altogether that were given to them by the same gods. And each nation has their own royal family and government. There are several other countries, but I don't think I can give you the rundown of all of them."

Meanwhile back on earth. Ishtarel tries to pry open the door but when he does, it leads nowhere.

"Damn! I need to find Tazama."

Ishtarel runs to his house to grab something from both the boy's room then goes outside and without any effort, he leaps into the air and flies at supersonic speed in the north. While flying he passes Springfield Illinois. In five minutes, he lands in Alberta Canada near a luxury cabin. And Out walks a man with light brown skin and messy beach blond hair wearing pajama pants with Canadians leaves on and a white t-shirt with the Canada's flag on it.

"Ishtarel how you been buddy? Long time no see. What have you been up to?"

"No time for small talk. I need your help. I need you to look into the future. I need you to use this to see if my kids are okay."

Ishtarel gives him some strands of hair from both his sons to give to Tazama. Tazama can sense the well-being of someone if he is contacting something that belongs to them. And if he focuses enough, he can see into the future of that person.
"Look into the future and see if my kids are going to be okay."

"What happened to them?"

"The door. I don't know how I don't know what and I don't know who. But the door opened, "he told the clairvoyant.

"What?! But how I thought you sealed it."

"I did but someone or something must have broken it and they've gone through it because I can't sense them anywhere. And you know I can't go through the door because the seal will be weaker." Ishtarel tells him.

"Okay give me the hair strands. Let me set up the thing. So, Ishtarel, how do you think the door opens?"

"I don't know. Tazama."

"Could it have been you know who?" Tazama asks.

"No. He couldn't. I definitely made sure he couldn't get here."

As Tazama sets up and starts his process his eyes start to glow, and he can see all the events that have transpired since his sons went through the door and how they are.

"So, what happened? What's going to happen? Are they all right?"

"The boys are fine; they're going to make it home safe. By what I saw it looks like they made some friends and are on their way to the valley. They'll be home in like a couple of days, maybe a week, maybe a week or two."

"A week or two?!"

"Well unless you want to go in there to get them, you'll have to wait. They'll be fine, they are your kids."

Meanwhile Back in the world of Palette.

"Look at that sign, it says that Hue city is only 3 miles away." Elon pointed out.

"Thanks, Pitou! We wouldn't have gotten this far without you. Wow, in only two hours and we're almost there." Said Jabari.

"Hey, look, Elon, Blaine and Galvan are drooling." Terri mocked them.

"We'll wake them up when we arrive in Hue City." Elon said.

"So, what's it like in Hue City?" Jabari asked Elon.

"It's one of the best vacation spots in the world, they have amusement, and water parks. They have all the finest restaurants and the best hotels in the nation."

"Wow, Jabari, can we go to the parks when we get there?" Kirby asks his big brother.

"I don't know Kirby. Maybe we can stay there to site see, maybe for like a couple of minutes but then we need to get moving. Hey, look I can see the city."

As they ride up to the horizon, they can see the entrance to Hue City. You can see all the attractions, a Ferris Wheels as tall as a ten-story building. Colorful lights across the city.

"Wow, it 's so big, so bright, so colorful! Can we stay a while longer to look around? Please?" He said with big ol eyes.

Trying to convince Jabari, Kirby grabs his brother by his arms, and stares directly in his face.

"Um, I guess we can stay a little longer than planned."

"What strange power does this boy have?" Terri asked.

"It's called being loveable on earth." Pitou answered.

"Oh, then I definitely have that power." Terri replied.

"I said "lovable" not punch-able."

# Book One
## Chapter Five
### City Lights

As they arrive in Hue City the view from within is greater than the view from outside. All the games, food, and rides excited Kirby.

"Ok two hours and we'll meet back here and then back on the road ok." Jabari reminded his brother.

"Ok. Come on, come on, let's go." Kirby said while trying to run off.

"Hold your horses' kid. We need to park the cart first." Blaine told Kirby.

"I look for a place to set it with Pitou and we'll catch up with you." Elon said.

"You sure Elon?" Kirby asked.

"Yes, I don't mind." Elon tells them.

Kirby takes out a marker and writes "property of..." And puts all their names on it.

"There now that are names are on it no one will take it." The little boy said.

They walk through the city towards the amusement park.

"I never thought I would be here, at least not at eighteen." Blaine said.

"Me neither but I always wanted to come here as a kid. When I was little, I would do small jobs around my village to try and raise money to come here but could never make enough." Galvan added.

"Yeah, same for me but then again my dad would never have the time to come anyway. He was always busy with the army." Blaine told them.

Jabari overhears the conversation and begins to think about growing up with only his dad and him trying to make sure they both had a great childhood.

"Well, I guess you two should enjoy it while we're here." Jabari told them with a smile.

"Welcome to Hue city park, here is your complementary park attire, I hope you enjoy your time." Said the park employee.

"Thank you, Nico." Kirby said, reading her name badge.

"Woah, they just give you free clothes." Jabari said while the employees give them a set of new clothes.

All of them smile and the group proceeds to enter the park. They go into the changing room and put on their new clothes; their clothes resemble that of Dashikis. They have the best time in the park Jabari takes Kirby on all the rides he's tall enough.

Elon watches Blaine and Galvan compete in every game. And off to the side, Pitou and Terri are gallivanting about. Watching the humans as they interact with each other and swiping food from unsuspecting vendors.

As time goes by, they have the time of their lives. While they are having fun, within the shadows the very same woman in grey is still following them. The fun time would soon be interrupted by another misfortune.

"Ok, Kirby it's time to go." Jabari told him.

"Aw already."

"Yeah, it's been four hours already Kirby and frankly all this fair food is making me sick. I'm going to sit in the cart." Terri said while trying to hold back from throwing up.

"Ok, so where is everyone else? Oh, there they are." Jabari asks.

"So, did you have fun today Kirby?" Elon asks him.

"Yeah, it was so much fun! Jabari, can we come back some time."

"Sure, but let's focus on getting home before we decide to come back." He tells his little brother.

Screaming people can be heard in the distance. As all of them converge on the scene they see a giant monster resembling the one they had fought recently but bigger. This monster seems to think more clearly than the others they faced. It is a dark blue giant; the monster stands 20 ft. tall standing on its hind legs with knees bending backwards with big arms that feel like rough crocodile skin. They clear everyone out of the way, so they can stop this beast.

"Kirby Stay here." Jabari told him.

"You know that I'm not going to do that so I'm going to help those people get out." He told his big brother.

"What? Fine, just stay away from the monster." Jabari tells him.

"Don't worry I will but how are you going to fight it, you left your sword." The little brother asks.

"I got it." Terri said flying with the shield and Pitou running in his wild fang form with the sword. "I was heading back to the cart with Pitou when we heard the screaming, so we thought we would bring your weapons. Your sword and Kirby's shield. Here catch."

"Jabari there are still people trapped, I'm going to go help them." Kirby told his brother while running off.

"Fine, just be careful. Elon you and I will take the right side, while Blaine and Galvan take the right, we take out the legs then go for the back of the neck."

They nod in agreement. While they take care of the monster Kirby, Pitou, and Terri try to get the civilians out of harm's way. As they do, a falling piece of metal nearly crushes a woman and her child, but Kirby uses his shield to cover the woman and child from the falling debris. He then leads them out of harm's way while carrying the shield over them. Terri flies two people at a time away from the fight and Pitou and rides people to safety.

"Do you think we got everyone, Pitou and Terri?" Kirby asks.

"Yeah, I think that's everyone, now it's up to your brother and the others to stop them now." Terri said.

"I think we missed someone. Look!" Pitou said.

Pitou nodded towards a man standing on top of the broken Ferris wheel with brown skin, brown hair wearing grey fingerless gloves, a light blue shirt, in a short blue trench coat that's open, with gray pants along with a holster for a thin long sword, and grey colored combat boots with a blue trim.

'What is he doing?" Terri yelled.

The man on top of the Ferris Wheel leaps in and slashes the neck of the monster bringing him down but not killing it.

"Who the hell are you?" Galvan said to the man.

"My name is Azuro. It looked like you could use some help there so I thought I would jump in. And you're welcome."

"Thanks for the help but that only slowed him down and we need to take this thing out before it gets towards the street and hurts someone." Jabari told Azuro.

"This one isn't like the ones from before this monster is more aware." Elon added.

"I weakened the back of the neck and it was covered with thick skin." Said Azuro.

"We'll let someone else take a crack at it." Blaine said.

At that point, they each took a shot at the back of the monster's neck . Blaine blazed down on the back of the neck and did nothing. Galvan struck his sword in the same area and nothing happened. Still, Elon comes from behind and stabs, but the skin was entirely too thick. Jabari sits their stun and tries to think of a way to beat this creature.

"Damn, we need something stronger." Galvan shouted out.

"No, we need to attack together but we need to find a way to get near his neck. Pitou, Terri come over here. Look, I need you to do this exactly as I tell you."

"What can I do to help?" Kirby stood waiting to know.

"Just sit back and make sure no one's in the way." Jabari tells him.

"I already did that come on let me does something!" Kirby said.

"Staying back and letting us handle this is something. Kirby just for once listens and stays back." Jabari said.

Jabari tells them the instructions and he puts his plan into action by telling Pitou and Terri to go for his knees. Then when it falls all five of them attack the neck but when they do, they break the skin just enough to break through the final layer.

"Damn it, it didn't break." Jabari thought in his head.

"Come on. We need to hit it one more time. It might heal itself." Elon said.

"I got to take this."

Kirby climbs to the top of the Ferris wheel then jumps down and takes his shield, jabs the edge of it in the monster's neck and it goes through decapitating the monster.

"Told you I could help."

"Kirby, your head is bleeding." Elon pointed out.

"Ahhhh owww. Jabari, it hurts. Make it stop!" He said, screaming.

"Didn't I tell you to stay back so you wouldn't get hurt? Come here and let's see it. It's not that deep, a little dirt in it, we'll clean it, come on." He told his little brother.

"What was that thing?" Azuro questioned the group.

"Long story guy but thanks for the help, I really appreciate it." Blaine told him hoping that would push him off.

"You're welcome. But if you can answer my first question and while you're at it. Who are you? Clearly, you and your friends are not normal." Azuro asked again.

"After everything we've seen in this world does normal even exist." Said Pitou.

"Look we can't explain everything and who are you again?" Galvan replied to Azuro.

"My name is Azuro. You and your friends aren't normal, you all are clearly not from the same place so why is there a rag tag group like you going around fighting these monsters? I'd overheard the one from you called Elon. Those two who I am assuming are brothers. The Clothes they were wearing before they entered the park and changed, I saw that their Clothes are not of the country or this world and the sword and shield they used no mere blacksmith made that I don't now explain." He said with a commanding voice.

"Listen here, pretty boy, we don't have to tell you anything, so how about you get lost." Galvan told him in a defying voice.

"Calm down. Listen Azuro was it? I'll explain everything, but you must calm down. Is that ok Jabari?" Elon said, trying to calm them down.

"Yeah, if it gets him to chill out."

"Why are we telling him?" Terri asked.

"Because he's not letting up and it doesn't seem like he's going to take what Blaine said and roll with it. You haven't noticed, look at him, the anger in his eyes, the tone of his voice, and the way he attacked that monster." Jabari said to Terri.

"Okay, that's a lot to take in. So those two are from another world. And you are trying to find them a way home, but you keep running into these monsters. And the little boy had a vision that he saw his home but bigger in a valley surrounded by mountains and the valley was covered in golden roses. And now you're heading to Zanatar's Valley." Azuro tries to sum it all up.

"Yes." Elon answered him.

"But I thought Zanatar's Valley was made up." Azuro said in confusion.

"Well despite everything we've been through nothing seems too farfetched." Blaine told him.

"So why were you so adamant on finding information about these things and us?" Jabari asks Azuro.

"Because one of those monsters attacked my village in Cerulean. It came from a merchant ship that docked at our ports. There was only one of them, but rumor has it that more of these things were spotted in Hue, so I came here to investigate. I'll find where they come from and destroy them, and you all seem to have had a similar problem running into these things. It is clear from what you told me this is no coincidence. So where are we off to now?"

"We?" Everyone asked simultaneously.

"It's clear you're all just going to keep running into these monsters while trying to get home so if I come with you, I'll find out where these things come from and we'll stop it. So, I will go with you." Azuro said, telling them what he is going to do.

"Well hold on there weren't hunting these monsters we are trying to help Jabari and Kirby get home." Elon told him, trying to clarify their goal.

"Yes, I heard you, but it seems that these things are attracted to you and I have a feeling if I follow you, I'll find the source and we can end it and get them home. Kill two birds with one stone." Azuro said.

It was clear that he was not going to take no for an answer, and he wasn't going to back off.

"No! I don't want to kill any birds!" Kirby said.

"He's a mad man!" Terri added.

"That's not what that means Kirby, it means to handle two things at once." Jabari told him.

"So, no birds will get hurt?

"Yes. No birds will get hurt." Elon tells him.

"Well, it's your choice Jabari what do you say?" Blaine said.

"I think it would be a great idea to have him on the team. We'll need all the help we get, and something tells me more of those things will come. It is like they keep coming like someone's sending them to us. And besides the more people, the better chance we have of surviving the next attack." Jabari agreed to let Azuro come.

"Hi, nice to meet you, my name's Kirby."

"It's also nice to meet you, Kirby." Azuro said.

"It amazes me how quickly kids warm up to people." Blaine told Elon.

"And vice-versa see how that guy changed his attitude?" Elon replied.

"Um, Kirby?" Azuro started to say.

"Yes." He replied.

"Your head is still bleeding a little."

He touches his head and looks at his hands and notices the blood. He then turns to his brother and lets out a scream.

"Jabari!" He said while screaming and crying.

"Didn't I tell you to stop moving so much! And Kirby you did a really good job today." Jabari said.

"Really?" Kirby said surprised.

"Yeah, I underestimated your ability to help but you have to understand the only reason I said to stay back is because I didn't want you to get hurt. But you have shown me you can handle yourself, so I'll try to give you more trust in your abilities." Jabari told him.

"Does that mean I can have a sword?" The little brother asks.

"No. Never. Not in a million years."

"Hey, we got the cart ready. Let us go when everyone's ready." Blaine announced.

Elon pulls Azuro to the side to have a talk with him.

"That crest on your hat it's not military. You're a noble man aren't you Azuro?" Elon asks.

"Yeah, why?" Azuro asked.

"Because nobles don't live in villages. Towns, and cities but not villages." Elon said trying to make sense of Azuro's reason for being here.

"Maybe not mine but a friend's. She was hurt badly by that monster and I need to destroy it." Azuro told Elon.

"Elon and Azuro. Come on, we're ready to go." Kirby told them.

"Coming." Both said.

"Elon, wait, I think it's only fair to ask you. Why are you here?" Azuro halted him.

"Let's just say I ran into them, heard their story and I just wanted to help them." Elon replied.

"What took you guys so long?" Terri asks.

"Nothing, just talking." Elon told him.

"What did you think they were talking about?" Galvan asks Blaine.

"Beats me."

As they load into the cart, they make their way to the next stop. Tint Town.

Chapter Six
Book One
Aziza's Will

"Elon, do you have the Atlas? How long until we get there?"
Jabari asked.

"By how fast it is going and the distance from Hue city to Tint Town I would say about four hours before we get there."

"Well since we take time before we Kirby I've been meaning to ask what's earth like?" Terri asked Kirby.

"Well, it's pretty boring compared to your world. No super powered people." Kirby said.

" So, question. Why do you and Jabari have powers?"

"Well, there is only one logical explanation for that." Kirby said.

"Kirby. We. Are. Not. X-Men." Jabari says before Kirby. Could say it.

"You don't know that!" the younger sibling replied.

"Who is X-Men?" Terri asked.

"Basically, like people from here but they're born with their abilities in their DNA. Wait. That gets me thinking, how are you guys able to do what you do?

"Well elemental manipulation can to humans over 1000 years ago. Legends say a rift opened in the sky and sprinkling snowflakes of life came down. And when they came into contact with people it gave an origin. An origin is the source of one ability to manipulate element energy and magic. Some had the ability to manipulate the elements, while others were able to use magic." Azuro explained.

"Wait so Jabari can use multiple elemental magic?" Galvan asked.

"No, I don't think so. I think he can manipulate more than one element." Elon said.
Galvan then interrupts. "Hold on I aint the smartest person in the world but I know for a fact people can only manipulate one element."

"We know that but clearly that's not that case for Jabari and I am assuming Kirby as well. That is why I think until we know what they can do, we go with the story that Jabari can use multiple magic." Elon said.

"Do you think your parents might know something?" Blaine asked.

"My dad might. Maybe he could explain."

"What about your mother?" Elon asked.

"She's not with us anymore. She died when I was seven, 12 years ago. I do not remember that much about her other than what my dad has told me. He talks about every chance he gets." Jabari said.

"She must have been something special to him if he talks about her to this day. I wish mine were like that." Blaine said.

"You mean your parents?" Jabari asked.

"Yeah, but my dad is an adventurer and comes and goes in and out of me and my mom's lives. And when he does come back, he never tells us anything about his adventures. It really makes me angry. That's why when I become a legend, I'll have a story to tell my mom that'll keep her on her toes every second." Blaine said.

"That's a great goal Blaine." Elon said.

Azuro noticed Galvan's look when mothers were being brought up.

"In about 20 minutes I will be there." Pitou answered the embarrassed boy.

Later they arrive in Tint Town and park the cart they stop to pick up supplies and look around.

"Come on Pitou and Terri. Let's go look around." Kirby said, jetting off.

"Hold on. Man, that kid has a ton of energy." Pitou and Terri said.

"Be careful and don't wander off too far. Let's look around and rest then meet back here in an hour. Pitou, go tell Kirby." The big brother told him.

They all agree then all of them branch off to see Tint Town and to look around. Kirby wanders into a pastry shop.

"Oh, wow look sweet, Pitou and Terri come here." Kirby said with a big smile on his face, wide eyes, and a watery mouth with drool.

"Yeah, they look so good. What are you waiting for to buy some."? Terri said with anticipation.

"I wonder what I should get." Said the little boy with excitement.

"Kirby you can't get a lot okay." His brother followed him in the store.

"Just one then Jabari?"

"Fine one but then that's it for you need to cut back ok. Excuse me um..."

As Jabari is about to order the girl behind the cash register turns around, she has long black and natural hair coming down to her hips, tied in a ponytail, dark brown skin with eight brown freckles around her cheeks four on each side, she also has light green eyes, and she speaks.

"How may I help you?" Said the beautiful young woman.

He was caught off guard by her looks, he stares at her with his cheeks turning a little red, and he begins to stutter.

"Uh hi um yeah Ms. Um Aziza"

"Hi, you were about to order." Aziza said giggling.

"Yes, um can we have two of those?" Jabari tried to order.

"Jabari, are you ok you look really compensated right now?" Kirby asks.

"I think you mean constipated Kirby." Pitou corrected him.

"Aw, is someone getting a little hot and bothered? Oh, la la." Terri teased.

"Here you go, you have a nice day and come again."

They leave the shop and Jabari has a dazed look on him from meeting the girl.

"Well, that was just... What's the word I'm looking for? Oh yes, hilarious, you could barely speak without stuttering." Terri teased.

"What's going on? Jabari, you love her. But you barely know her, you can't fall in love with someone you barely know. Who does that?" Kirby questioned and stated.

"Kirby I'm not in love with her, she's very pretty and seems nice but I don't love her. Come on, let's go look around somewhere else."

The scene cuts to the bar where Blaine and Galvan are having a drink and talking, then Elon and Azuro walk in and sit next to them. Azuro looks at Galvan and remembers how strange he was acting on the ride here and Elon wondering what Blaine meant by what he said on the way here.

"So, what was wrong?" Elon asks the buzz pyromancer.

"When?" He replied with his whole speech slurred.

"When we're talking earlier when we were on the road you said 'She must have been something special for him to leave that position. I can't imagine doing something like that.' What did you mean by that?" Elon asks.

"Have I told you guys about my dad?" Blaine asks.

"No not really, you mention that he was in the army. Do you want to talk about it?"

"Well, he's in the army, actually one of the highest-ranking generals people call him the 'Earth Scorcher'. He loved fighting for his nation more than anything. Even my mom couldn't take the fact that he loved being on the frontline more than being with us, so she left and took me with her. I was only seven when we left, I would hear her cry at night sometimes and I would go to comfort her. My goal in life is to achieve my dream but to also have my family by my side while I'm doing it, I'm going to do what my dad never did." Blaine droned on while slurring every other word.

"Blaine, I had no idea. I'm sorry to hear about why your parents split but I'm glad you have no desire to let it happen to you. I hope you achieve your dream and become that legend." Elon told him.

"Thanks, Elon." Blaine said.

"Real men don't share feelings unless they're drunk. That way they don't seem weak." Galvan said with a drunk hiccup then slurred speech.

"How many drinks did you have?" Azuro asks, looking unsurprised but concerned.

"I don't know. What's that number between 9 and 11? Add 5 to that."

"Well, that's enough for me to ask you this. Why were you so defensive early on the ride over here?" Azuro asks the inebriated Galvan.

Galvan started the story "Because when I was younger, I was always thought to treat women with respect by my dad. One day our farm was attacked by bandits. They destroyed all our moms' crops. (Drunk Hiccup) But we still had to pay taxes despite that we didn't have all the money, so when my dad went to ask them for more time, they took the little money we could offer and said they'll let it slide. My dad and I just thought they were being reasonable but later we were told the truth. My mom told my dad that she did "somethings" so they would give us some slack. I can remember the look on my dad's face when she told him."

Galvan continued "I've never seen him so disappointed but the next day he went on like nothing happened, my mom too. Later, that night I overheard them talking. She asked him if he hated her. He said no he still loved her, and he forgave her, he just didn't trust her anymore. (Hiccup) I always wondered how you can love someone but not trust them, there are women who get my attention, but I can't love someone if I can't trust them and if I do love them and they did what my mom did I don't know if I could still love them."

"She only did it to help out the family, it's not like she didn't love your father." Azuro tried to explain and convince him that people who love you do what they can to help make sure you're good.

"It doesn't matter she embarrassed my dad and brought shame upon our family. It's not like I hate women. I still follow my dad's teachings but if the woman I love cheats on me I wouldn't love her after that." The impaired lightning swordsman said.

"Sorry to hear that."

"It's fine I guess, to be honest I don't know who I'm angry at my mom for cheating or my dad for saying he forgave and loved her but still doesn't trust her. To this day I'm still confused." Galvan said to Azuro.

"Well, I hope that never happens to you and that one day it will all make sense to you. And whoever you end up with isn't put in that situation." Azuro said, trying to cheer him up.

"Thanks. Hey, guys do me a favor and carry me to the cart, I don't think I can't walk right." Galvan asks.

"Are you serious? Why did you drink so much to the point you can't walk straight? Get him and let's go look around some more." Blaine said while stumbling.

Meanwhile Jabari and the others walk through the park in the middle of the city. The park is so nice there are so many beautiful flowers of different colors. The tree holds different types of birds and other animals running through the treetops. And a fountain in the middle of the park. It makes all of it seem so enchanted. While they enjoy their time in the park Jabari turns his head and sees the girl from the pastry shop looking scared while holding a brown paper bag out of curiosity, he follows her and right behind him is Kirby. They follow her into an ally where she meets a large intimidating man. He walks towards her and he speaks.

"You got my money little girl?" The man says.

"Only if you got something for your breath. Here it is, Lug , now this is the last payment, you'll leave my family and I alone now." She told him to cover her nose.

Lug takes the money and begins to laugh saying "You'll pay as long as I say so."

"No, we had a deal! I made all the payments and that was it." She shouted.

"I think you need to keep the payments up and be grateful that I don't wreck your parents' shop doll face." Lug tells her.

"We can't keep these payments up or we're going to lose the shop then you won't get any money." She yells at him.

"Did I ask you that?" He replied.

"Why are you doing this? Just go get a job like everyone else! Oh, that's right you probably don't meet the requirements, we all know you're not the brightest." She scolded him.

"Hell, you say?" He said with anger.

He winds up striking her and she balls he fist, and it begins to glow but before either could do anything Jabari steps in and bashes him in the head with the hilt of his sword and punches him in the face.

"What the...?"

"It's you!" Aziza said shocked to see Jabari.

Jabari stands over lug with a menacing look on his face, he walks around to his face and takes his sword, puts it directly in front of lugs face and tells him "If I ever see you bother her or anyone else, I will personally break you in half." Then Lug runs away but warns them that he'll be back.

"You watch yourself punk I'll be back with my boys." Lug said.

"You're the man from early with his little brother. Why? Why did you help me?" Aziza questions Jabari.

"Because he was about to hit you and I couldn't sit by and let it happen. Who was that guy?"

"Lug, he and his gang go around telling people to pay them money for protection from himself. And if not, he was going to hurt them, their families, and their business. And now I think he's going to want more than money when he comes back.

Don't get me wrong I'm very grateful for what you did but I think you made it worse. He's going to be back with more thugs, and I don't think you can fight them all on your own." She explained.

"But that's the thing I'm not on my own. I have friends with me who can help you with your problem." Jabari tells her.

"Wait, you don't mean your brother, dog, and rabbit, do you? I mean I appreciate the optimism."

"No, I have friends who would be glad to help." He reassures her.

Kirby runs over and asks, "Hey again, are you ok?"Aziza responds in a calmed voice telling him she's fine thanks to his brother and tells him he's very lucky to have him. Then she asks him what they are going to do. He tells her that we need to find his friends and plan an attack. While they look for the others Jabari asks about Lug.

"So, where did this guy Lug even come from? He doesn't even look like he's from this town."

"I don't know where Lug came from, but he appeared in town a little over four months ago. Bullying the town folk pushing them around. He collects money for protection for the townspeople from him. People here are on the brink of losing their businesses and their homes because he keeps taking money. But I'm going to make sure he stops, no more paying him, and that's why I have something for him. I've been practicing magical spells in secret, but I know I can't beat him by myself."

Later, after she explains the story of Lug terrorizing the town, they eventually run into the others and explain what's going on at the pastry shop. They all agree to help Aziza fight the thugs and save the town. They devise a plan for the six of them Jabari, Aziza, Elon, Blaine, Galvan, and Azuro to fight the thugs and Kirby, Pitou and Terri will defend her parents and her shop. All six stand outside the pastry shop waiting for Lug. While they're talking, the townspeople board up their homes and shops when word spreads of Lug coming back.

"There's nothing to worry about now that we're here and we would be glad to help with these thugs." Blaine said, assuring her.

"I can't stand when scum like that hurt innocent people, let's teach them a lesson." Elon added.

"See told you they would be happy to help." Jabari said.

"Thank you. I really appreciate all of you coming to my help. We'll finally be able to put an end to Lug." Aziza says with a smile on her face.

"What's wrong with Galvan, Azuro? Why does he look so sad?" Kirby asks.

"He had too much to drink and now he's a little dizzy." Azuro answered.

"What could someone drink so much of that it would make them fall flat on their face?" Kirby asked.

"Um, he drinks the same thing Uncle Tazama drinks when he comes over." Jabari told him.

"Oh, Dizzy Juice but he needs to wake up." Kirby said before yelling in Galvan's ear to wake up.

"Kid! Come on, my head is killing me." He said waking up.

"Then next time stop before you hit 15." Azuro told him with a scolding tone.

"Hey! I was in my emotions." Galvan yelled, giving an excuse for drinking.

"I thought men didn't talk about their emotions." Azuro contradicted what Galvan said to him earlier.

"My dad says to my uncle that when he drinks too much dizzy juice is learned his limits." Kirby tells him.

"Sweetheart we need to leave the store, those hooligans are on their way to destroy it." Aziza's Dad and Mom said with worried looks.

"Don't worry these men are going to help us with that, they are going to stop those thugs right in their place." Aziza said, trying to calm her parents.

"They're here, I can see them coming." Terri said looking outside.

Kirby looks out the window and sees Lug and his gang; there are about fifty of them outside, maybe more. Before Jabari walks out, he tells Kirby.

"Kirby stays here with Aziza's parents and tries to keep the thugs away from the family." Jabari orders Kirby.

"Aye aye you can count on me." He told his older brother.

"Aziza, where are you going?" Her parents ask.

88

"I'm going to fight with them. I've been practicing magic to stop Lug for a while now."

Lug can be heard screaming threats from outside.

"So, you're still here, thought you would have run away but it looks like you stayed to get your ass handed to you." Lug said threateningly.

"So, this is punk huh? This will be quick." Blaine said.

"You're right this will be quick. Get them boys!" Lug said as he ordered his men to charge.

The thugs charge at Jabari and the others, but the thugs stand no chance. We see our heroes beat them back one by one but when you knock down one another take its place. Aziza doesn't hold back and attacks, letting loose a blast of an indigo-colored energy knocking back several men. The boys join in the fight and help her fend off the thugs.

"Wow, they're beating them back like it's nothing." Pitou said.

"Yeah, but there are a lot of them out there hoping they don't tire out." Terri added.

While they were watching the fight unfold some of the thugs were able to sneak in from the back. Kirby reacts quickly by throwing his shield and knocking out 3 of them. Terri takes on two of them by growing his two large ears and grabbing them and slamming them against the floor back and forth. Then he tosses them out and Pitou grows into his Wild fang mode and tackles multiple thugs. All three are doing their best to fight back all the thugs that are getting in.

But then one of the thugs grabs Aziza's mom. She screams, and this causes Kirby's eyes to glow and him to see a woman standing in the field of golden roses. In the vision, the woman turns, and Kirby almost sees her face, but the vision cuts off. Kirby then screams to let her go. But the thug is then blasted by a bolt of bright indigo colored energy.

"Kirby, you and the others get them all in one area."

Kirby, Pitou and Terri throw all the thugs in one pile and Aziza fires a barrage of bullets at the pile of thugs sending them flying through the wall across the town. Everyone's attention is on her as she walks out with her hands growing. She tells Jabari and the others to get back and she forges a mass amount of bullets and fires at the thugs.

She decimates them leaving them unconscious and scared. Lug sees and begins to charge with a giant club, she blasts it out of his hand, leaps over him and as she does, she fires a fury of smaller blast. This knocks him to the ground, and she walks up to him and speaks.

"Listen and listen good Lug. You are going to leave not only my family alone but this whole town. I'm sick of living in fear of one day you'll hurt someone so I'm going to help you leave."

She musters up enough power to blast them all, sending them flying. She then drops to the ground tired. Jabari rushes to her side.

"Hey are you ok?" Jabari asks her.

"I'm good. Thanks." She replies.

"Kissy kissy." Terri teased.

As the dust settles, they help rebuild what was destroyed in the battle. Neighbors come by after the fight to say their thanks and praise Aziza for her help.

"Seems like you didn't need my help after all." Jabari says flattering her.

"Don't flatter me. That was my first fight and I was tired after a couple of attacks. I guess I still need a little training." She says with modesty.

"Well, I guess those guys won't be back for a while." He told her.

"And if they do, we'll be ready. The townsfolk wanted to learn how to defend themselves just in case, so they all decided to learn some magic for defense. But if I need a little help is it okay if I call you and your friends again?" She asks him to blush.

"Yeah, that'll be great, but I don't know what to call it."

"I can help you with that."

They follow her to a store that sells a communication device called a Comtrix.

"It's called a Comtrix. People use this to talk to each other and send messages. I can't believe you don't have one. I could get one for each of your friends." She explained.

"That'll be great thanks." He spoke.

All of them show her their gratitude for the gifts.

"No problem. Here I'll show you how they work. Just speak your name and place your fingerprints on them and your setup.

To add someone let them put their finger so your prints are in contact and there I am." She explained to her new friends.

"Thanks, so I put my thumbs here and you can call me?" He asks.

"Yeah. So, I call you when I need you and you can call me when you need me." She told him.

"Yeah, or when you want to you can." He spoke.

"Thank you. You were amazing to help me in my time of need when you didn't have to. Where are you guys going anyway?" She thanks and asks him with a smile on her face.

"We're going to Tone Town."

"Oh, are you participating in the tournament?"

"I don't know. Didn't even know there was a tournament."

"Yeah, all the strongest fighters gather there to test their strength in a basic tournament style competition. And there is a major reward. You should join, you could win, I know you could.

"Thanks, I'll think about it."

"If you do, I'll be there cheering you on. I wasn't planning on going because of those punks but now that they're gone I can. So, if you do join the tournament I'll be there, sorry I'm keeping your friends waiting."

"It's okay so it was great meeting you Aziza."

"You are too."

As our heroes say their goodbyes, they make their way to Tone Town to where a tournament of fighters is being held and from the shadows, the woman in grey who was watching the whole thing speaks.

"Wow, following these guys has been fun, can't wait to see more of these guys in action."

Book One
Chapter Seven
The Woman in Grey

Our Heroes make their way towards lake Lacata Pitou ask "Hey, does anyone else notice the lady in the grey cloak following us or is it just me?"

"No, you're not the only one I've noticed ever since we left Hue City. I thought it was just a coincidence, but she's been on our trail ever since then I thinks it's time to confront her. You can come out now we all know you're there." Elon told him.

"What? But how?" The woman asks, hiding in the shadows.

"Who are you and why are you following us?" Azuro question.

"Did you know anything about her?" Blaine whispered to Galvan.

"Nope but let's pretend we did." Galvan said.

"So, you knew I was here? Why didn't you say anything before?" She asks.

"Waiting for the right time. Now, who are you?" Elon demands from her.

She steps out the shadow and takes off her cloak to reveal herself. A medium tall dark brown woman with dark black short hair with white bandages wrapped around her arm.

"My name is Cornelia, I've been following you for a while now, about time you notice."

"Why are you following us lady?" Jabari asks.

"I got bored seeing you guys fighting that shadow thing and was curious. So, I started following you from Shaden." Jabari says.

"Shaden? That's not following us, more like stalking us." Pitou says.

"Hey, I'm just your average witch, who got curious about a group of men, a kid, a dog, and a rabbit who were fighting these monsters and I got invested in the story. I wanted to see what happens next." She tells them.

"Witch? But you don't look like a witch. You look nice." Kirby said.

"Oh, really and tell me little boy what witches look like in your world? Oh yes, I also eavesdropped on your conversation so, no need to catch me up. You guys aren't the quietest people just, so you know." She speaks.

"Hold on, what do you mean 'No need to catch you up'?" Elon asks.

"I am coming with you guys. I came here this far and might as well see what happens in the end."

"So, a witch from out of nowhere just decided to follow a group of people out of curiosity. For all, we know you've been the one sending those things after us." Azuro scolds her.

"Sorry sweetie, that's not my style or magic. I use hex and I'll just join your little group so; you won't suspect me of being a creeper" She said.

"Fine by me." Jabari said.

"Hey, you trust this lady. We're just going to let her follow us?" Blaine asks.

"If she wanted to do something, she would have done it by now, I think she is good and besides if she tries something there's more of us then there are of her." Jabari said.

They all make their way to the port for the ship to cross the lake.

"We're back with the tickets." Elon said.

"The boat leaves in twenty minutes so let's all of us make sure we stay together and get on when it comes." Jabari said.

"Kirby, do you trust this lady too?" Terri asks.

"I don't know. Let me try something. Excuse me Cornelia, can I ask you a question?"

"Of course, you can cutie."

"Who's more adorable, Pitou the dog or Terri the rabbit?" Kirby asks the Witch.

"Kirby I must ask you. What is that going to prove?" Pitou asks.

"Well, this is a hard question. But I would have to say the little boy asking the question is the most adorable." She answered.

"She's good with me." Kirby said as he gasped at her answer.

"Really? What would you have done if she would have chosen me or Terri?" Pitou asks.

"I mean even your name sounds cute. Kirby. Your mother must have known you were going to be an adorable little boy." She told him.

Kirby's eyes got wide and bright and a giant smile appeared on his face.

"Hey um Jabari we might have a slight problem. We are all out of money." Blaine tells Jabari wondering what we are going to do next.

"What!? But how?" Jabari asks.

"Well, we did go through three towns, supplies, the cart, and these tickets." Elon explains.

"But we still have the cart, so we should be able to make it far." Azuro says trying to find the bright side.

"Not with these wheels we won't. They are practicing falling off. Considering how fast Pitou runs in his wild fang form I'm surprised it stayed on this long." Blaine says as he examines the cart as one of the wheels falls off.

"Really you all should take better care of your things. How are you going to get the money to buy new ones?" Cornelia asks the group.

"Can you just make money with your magic?" Terri asks Cornelia.

"Don't you think I would if I could? It's illegal for witches to make money with magic. No, I spent it all following you all. What about the Tournament?"

"The tournament? What about it?" Jabari asks.

"Look, there is an award for coming in first 500,000 Hueleon. That's more than enough to buy a new cart." Jabari said with excitement.

"This is great. I've been meaning to fight someone who will give me a real challenge." Blaine said with a grin on his face.

"Not only that if we're all in it will give us a chance to see which out of the five of us is strongest. We'll go against each other, and it will finally give us our chance to fight without any interruptions." Galvan said hoping to go against Blaine.

"I'm lost to see how their only concern is fighting each other and not winning the money for the cart." Azuro comments on their excitement with an unamused tone.

"Yes, even though the last time they tried to fight nearly cost us money and almost decimated a valley." Elon said to Azuro.

"So, it's settled. When we get to Tone Town, we'll enter the tournament and win. Hey, you guys, the boat is about to leave. We should get on board. Come on Kirby." Jabari told everyone and called his brother.

"Coming." He spoke.

They all head towards the boat that resembles an old steamboat and get ready to load as they do. Kirby sees a familiar face in the crowd. It's Yamato! He sees Yamato heading towards the trail around the lake.

"Hey, Yamato over here, the boat is this way. Why is he going that way?" He asks out loud getting off the boat.

"What are Kirby doing? Get back on this boat." Pitou demanded the little boy.

"I'm going to get Yamato, he's going to miss the boat to Tone Town. I'll be right back."

"Hey wait. Pitou talk some sense into your human." Terri told him.

"Kirby, get back here if the boat leaves and you're not on it your brother will have a heart attack. Coming back with one of you will be hard to explain to your dad." Pitou said, trying to convince him but to no avail.

"I'll be back, and he'll be fine."

"Come on let's follow him if he doesn't make it back at least he won't be alone." Pitou said as he jumped off the boat after Kirby.

"I am never having bunnies. Not if they stress me out like this."
Terri said, jumping off the boat following those two.

"Hey, Yamato, wait up, you're going the wrong way! You're
going to miss the boat! Hey, stop. Where did he go? Oh, there
he is." Said Kirby with an optimistic face.

As they walk towards Yamato, they notice he has his back
turned. They hear him muttering to himself soon the muttering
turns into loud arguing with himself.

"Stop it, do you hear me? Stop it! Damnit why won't you stay
down. I'm the one in charge, not you! I refuse to let you even
try to take over" Yamato yelled but one was there but him.

"Who is he talking to? There is no one there." Kirby asks.

"I don't know. Can you see anyone?" Terri said with a scared
look on his face.

"It's clear that he is talking to someone that we just can't see.
You may not feel it but there is a presence here, an evil one."
Pitou said ominously.

As they approach him, they see an ominous dark purplish glow
from Yamato swords and then the glow engulfs his body. Kirby
speaks to them.

"Yamato, are you ok? Who are you talking to? Is it someone we
can't see?"

As they get closer the area gets colder, a chill runs down their
spines. Yamato turns his eyes glowing red and he has black
markings all over body and speaks with a demonic voice that
sends terror into the hearts of the three.

"Hello, little boy. Why are you wandering this trail all by yourself?" Yamato said with a distorted voice and a sinister smile on his face.

Pitou jumps in front of Kirby telling him to get back and stay behind him. Kirby stands there with a terrified expression on his face not believing that this person is the same Yamato as before.

"Oh, a little doggy. Who else?" Yamato asks them.

"Terri? Terri? Where are you?" Kirby asks.

Terri responds from behind the tree with a "Hey. Still here just not to close."

"What are you doing behind the tree Terri?"

"Sorry but that voice and him talking to himself, that's too freaky for me. Besides, you just said there is an evil presence here. When we first met him, he was so calm and nice. What happened?" Terri said, panicking.

"Let's just say he is taking a break. I'm in charge for a while. I'll be happy to take a message." Yamato said still with a demonic voice.

"No thanks um we'll tell him the next time we see him." Kirby said.

"Well, in that case, you can take that message to your grave." Demonic Yamato said as he drew his sword which let loose an evil energy that causes the forest animals to run away.

"Run!" Kirby said, bolting in the opposite direction of the trail.

All three of them make a run for the pathway back to the boat. But Yamato cuts them off by cutting down several trees to block their path. As Yamato is about to strike, Kirby takes his shield and throws it at Yamato's chest, it throws him back, but he gets up right afterwards and charges. Before he slashes down on them Kirby's shield starts to glow and a golden light shines blinding Yamato. After the light shines, the black marks disappear from Yamato's body and he passes out.

"What the heck was that all about? Why did he attack us? Why was he covered in marks?" Terri asks frantically.

"I don't know but whatever you did with your shield it stopped him and made that purple aura disappear. Don't go just yet, Kirby." Pitou said.

"I just want to make sure he's ok, he's not moving."

"He's ok? I'm sorry but was he about to get massacred no we were." Terri said.

They surround Yamato wondering what happened to him. They poke him with sticks, and he begins to wake up. He is dazed and confused and questions where he is.

"What happened? Where am I? Oh, it's you, the little boy from Drawlins and your little dog and rabbit. Your name, it was Kirby wasn't it?" Yamato asks in confusion.

"Yeah. Are you okay? You were acting weird just now." Kirby told Yamato.

"That's putting it mildly. No, I mean that's really putting it mildly." Terri said not satisfied with how Kirby described it.

"What happened? Did he come out? Did he hurt you?" Yamato asks with fear in his voice.

"No, maybe it scares us a little." Kirby responded.

"A little?!" Terri yelled.

They explained to him that he wasn't himself and they could tell that was not him. Embarrassed for not being able to control himself he begs Kirby to forgive him. He accepts his forgiveness with a big smile on his face and tells Yamato not to worry about it. Now that Yamato is all better, Kirby brings up the boat to Tone Town and their participation in the tournament. They all race towards the port but as they do, they see that the boat has already left and is almost halfway across the lake.

"No, we missed it." Kirby said with disappointment in his voice. Yamato apologizes again for causing them trouble and making them miss the boat.

"I'm sorry this is all my fault, if I was just in control for a little bit longer you wouldn't have missed the ferry because of me." Yamato apologized again and asked for forgiveness.

Kirby says it's okay because Yamato was his friend and friends look out for each other.

"It's ok Yamato boats come and go but friends need to look out for each other." Kirby said, trying to cheer Yamato up.

"You consider me a friend?"

"Yeah, and besides there are other ways to get to Tone Town. Terri, can you fly us to the boat like one at a time?" Kirby said, throwing out ideas to get to the boat.

"Yeah, but it would take way too long if I took one at a time. I'd come back for the second person. The boat would have been past the halfway point and I can only flap my ears for so long. Can you swim us across in your wild fang form?" Terri asks Pitou.

"It would take too long. I can run us through the trail. I'm pretty good at my speed. It would take a couple of hours and we would still make it a day before it starts."

"Ok let's go." Kirby said.

Pitou transforms into his wild fang form and Kirby and Terri hop on. Kirby tells Yamato to get on, but he is unsure if he should come, he has caused so much trouble for them already. Kirby reassures him that because they are friends, they help each other and then tells him again to get on.

"Let's go." Pitou said as they all got on, they jet off on the trail, Pitou running as fast as he could to get to the other side of the lake before the tournament started. An hour and a half go by before they make it to the halfway point but by then Pitou is tired.

"Oh, Pitou, are you okay?" Kirby asks. Pitou responds panting, "Yeah, just a little tired. I haven't run that fast in a while." Pushing himself to get to the other side Yamato offers to carry Pitou until he is back at full strength. Pitou then reverts to his smaller form and Yamato carries him in his arms.

"Thanks for carrying him Yamato. Hey, Terri, can you fly to the top of those trees to see how far we are?" Terri soars to the top of the trees and tells them they have passed the halfway point. Kirby asks about the ship and where it is. Terri tells them that the ship hasn't docked yet, they're close but still on the water. Terri says he thinks he can see Kirby's brother on the boat from here. Kirby tells them to let's keep going forward. As they do, Yamato asks about Kirby's older brother.

"Kirby, I didn't know you had a brother." Yamato said.

"Yes. Why?"

"Did you tell him where you were going before you got off the boat?" The swordsman asks the little boy.

"Now that I think about it, I don't think I did, it didn't really cross my mind to tell him where I was going. Probably should have told him that."

Meanwhile on the boat. Jabari is unaware that Kirby is not on the boat. The scene cuts to Galvan throwing the ferry upside down. He groans in pain screaming "Are we there yet?"

"No, almost but no, not yet. Why are you even throwing up?" Azuro asks.

"Because I was hungry, and I saw some food the kitchen staff were offering."

"Hey, where's Kirby, the dog, and rabbit?" Ask Blaine.

"I don't know, I know they were on the ship when we were about to leave. Maybe they're just exploring." Said Elon.

"Wait, I see them on the deck sitting in those chairs." Said Jabari.

But what Jabari doesn't realize is that those were old women who had hats that resemble the top on Kirby and the other's heads.

Now back to Kirby and the others as they make their way through the trail, but Yamato senses an unwanted presence. He tells them to move faster, Kirby asks what's going on, Yamato looks around and tells them that they need to get out of here. Yamato then grabs Kirby by his waist then speeds off down the trail. Springing from the trees a blue shadow begins to chase them. This shadow that runs after them is the same one that pulled Kirby through the door.

"That one right there. That's the one that pulled me through the door! Terri look isn't it?" Kirby said.

"I don't know I'm too busy covering my eyes in fear to look at Kirby." Terri said with a terrified voice."

The monster fires a light blue energy stream and knocks Yamato off his balance, all of them go off flying. Yamato, Pitou and Terri land on solid ground, but Kirby flies off into the air. He then lands on a steep hill and starts rolling down it, the monster leaps into the sky and sees him. The monster then dives down for an attack right before it can do anything the monster is cut down by a man with a bow and arrow. The man has albinism skin and pale blond wavy hair. The man then picks up Kirby off the ground and asks him if he is ok.

"Yes, I'm fine. I've been asked that question a lot."

The man introduces himself as Ivorious, Kirby says thanks for saving him and Ivorious asks Kirby.

"Why is he out here by himself".

Kirby responds that he is not by himself, that he is with his friends, and then points towards the top of the hill. Yamato stands at the top and asks where the monster went.

Pitou asks, "Are you ok, Kirby?"

"Who the hell is this guy next to Kirby." Terri asked.

"Ivorious killed it. I'm fine he saved me before it could hurt me. And his name is Ivorious but that's all I know about him." Kirby explains answering all the questions.

"Thank you for helping him. I really appreciate it." Yamato says to the man.

"No problem, I'm glad to help but if you don't mind me asking, were all of you going to the tournament?" Ivorious asks.

Yamato tells him yes that they are on their way to the Tournament until that monster ambushes us. Pitou tells them that he might have enough energy to run them all the rest of the way.

Kirby cheers with excitement saying, "Now we're going to make it, Pitou transforms, and everyone gets on". Ivorious looks at them all and Kirby asks him if he needs a ride.

"Um, is it safe? There isn't even a saddle." Ivorious said nervously.

"Of course, it's safe. Pitou's the safest form of travel I know." He convinced Ivorious to take the ride.

"Okay." He spoke.

Pitou makes sure all of them have a good grip and he tells them to hold on because they are not stopping. Pitou jets off down the trail faster than before moving so fast he leaves a slip stream behind him. Ivorious asks Kirby "Is this what you consider safe?" And Kirby responds causally with a "Yes. Yes, I do."

Terri says all the bumping from the ride is making him sick and Pitou tells "If you throw up on me, you'll regret it." Pitou speeds start to go up trying to beat the boat to the dock. Pitou is running so fast that Terri almost flies off but is caught by Kirby. He leaves a slip stream so powerful it bends the tree back and within 30 minutes arrive to Tone town tired and used up. Pitou reverts to his smaller form and speaks.

"I think I really over did it this time and I need a day to sleep" Pitou states.

"Shush you rest, and I'll wake you when we find something to eat." Terri says, closing Pitou's eyes.

"We need to get to the port to meet my brother. You two should come meet him and the others. Gosh, I hope he isn't too worried. At least I'll have adult supervision." Kirby said, running to the port with everyone behind him.

Ivorious tries to regain his balance after the ride, saying he can't believe that little boy travels like that and remains unaffected by it. Yamato tells him that it's his first time too and it's not so bad. But this time he doesn't feel so well. Both their faces turn a little green like they're about to throw up, but they swallow it. Meanwhile, the boat begins to dock.

"There's the port, I'm going to get Kirby and the others." Jabari tells the group but in that same moment Elon points out that he thinks he sees Kirby and the others at the port. This causes him to look at the port and see them but is confused. He thought they were over there in the chairs for the whole time.

"What!? But isn't that him sitting over there? How can they be over there at the dock?" He says in disbelief. He runs over to where he thought they were sitting and looks and sees the old women.

"Sorry son, did you say something? I couldn't hear you." The old woman said.

"I guess you left him behind." Said Cornelia and this caused Jabari to freak out in a hilarious way talking about how he is a bad brother.

"I forgot him. I forgot my little brother and didn't even notice? I'm a horrible brother."

Blaine tries to make him feel better by telling him that they all didn't notice so he shouldn't feel too bad. But Elon tells him that doesn't really help. The ferry arrives at the port and Jabari runs off to apologize to his brother.

"Kirby I'm so sorry I forgot you. You must have been so scared, I'm sorry." Jabari apologizes to his brother.

"Don't feel bad I was safe, I had adult supervision." He said pointing at Yamato and Ivorious.

"So, you're not mad at me?" Jabari asked.

Kirby thinks to himself that he shouldn't tell Jabari that he ran off the boat.

"It's ok. I'm fine, thanks to my friends. I'd like to introduce you to Yamato, the guy from before who knew about pandas and my new friend Ivorious. Ivorious saved me from another one of those shadow beasts."

Jabari says, "Thank you both so much for taking care of him." Terri clears his throat to try and get some attention and Jabari says thanks to Terri and Pitou for their hand in it too.

"There is no thanks needed, I owe your brother for saving me earlier. But we must get going if we want to make it in time for registration." Yamato told Jabari's group.

The whole group makes their way to the registration desk. All sign up except for Kirby and Cornelia. They receive the information for the tournament and they stay in the rooms for free for the duration of the Tournament. But from a far Jabari hears a familiar voice calling his name. "Hey Jabari" can be heard from a distance, he turns to see Aziza from the Village before. He smiles as he calls her name Aziza runs then jumps into his arms hugging him.

"It's so good to see you again." Jabari said with a big smile on his face. She replied it's great to see him as well.

"Have you registered? I can't wait to see you win this whole thing. Oh, and I hope you guys do well too." She speaks.

"Now that we're all registered, how about something to eat? It says here that the inn we're staying at has a diner. Would you like to join us, Aziza?" Jabari asks.

"Sure." She replied.

"Yeah, I'm starving. And I was not looking forward to that boat food." Blaine added.

Galvan says "Don't remind me. I can still smell the food before and after I ate it." As he tries to hold back from throwing up. Jabari then asks Yamato and Ivorious to join them for dinner.

"Yes, come on please." Kirby insisted.

Both men agree to join the group for dinner. They all go to check and relax. They get a table big enough for them all and after 45 mins Jabari asks Yamato...

"Yamato, can I ask you a question?" Jabari asks, Yamato says of course and then Jabari continues with his question.

"When my brother met you the first time, he mentioned you knew about pandas. How do you know about them?" He asks Yamato.

He then responds by saying "Yes the Wilva, your brother mentioned how it looked like a dog crossed with a panda."

Jabari then continued with the conversation "Yeah I was wondering where are you from exactly? If you know what a panda is."

"There are a lot of them in Japan where I'm from." Yamato told the group.

With shock Jabari says, "So, you're not from this world either? You're from Japan?"

Yamato then replies with "No I'm not and judging by your expression neither are you. You're shocked that I'm from Japan, I see?"

Surprised by this revelation Jabari goes on to say. "I thought Kirby and I were the only ones. Also yeah. So I guess that means you were a slave taken there."

"Yes I was taken from my home country at a young age, I think 4. I was taken by Spaniards to Japan where I was made a servant to a minor noble family. I worked off my debt by 16 and left on my own to travel the country" Yamato said explaining his story.

"Wait, what's Japan? What's a panda?" Galvan asks in confusion.

Azuro answers by saying, "I'm guessing that Japan is a country in your world?". Then Yamato responds saying yes that Japan is his country.

After encountering this information Elon sums it up by saying "That would explain why Kirby and he knew what a panda was and nobody else."

After getting an answer to his first questions Jabari then goes to ask, "But Yamato if you're from our world how did you get here?"

He answers. "I don't know one minute I'm in my world fighting a dual blade wielding samurai. Then the next minute when we both attacked and the blades collided a portal opens up and pulls me in."

Kirby stares at Yamato with his jaw dropped and says, "Woah that is the most awesome story about being sucked through a portal while fighting someone I ever heard."

"Yes. I had a feeling you and your brother were not of the world. So where are you from?" Yamato asks them.

Jabari tells them "We're from Virginia in the United States." But Yamato looks at him in confusion and asks.

"The United States? I think I heard of such a place before. It's fairly new isn't it?".

"Well no. It's been there for a while, it's called the melting pot of the world." Kirby says.

"I have heard of this place, but I thought people of your color weren't citizens in Virginia. It is one of the territories named in the US. I heard from a friend that savage invaders from Europe came and wiped out most of the indigenous people there." Yamato tells Jabari and Kirby.

"Wait what? Yamato what year was it when you pulled through the portal?" Jabari asks Yamato after being shocked by what he said.

Yamato tells them "It was the time of the Edo era 1665." Both Jabari and Kirby stop and look at Yamato with shock and scream "Whaaat!?"

"1665? As in 1 6 6 5?" Kirby asks to make sure he heard Yamato correctly.

He responded again by saying yes in 1665. "Are you telling me the portal that pulled you here snatch you're from a different era in time?" Jabari asks in massive confusion wondering how this could even be possible.

"Wait, are you not from the same time as me?" Yamato asks.

And Jabari replies with "No. My brother and I are from the year 2017." Then Terri stops the conversation.

"Wait!" Terri yells and Pitou asks, "What wrong?", then Terri starts to count "1 2 3 carry the 2 that are 352 years apart. I just wanted to see if I could do the math."

"But how can a portal pull both of you in from different times to this point of time in our world?" Elon asks after hearing all this information. But to all the information that has come to the surface. Ivorious and Aziza sit in their seats looking entirely lost throughout the whole conversation.

"Wait I'm so confused right now can someone please explain to me what you are all talking about?" Aziza asks, and Ivorious adds with a "Me too."

Jabari explains everything so far to Aziza and Ivorious about what has happened so far.

"I don't know what to say other than wow. I never heard of people from other worlds before." Ivorious replied. Aziza agrees and decides to step outside right quick Jabari follows her worrying how this news has affected her. Aziza walks outside with Jabari following her.

"Aziza. Hold on. Wait." Jabari is trying to catch up to her.

"When were you going to tell me? What about what you said back in my town? You said you would come back and visit but how will you do that?"

"Aziza, I swear I was going to tell you. When I found a way home, I was going to call you and say goodbye. And that sounds way worse than I thought I would."

"So why are you competing in this tournament if you need to get home?" She asks.

"We need money to buy a new cart because the old one has broken wheels. We are going to try and win the money."

"And these monsters that keep attacking you, where did they come from?"

114

"I don't know. They pulled us here, but I don't know why."

"Well, I guess we'll find out together."

"What?"

"I'm still a little upset that you didn't tell me everything from the beginning, but I want to repay you for helping me. It is the least I can do. But promise me something."

"Sure."

"When you get home, back to your world, promise me that if there is a way for you to travel back and forth to this world that you'll come and visit. You know because you're a cool person. And I would like to see you again if I can. And if not call on the Comtrix. Pretty sure it works across worlds maybe."

"I will. I promise."

"Good."

"So, do you want to go back in?"

"Sure."

"But I have a question: why'd you come all the way to see me?"

"Well after the whole Lug situation we beefed up our security and I wanted to see the Tournament to learn new ways to protect my town by observing everyone."

As they walk through the door and everyone has their ear to it. Jabari has an irritated face and says, "Come on guys really!" Blaine tells him "We were worried.". Then Terri says, "No we were not, we were being nosey."

"And hey Ivorious, Aziza keep this between us, you know about me and Kirby being otherwordly." Jabari told both and they both agreed to keep it between them.

Later, everyone is off to their rooms to rest for tomorrow. Kirby shares a room with his brother and is wide awake. He tries to wake him up because he can't sleep.

"Hey Jabari." But Jabari is still sleeping so Kirby calls his name again but still no response. This next time Kirby does a quick little shout "JABARI!"

"Kirby come on I'm trying to sleep and go to bed after everything you did shouldn't you be tired." Jabari tells Kirby while being half awake.

But Kirby questions his brother about the conversation that he had with Aziza "I overheard what you and Aziza were talking about.".

"Overheard or eavesdrop?" Jabari tries to correct his little brother for his actions earlier.

But he responds "You say left I say opposite right. But was what you said true? If there was a way, we could travel from both this world and ours, would you come back and visit?"

"Yeah. Why?" Jabari asks.

"Can I come back too? I really like it here but not enough to live here but to visit. I'm making a lot of friends, the friends we have now are nice and I want to come back after we find a way home. So, can we come back if there's a way back?" Kirby said in a fast pace.

His brother sees how he feels about this new world and everyone here. He tells Kirby. "Of course, we can.". "Yeah. And besides if the door we came through goes nowhere in our world then it must lead back to this world." Kirby says before closing his eyes but is woken up by Jabari and asks to repeat himself.

"Wait what did you say?" Jabari asked Kirby. "The door we came through, it appeared out of nowhere and when I opened it led to nowhere but the wall. I went outside to check but there was no other side to the door. I'm tired goodnight." Jabari looks up to the ceiling thinking to himself not once did he question if his dad knew about the door.

# Book One
## Chapter Eight
### Let the Tournament Begin

The next morning is the day of the Tone Town Tournament. The arena is packed, the crowd is ready for some action, and the fighters are fierce. As the participants get ready Kirby, Aziza, Cornelia, Pitou, and Terri sit in the stands next to the commentator's booth when one of the commentators Torre comes out and asks them for a favor.

"Hey, do the three of you mind coming in here to help me comment that my partner couldn't make?" Said the commentator.

"Um what do you guys say?" Aziza asks Cornelia and Kirby, they both say yes and all three agree to help. Terri and Pitou decide to sit it out and watch. The commentator introduces himself as Torre; he gives them the rundown of being a commentator.

"Come on in. Okay all you need do is give commentary. Got it?" And they all reply, "Got it."

Loud and excited Torre starts the Tournament by speaking into the mic "Ok Hello ladies and gentlemen are ready to see some of the world's best fighters duke it out for the grand prize."

The crowd cheers so loud it rocks the whole stadium. "Today kicks off our semiannual Tone Town Tournament. Today commenting with me are two lovely ladies Aziza and Cornelia, and a kid named Kirby.".

Kirby pulls Torre over and asks, "So all I do is talk?"

"That's right, Dark child. All you do is give a comment or opinion on the fighter."

"I hope you're all ready for fighters of all kinds to show you what they are made of!" Aziza shouted into the mic hyping up the crowd.

"We got fighters from all over from Vermillion all the way to Frostas. Which is befitting because we know that you all have come from all over the world to see this." Cornelia said in a monotone voice, but the crowd doesn't care how she said it because they're still cheering.

Kirby joins in "So cheer your hearts out for your favorite fighters because I know I am."

Torre introduces the first group of fighters. "This fight is sponsored by Giovanni's Water. Purified water so good the gods approve it. When your name is called please step out into the arena. Now Let's Introduce our fighter, since we have twenty-four fighters, we 'll introduce them by countries first from the Vermillion Nation. Self-proclaimed flame swordsman Blaine. The man-beast who was raised in the woods of the Vermillion who survived off his primal instincts Warrick, watch out for those claws' folks. Then the witch of fire, enchanter of flames she is Lizzie. And finally of Vermillion watch out for sticky fingers folks here he is Dion but seriously hide your wallets.". He then tells Kirby to take it from there by reading the paper.

"From the Celadon nation, we have Elon, a pike man with medical training. Emerald Marksman Luroc, then a mage with her pet cat Kelly is Nina. Last up for Celadon is the so-called Bandit of the woods Yaza." After Kirby Aziza introduces the next.

"Now from Cerulean nation Azuro, a saber swordsman of a high aristocratic family, the sapphire dragon knight himself Zeke. The pirate Verkyra, and then some girl power. The gunslinger girl Rachel and her sister Nakeya!!!" She finishes and points at Cornelia. Cornelia looks bored trying to sound excited but goes for it anyway.

"Acacia if you're here make some noise for Swordsman Galvan, Tactician Wallace, Sky pirate Voltnus and Mayla who I'm assuming is a dancer by how she's dressed." She said in a monotone voice but that didn't change the crowd's attitude.

119

Then suddenly Kirby looks at the second person that Cornelia called. Wallace and Kirby jumped.

"Hey, I saw that guy before.", Who Aziza asks, "Wallace. I bumped into him a while back.".

Torre continues "Now from the Ebony nation Ebondre just look at that face folks isn't he just scary looking.". Ebondre looks dead into the Commentators box and glares at Torre and he gets scared, ducks down and screams. "Don't hurt me!".

Aziza comments "Woah who knew that you could make someone squirm with just a look."

Then Cornelia tells Torre "I suggest if you value your life don't say that again.". Kirby makes eye contact with Ebondre and waves his hand and says "Hi!", everyone is surprised and looks towards Ebondre for a reaction. Ebondre then nods his head toward Kirby then walks to the center of the arena.

Torre then gets up from behind the desk. "Well, that was surprising back to the roll call Lex, there's not much on him, he's a real closed off guy.". As Lex's name is called, he looks into the stand to see a white man with ivory hair, yellow eyes, and a sinister smile looks to him and nods his head. Torre continues "From the Ivory nation Ivorious and Lunalana. I don't know much about Ivorious, but I know that Lunalana loves stabbing people with that lance of hers. Man, she sounds crazy."

"Ivorious is cool too, he took out this monster who was trying to snatch me." Kirby said then Torre added "Well I hope he is strong enough to handle the fighters here. Now to introduce everyone else, From Acajou nation Brock! From the Cyan nation, Winn! From the Pewter nation Chrome! Pryce From the Frostas nation! And last up are fighters from places I never heard of Jabari From Virginia. Shyera from Ethiopia, Yamato from Japan, Dia from Brasil and Keyon from Lybell village."

"What? Another person from Japan? And someone from Ethiopia? What's a girl from Ethiopia doing here?" Jabari said with a shocked look on his face.

"I'm assuming that the girl from Ethiopia is from your world too." said Azuro.

"That second girl she's from the same place Yamato is." Blaine said, turning to the group.

Elon adds "Which means she is from Jabari's world too, along with the other girl from Ethiopia."

"Hey Cornelia. How do you think those two girls got here?" Aziza asks Cornelia "I don't know up until now I thought Jabari, Kirby, and Yamato were the only ones." Both ladies look just as stunted as the others.

"These fighters came to show you who's the best and to walk away with that money to prove it." Torre yells in the mic. Kirby tells him he is not really worried about who's going to win because he already knows his brother, or his friends are going to win.

The other fighters look at Jabari and the others, making them targets.

Jabari says thinking to himself "Kirby I love you and I know you're being supportive but don't put a target on my back."

But Blaine has a different approach on the attention "Thanks kid. Now they won't hold back."

"Now that we introduce fighters , let 's get down to business to see who will be in our first match." Torre said ready to begin the tournament.

Everyone turns their heads to the screen; they look at the brackets to see who everyone is fighting. The screen reveals the first match will be Jabari vs Dia.

"That's your brother Kirby?" Aziza told Kirby. "Yep, that's him and he's going to win." He said having no doubt in his brother.

"He's going to have to prove you right in the very first match. The match will begin in one hour. Fighters prepare yourselves." Torre told him.

"Of course, I'd be first." Jabari said with a not so amused tone. Blaine tries to cheer him up by saying that when he wins, he'll be able to fight him.

"Hold on you got to go through me first. Before you can fight him, you have to beat me first." Galvan told both with overwhelming confidence.

"You do know before both of you fight him, you must defeat your first opponents." Said Wallace, the man who Kirby bumped into before in Shaden Town.

"Warrick no go down without a fight. You need to beat Warrick first." The beast man from the Blaine nation said, speaking like the hulk.

"And because of your cockiness I will take joy in beating you then you flame swordsman and then you Jabari." Wallace added. "I didn't even say anything." Jabari said with a confused look.

122

"Hey, Oh, so your friend thinks you'll win without a challenge? That's not really a nice thing to say." Said Dia walking up to Jabari. Dia is a medium tall woman with dark brown skin. She's wearing a dark purple dress with orange and pink accents.. Her hair is in a neat little bun, she has a thick full hourglass figure.

"You are cute, but you know what would make you look cuter?".

"No. What?". Jabari asks the young lady.
Then she answers, "You, on the ground and unconscious."

"Of course what else would be the right choice." Jabari said, throwing his hands up in the air.

Tensions heat up as the others are amped up to fight. The group meets up in the waiting room preparing for their fights.

"She said what?" Said Azuro.

"She said that I would look cuter covered in blood and started laughing like it was nothing then stopped and said see you later. She's crazy." He said pacing back and forth nervously.

"The announcer said she was from Japan. Yamato, is she from your time?" Kirby asks him "I don't recognize her. But from her clothing she looks like she is from my time."

There is a knock on the door, it opens, and a woman walks in. She has naturally nappy white colored hair, dark skin and stands at a medium tall level with a full figure. She has on glistering silver armor and a long sword with a silver handle. "Excuse me. Are you Jabari?" She asks.

"Yes? Aren't you Shyera?" He asked back.

"Yes, I came to warn you not to fight Dia. Drop out of the match, that woman is dangerous."

"What? Don't you think you're overreacting a bit?" Azuro jumped in to say.

"No, this girl is otherworldly." She replied.

"What do you mean?" Jabari asks, wanting her to clarify.

"Do you mean like you?" Yamato asks.

"I saw her when she came to this world a couple of months ago. She was drenched in blood and half naked in her clothes looking like she got into a fight." Shyera told them.

"You saw her come to this world? Like when she fell through a portal?" Jabari asks, wanting to know more.

"Yes. I fell into this world a couple of months before she did. While I was here, I made a friend. She's a chef in her country. While I was there, I made two other friends, they were both sisters. I was with them when we saw her. We were in the fields talking to each other when she came into this world. She is not a normal person the moment she saw us she lunged at us and tried to kill us. She's crazy, she's unhinged, she's deranged, and far too dangerous. And when we got away from her, we ran past a group of bandits and when they came across her she killed them. Drop out." She explains trying to convince Jabari.

"Jabari can't drop out. I talked to the crowd about how great you are, you have to fight, at least try." Kirby said, trying to convince his brother.

"Really Kirby that's what you're worried about? Okay I'm not dropping out." Jabari said.

"Are you listening to me? She is insane, she will kill without hesitation." Shyera said, trying to make sure she got her point across.

"I'll be fine. I'll just keep enough distance between me and her, and besides, we need that money for a new cart." He tells her.

"Fine then but she also throws her fans for long distances so be wary of that. And whatever you do, don't bleed in front of her. It will only make her more vicious when she sees it." She tells her.

"Wait before you go, I need to ask you a question. First when you came through the portal, how did you get pulled through?" Jabari asks dying to know.

"I am originally from Ethiopia. But while traveling to other countries I was captured by colonists and they took me to a foreign land. I was a slave back in Britain, I was tasked to clean the home of my former captor. One day I came across a powerful sword while doing so. I pulled it from its sheath. My captor caught me and tried to punish me for messing with his things, but the sword began to glow, and a massive portal opened and sucked me in. I woke up covered in armor and my hair had turned white."

"Similar to Yamato's story, both of you were just in your own time and a portal just opened."

Elon comes in to tell him his match is about to start, so Jabari gets up and tells the group he'll do his best. His brother tells him he is going to do great and the others also give words of encouragement before his fight.

"Will the fighters please approach the arena for your match?" Torre announced on the intercom. Both Jabari and Dia approach the arena from opposite ends of each other. Dia steps out in a Japanese style dress with her fans concealed.

Torre explains the four main rules. "In the right corner we have Jabari. And on the left we have Dia. Here are the rules: 1. Fight ends when one gives up or is incapacitated or unconscious. 2. Once someone gives up the fight is over. Absolutely no overkill. 3. No killing your opponent. We want to see a fight not a murder. 4. You have limited grounds of the arena to fight, go out of bounds the match is over. Now let the first match of the Tone Town Tournament begin."

The crowd is cheering, the blood is pumping, and the tension is high. Dia pulls out her fans and opens them and strikes a elegant pose. "Hey there, handsome. I see you got a nice sword there. So how many people have you cut down with that?" She said while licking her lips waiting for his answer.

"None I don't kill people. Only monsters." He tells her to beware of the warning given to him by Shyera.

"Oh, come on, don't give me that. Besides monster is an interchangeable term, to a mouse a cat is a monster, to a cat a bear is a monster. It all depends on the person's view. Come on cutie, are you telling me you got that big old sword and haven't hacked someone? I don't believe you but if you haven't killed anyone, I bet if you did, you'd enjoy it." She said with a wicked grin and lifeless eyes.

"No, I don't. What kind of person takes joy in killing?" He asks her.

"I do. Back where I'm from it's required for a pretty lady like me to defend myself but participating in it gives me a rush. Back in my world I killed soldiers, thugs and a plethora of intimidating men. The thing is they never suspected me. Before I came here, I slaughtered an entire gang. And when their blood falls, I can't help shrieking with joy and pleasure. But do you know what really gets me off, I dance in the pools of their blood, surrounded by their bodies, an audience of corpses."

" What do you think, fellow commentators?"

"She is very passionate about fighting or this bitch is just flat out crazy." Cornelia said being honest.

"I think she doesn't know what she's up against, she's going down. You can win this Jabari!" Aziza says cheering on Jabari.

"I thought commentators were supposed to be unbiased." Cornelia said poking fun at Aziza.

"He might be in danger but he'll pull through." Kirby spoke.

"So that's your little brother?"

"Yeah why?"

"He's a little cutie just like his older brother was."

"Why are you talking in the past tense?"

"Because after I'm done with you, your face won't be so pretty."

Dia jumps in the air at an amazing height, takes her fans and throws them at Jabari, he nearly misses them. He thinks he is fine but seconds later cuts appear on his face and arms. Her fans then boomerang back to her.

"Damnit!" He yelled and then said, "That crap actually hurts."
He screams.

"Stings, doesn't it? Don't fall now, it's not over yet!" She said
laughing maniacally.

She goes in for a close-range attack with her fans but Jabari
counters with parries to each one of her strikes with his sword.
Then he goes low and jabs her in the stomach after that she
combos with an elbow in the face causing her nose to bleed.

"Nice attack there, he waited for an opportunity Kirby your
brother doesn't disappoint." Torre said with enthusiasm for
Jabari landing a hit. "I told you. My brother is amazing." Kirby
said but was interrupted by Aziza pointing at Dia "Hey what's
going on with her?" and Cornelia thinks she is having a seizure
on the field.

"Oh my god. There is so much blood. You caused me to bleed
and I have never been so happy. The only person who has been
able to do this is a stupid sword wielding bitch. I'm talking
about you Shyera. Now let the fun begin." She says as her
lifeless eyes become wide open and full of a sinister look.

Dia's eye widens"Let's dance!" She leaps into the air then she
hurls hundreds of dark energy feather constructs from the sky
raining down on him. Jabari uses his sword to fend off some
but, in the end, he is badly wounded by her attack then falls to
the ground lying on his back.

Kirby, Aziza, and Cornelia look from the booth and their
worried statements go into the mic and echo through the arena.
Kirby screams "NO!", Cornelia says "Oh my god.", and Aziza
yells his name in the microphone to get up.

Dia then gets on top of him and says "Poor boy. Does it hurt? Don't worry I'll make it better."

Torre is on the mic asking, "Is Jabari down for the count?"

Kirby jumps up on the mic and tells him "No. He's not! Get up!" and Kirby isn't the only one all his friends cheer him on. Aziza says, "You can win this!", "Yeah screw being unbiased, kick her ass!" Cornelia shouted.

Blaine shouts from the stands "Get up you can't lose, if you lose then I can't fight you!" And Galvan added "Yeah what he said." Then Azuro looks at both men and says in a sarcastic tone, "I'm glad you want our friend to win for the reason of fighting you."

"Your friends are so annoying, they're making me look like a bad guy. I mean I can tell that you like this kind of position that you're in." She said teasing.

"What makes you say that?" He asks.

"I got a feeling most men like being under a woman." She spoke.

'Is that feeling you got in your head?'

She stares at him in confusion then Jabari grabs her by her shoulders and repeatedly head butts her knocking her off. He then takes the back end of his sword and swings against her holster knocking her weapons off. He charges in and swings his sword down on her as she parries it with her fans. He sweeps her legs with the sheath of the sword then follows with a combo of a strike to the neck with his hand, punch to the stomach, and then takes her arm and tries to throw her out of the ring but she plants her feet on the ground right before she's out but struggle to get up.

"Oh, how the tables have turned, Jabari has gotten the upper hand." The commentator Torre announces as the crowd goes wild.

She gets up and starts to speak "What a shame it is, your brother will be all alone with no one to protect him. Because I'm going to make you can even protect yourself. Then maybe I'll have a little chat with your little brother to keep his mind off your life-threatening injuries. But then again he's annoying so I might have to..."

Before she finishes Jabari's, eyes begin to turn white and his voice becomes distorted. "Shut your mouth, don't you ever speak about him." She looks at him with a stun look "What the hell, what's with your voice?" She asks with shock and fear in hers.

As Jabari gets in his stance his cuts start to heal. He radiates a multiple of auras, in this order from head to toe. Red like fire, green like flora, yellow like lightning, blue like water, and white like light. But as everyone focuses on the fight Ebondre, Brock Chrome, Pryce, and Winn notice Blaine, Elon, Galvan, Azuro and Ivorious's eyes are glowing with the corresponding colors of Jabari's aura red, green, yellow, blue, and white.

Then Jabari raises his hand and goes to approach her. She takes her fans and tries to cut his hand off, but they break as he bats them away with his sword, he then touches her on her forehead. She flies back into the wall then falls to the ground incapacitated. At first the crowd is in awe, then cheers start to roar from the crowd.

Kirby, Aziza, and Cornelia jump and shout at the same time "Yes, he did it! He won!" Both Blaine and Galvan said, "I knew he could do it and now I can fight him."

Elon says to Azuro "I'm starting to think the only reason they stuck around this long is just so they can beat Jabari and each other up."

Then Azuro says "That makes the most sense when it comes to them."

"Amazing, insane, and I still can't believe it! He took a beating and came back and took the victory! The winner is Jabari! He will move on to the next round!" Torre announces.

"Man, what just happened and my cuts they're all gone. And I won."

Torre announces to the next fighters "Okay the paramedics will now take Dia to the emergency medical center. Jabari looks fine so, while our janitor cleans the field, the next fighters will prepare and that is Chrome and Lex."

Book One
Chapter Nine
Master's Toy

The group gathers in the waiting room excited about the results of the first match. Kirby is jumping around all excited telling his brother he knew he could do it.

"That was amazing, how did you do that?" a hyper Kirby asks.

"Yeah, you never told us you could use your magic like that." Aziza said.

Still lost in the fight between him and Dia. "I didn't know either. Hey Blaine, Elon, Galvan, Azuro, Ivorious did you guys feel that power too?"

All of them said yes.

Aziza asks Jabari "What are you talking about?"

Then he explains what happened right before the end of the fight "When she talked about Kirby being alone and me not being able to protect him something in me exploded. I could suddenly feel all the intense power within me. Not only that I could feel the presence of all five of you like you were fighting with me somehow. When I black out, I had some sort of out of body experience. I saw my body fight her but then it went black again. I was standing on an obelisk surrounded by ten other ones and the five of you were on them."

"But wait, you said ten. There are only five people you named." Aziza said.

"I know but the others were those guys Ebondre, Chrome, Brock, Winn, and Pryce. I don't know why but they were just there." Jabari told the whole group.

"Maybe we can worry about it later. The next match is about to start, maybe it will take your mind off it." Cornelia said.

All leave the waiting room to see the match but as they did Ebondre hid in the other room where no one noticed him and heard everything. Everyone heads to the stand to watch the match when they sit down, they notice Brock, Winn, and Pryce are sitting next to them and Ebondre walks up and takes a seat close to them. And he stares at Jabari.

Aziza notices Ebondre's glare "Jabari did you do something to that guy?" she asks Jabari wondering why he was getting dagger eyes from Ebondre.

"No, I never even spoke to him. So, I don't know why he's looking at me like that." He told her; she then asks isn't he one of the other people Jabari saw in his vision? He responds, "Yeah along with Winn, Pryce, and Brock over there."

"Well, he's staring at you like you stole something." Terri said, popping out of nowhere.

"What's wrong? Is there a problem?" Blaine asks.

Pitou explains the situation. "Well apparently, Jabari has caught the attention of Ebondre but maybe not in the friendliest way." "Don't worry I got this. Hey, you got a problem pal?" Terri shouts at Ebondre. Pitou tells Terri to control himself and not to call attention to himself.

"If you know what's good for your rabbit, you'll listen to that dog. Shame if you end up in a stew." Ebondre threatens Terri causing Terri to hide behind Jabari and say, "Aw man when I am going to learn to keep my mouth shut." But Galvan gets up and says "Hey, no one threatens the rabbit but us. You got to earn that right."

Ebondre calls him dunder head and tells him to be quiet, this causes Galvan to get up and dare him to say it again but Blaine interferes. He tells Galvan to calm down and not let Ebondre get to him. Then Ebondre tells Galvan to listen to Fire Pit referring to Blaine and this gets under his skin and now both Blaine and Galvan are irritated with Ebondre.

Azuro jumps in "Both of you chill." And Elon agrees with him telling both they are falling for his antagonization. Cornelia says to all of them "Or do we need to remind you that fighting outside the ring can lead to you getting disqualified. Then you won't be able to fight Jabari.". Ivorious adds to her comment "She right don't get kicked out when you haven't even fought in the tournament yet."

"Look we don't want any trouble; we came to participate and watch." Jabari said, trying to calm everyone down and Aziza adds, "Yeah there is no need for hostility." She said with a chuckle trying to lighten the mood.

Ebondre Glares at Jabari. As he does, Kirby walks up in front of Ebondre and gets in his face. Brock, Winn, and Pryce watch and so does everyone else to see what Kirby does. Kirby takes his hand and bops Ebondre on the head and speaks. "Stop being mean to my friends, what you're saying isn't very nice, it's wrong to call people out their names. It's wrong like a fire pit and thunder head. I think you owe them an apology."

Everyone is shocked. "You know what? You're right I shouldn't have called your friends out their names and I apologize for that."

Kirby then says "Good. Sorry for being rough and bopping you on the head but I felt like it was needed. I hope I didn't hit you too hard." He said while rubbing Ebondre 's head where he bopped him. "I'm fine and you were well in the right to stand up for you friends."

Torre's voice can be heard on the intercom "I Hope you're ready for the next match!"

Jabari looks and says, "Hey Kirby I thought you Aziza and Cornelia were commentators."

Cornelia says, "Honestly I got bored with it and left." And Aziza says, "Yeah and besides, he does a great job all on his own." Terri says in a pity voice "Well at least you tried."

Cornelia says clarifying "We didn't fail! We stepped down!" Aziza says, "Yeah we didn't want to interfere with the flow." Kirby says "Meh I'm okay with it. I had fun while it lasted but I rather spectate than commentate."

"Now let are fighters please step into the ring entering from the right we have Chrome. And from the left corner is Lex. Chrome is from the Pewter Nation and Lex is from the Ebony nation."

As both fighters in the arena Chrome walks in with an arrogant smile toting a massive steel Mace. He is wearing a fur demon pelt draped around him exposing his chest then wearing grey combat boots and pants, and he has greyish silver hair. And from the other end we see Lex walks in with a mask that covers his eyes, with purple lens for him to see though, he has armor from head to toe with a black purplish style along with some gold highlights around the armor. He then proceeds to unsheathe his two double edge swords.

"Now you know the rules, let 's begin the match." Torre says.

Chrome "Hey take off the mask I want to see your face when I beat you." He said with an arrogant smile.

"You lack humility, but I will give you a dose of it." Lex says to him as he pulls out both his swords. He then runs at Chrome at full speed hoping to land a direct critical blow. Thinking that it would take a while for him to get a good start up swing but that's not the case.

Chrome screams "You're fast but not enough to get me!" Chrome picks up and swings his Mace with ease. Lex, having to act in the moment, uses both his blades to block it but takes damage when they push up against him as he flies back. The crowd is amazed, despite how heavy it looks he picks it up with little to no effort.

Chrome was fast to throw off the first attack, but Lex keeps coming with attacks from all sides. Lex sees an opening and goes for it and strikes the left side of Chrome, but he takes no damage. Lex retreats in confusion, Chrome explains.

"You're probably wondering why your attack did nothing. We'll see here my pelt it's made from metal and demon scales

136

making it as if it were armor and so are my pants. The only exposed area on me are my arms and chest so if you want to do any damage you got to aim here."

Aziza, looking confused, asks "Why would he give away his secret like that?" Jabari gives his idea of why we would tell him this information "He probably wants to make Lex think he can only be hit in those two areas." His brother Kirby asks "Really?" Jabari goes on to explain "Think about it if Lex thinks the only areas he can hit are his chest and arms then he knows what areas to protect because Lex will go for those areas only. And that could leave Lex open for attacks."

On the battlefield, Lex calls Chrome out on his trick. "How stupid do you think I am to fall for such a simple trick like that? Do you think I'm a moron? I know you only said that because you want me to only go for your arms and chest. I'm not stupid."

Chrome shrugs his shoulders and says, "Well it was worth a try."

Lex looks into the stands directly at the man with the white hair, yellow eyes, and sinister smile, then the man looks down and mouths the words "Finish this". Lex then nods. "He wants me to end this." Lex said out loud, this caused Chrome to look at him in confusion and ask " He? What are you talking about?" Lex looks at him and tells him "You want to be conscious to even understand." The hilts of Lex's swords start to form into skulls, he then forms an V with the swords and slash's a malevolent dark V blast at Chrome. It connects with him and explodes. The crowd gasps!

The crowd watches in awe as the smoke clears. Torre then speaks into his mic "Hey are you still alive? What the...? He is still standing, oh my gods and goddess, how did he survive!"

Lex stands in front of Chrome looking stunned. He was able to block his powerful attack. "How's that impossible?" Chrome tells him why his attack did nothing. "It's one of my special abilities. Once in a while it can absorb a powerful physical attack with my Mace, and I can deal the force back twice as much."

This terrifies Lex and screams "No!" Chrome replies "Yes, this means you lose!" Chrome takes his Mace and smashes the ground; this sends a shockwave of metal pillars shooting out of the ground. Then one strikes Lex in the chest knocking him down. As he does Jabari's eyes start to glow gray, Torre announces that Lex is unconscious, and the winner is Chrome.

Aziza and Kirby both call Jabari's name, shaking him, trying to snap him out of this trance-like state. He wakes up dazed. Blaine asks, "Hey you okay man." Jabari responds that he is fine. Ebondre, Winn, Pryce, and Brock notice this but they say nothing. Torre speaks in his mic, "Give a round of applause for our contestants, medic take Lex, there will be an hour intermission before the next fight."

The group heads to one of the waiting rooms and talks about what happened. Elon asks "Was it another vision? What did you see?" Jabari tells them, "The obelisk I saw is one of them." Azuro states that "When Chrome used that attack your eyes started to glow." Then Cornelia tells him "Clearly there is some sort of connection between you and those others." "But why, Jabari's never met them before." Ivorious pointed out.

At this time Ebondre, Chrome, Pryce, Brock, and Winn burst in. Ebondre just straight up asked Jabari "Alright I had it. What's with you and the eyes huh?" Jabari says "I don't know. It just happens." All five tell them that they heard everything, and they want an explanation. But the group sits there, darting their eyes at each other, thinking how they can explain all this.

138

Ebondre goes up to Jabari and grabs him by his arm and demands an answer, then this causes Blaine to get up and grab Jabari's other arm.

Cornelia tells Ebondre and the others to back off, Aziza tells everyone to calm down so that they can try to explain. Then Terri pulls out a metal pipe and says "The time for talk is over now! Go for the jugular! I'll go for the kneecaps with this.". Pitou with a shocked face asked Terri "Where did you get a crowbar?"

During all the confusion the ten of them Blaine, Elon, Galvan, Azuro, Ebondre, Ivorious, Brock, Winn, Chrome, and Pryce, their eyes glow. In a flash of light everyone who was in the room witnessed the same vision as Jabari does. All together they see three visions, in the first one they see eleven human shaped silhouettes and one silhouette has its back turned to the rest of the ten.

In the second vision ten people stand in front of Jabari and Kirby. In the third vision, they see Jabari standing with his sword on an obelisk with Kirby and his shield and in the vision, they are looking in a mirror, seeing their reflection. Seconds later they wake up.

"Woah what was that?" Kirby said waking up was lost from that vision.

Everyone begins to wake up and tries to figure out what they just saw. Aziza wakes up rubbing her head "My head is killing me and Cornelia you fell on top of me get off." She said trying to push a semi awake Cornelia.

Jabari asks if everyone is okay, they said yes with a groan. Questions fly from everyone in the room, "what was that?", "Why did we see that?", "What does it mean?", and everyone is lost. They are clueless to what just happened, and this angers Ebondre even more, because now he has more questions and wants answers, but no one has one.

"Alright explain yourself now. What were all those visions about? Tell me now!" Ebondre said, grabbing Jabari's shirt demanding a response.

Jabari looks him in the eye and says with a deep voice letting him know he has had it with him. "Look, I don't know why I'm having these visions. I don't know why you guys are there but what I do know is that I can't make them happen on command when you guys touch me."

Ebondre claims that Jabari isn't telling them everything. But he says he's not worried the truth will come out of you eventually. They all sit there thinking "What do you think he meant by that?"

Feedback from the intercom starts and you can hear Torre voice "Will are next fighters please report to the arena."

Cornelia asks, "How long were we out for?"

Pitou's response "Looks like the whole hour."

They all get up and go to the stands, they get to their seats and Ebondre and the others are waiting on them.

Cornelia says, "Look who's waiting. What do you guys want?"

Brock responded with "Nothing but the truth."

"Alright for our next fight we will have Keyon vs Luroc." Torre's voice echoes through the arena. Both fighters' step in on Keyon , a medium-tall black male with short sterling silver

140

hair with black tattoos all around his body carrying a silver long sword. Luroc a black man standing a couple inches shorter than Keyon, carries a bow and arrows.

Torre announces "Are you ready? Fight."

With an overconfident attitude, he says "Prepare to be amazed, the woodsman archer is ready to take home a victory. Sorry you came all this way for nothing pal." Luroc takes three arrows and launches them at Keyon but he grabs them and snaps them in half and knocks Luroc out.

Torre then speaks into the mic, "Well that was over quick, fast and in a hurry. The winner is Keyon." On the ground Keyon picks up Luroc and tells him not to waste his time. Torre then tells the next fighters to come on down and someone to get Luroc.

Galvan says, "Damn that was sad to watch." Azuro agreed saying "Yeah and he bragged so much about himself then lost." "I was rooting for you wannabe green arrow." Kirby shouted, and Terri asked, "Who's that?" And Pitou replies with "I'll tell you later." Torre then tells the next fighter to come down "Here we have Winn vs Dion. "Winn , are you okay?" Speaking into the mic. Winn stumbles on to the arena with a bottle in his hand. He answers with a slurred voice "Yeah I'm awesome, great, someone hold my beer." Torre asks, "Is he really drunk?"

Brock says in an angered voice "Is that dumbass really going out there messed up like that?" Winn stumbles to set his beer down "I'm going to set it right here. Stay beer." Winn bumbles around with his Boomerang. He is a light skinned man with short black hair, wears a long sleeve sky blue armor and matching pants. "Alright, I'm (hiccup) Ready! Let's do this." Dion asks, "Are you serious he shouldn't even be allowed to fight?" Looking towards the commentator booth for an answer

141

Torre opens the official rule book and says there is nothing in the rulebook that says he can't fight while drunk. So, the fight will continue. Dion thinks to himself that he's going to end this fast. "I can't believe I can't showcase my skills because you come out here drunk." As Dion runs towards him Winn takes his Boomerang and jabs Dion in the head, face, and stomach. Dion looks stunned and confused because he doesn't understand how he could be able to attack while being this drunk.

"How did you do that?" Winn tells him "Just because I'm intoxicated doesn't mean I can't fight. When I'm drunk my body is looser, so I can move more like the wind. And if you like that check this out" Dion blurts out "Bull crap, no way alcohol is making you fight better and no I didn't like it, you broke my nose."

Winn takes his Boomerang, pushes a button and opens a large fan on top. He waves it up to launch Dion 30 feet in the air, then jumps up over him then slams him back to the ground by waving the fan again downwards knocking him out. Torre then says, "And at the end of the fourth match Winn is the winner. And is he crying? He won. Why is he crying?" "I knocked over my beer." He said with a crying voice with tears in his eyes.

"We'll get you another beer, just stop crying. Let's move on to the next fighters. Which are Azuro and Zeke." Torre said. As both fighters step out from the corners, Azuro can hear the roars of his friends. Zeke a white man standing the same height as Azuro wearing royal blue drake armor, with the helmet covering his face in the shape of a dragon head. Carrying a large two-pointed lance.

Zeke steps up and says, "Before we begin our match I would like to apologize to your little friend." And Azuro asks "Why?"

Zeke tells him " Because he's expecting you to win and I don't plan on letting that happen."

"Looks like everyone in this tournament is out for us." Ivorious says.

Cornelia tells them "Now you have more motivation to win."

Galvan agrees with Cornelia "Good that means we will have to give it our all out there."

Blaine added, "And I didn't come here for an easy fight anyways."

"Wait I thought you guys entered for the money a new cart." Aziza said.

Terri adds "Now it's about victory, the fight, and the love of battle."

As the match begins, both fighters stand and glare at each other, waiting for the other to strike first. Zeke jets forward towards him and for someone wearing armor he was fast enough to cut Azuro on his arm tearing his sleeve. Azuro says "Shit! You're fast but I'm just as fast." Azuro says that a piece of Zeke's armor falls off and Zeke is shocked but impressed. "Hm. I can see why the boy has the utmost faith in your fighting abilities. But I shouldn't be surprised by the way your friend fought against that Dia girl. This should be fun so don't hold back." Zeke told Azuro and the response saying, "I never planned to."

Zeke hurls his lance at Azuro, he dodges it but when the lance lands it turns into water. Then water returns to Zeke's hands and it reforms the lance. The crowd is in shock, they are amazed because they have never seen such a thing before. Zeke tells Azuro about his weapon "The sea serpent's lance, it was forged from the scales that came from a water serpent. I got this from my father as he did from his and so on from the day it was created." Azuro tells him "I can handle it."

As they look dead in each other's eyes, they scream. Both men run towards each other and collide in the middle of the arena. Pieces of armor and articles of clothing are blasted off. Azuro and Zeke are at a stalemate going back and forth trying to get the best of one another. Blades clash with one sword and one spear, trying to get the upper hand on his opponent. "Don't tell me you're tired already." Zeke said laughing and breathing heavily as his make breaks off. Azuro, laughing and breathing heavily as well, says, "I can do this all day, but I'd rather end this now."

Azuro then takes his middle and index finger and starts to draw in the air, they begin to glow. Then water starts to appear and little jellyfish like creatures start to form from the water, he sends them to attack Zeke. The jellies sting him and paralyze him making him unable to continue. "You are an amazing fighter, but you could use some practice." Azuro tells him. Torre declares Azuro the winner and the crowd cheers after an amazing battle. Azuro walks up to Zeke with a bottle and tells him to drink this but Zeke tells him he can't move.

Azuro pours a serum into Zeke's mouth. "Bleck! It tastes awful. But hey I can move now." Azuro tells Zeke what he just swallowed was a potion that cures the paralysis. Torre says into the mic, "Sportsmanship at its best." Azuro helps Zeke off the field and into the paramedics. Azuro walks up to the group and they congratulate him on his win. But the feeling of celebration left as it came when they saw the next matchup. On the screen, it shows Ivorious Vs Ebondre

"Oh man it just had to be him." Jabari said as sweat dripped down his cheek. Blaine tells Ivorious to go down there and kick his ass. And Galvan tells him to show him what he's made of. As Ivorious walked down the stairs to enter the field he made eye contact with Ebondre. Moments later they both step into the arena, the group is in suspense. Ebondre rolls in with a menacing looking black and purple Scythe. Ivorious pulls his sword with a gold and silver color scheme.

Torre tells them both to come down and to let's begin the next match. It was Ebondre vs. Ivorious and Ebondre still had the same look in his eye from before.

Ebondre tells him "I don't know why you and your little squad are here and I really don't care. I'm going to make an example out of you and maybe your leader will keep out of my head. And if not, I'll teach him myself when I fight him." Ivorious tries to talk to him "Look there is no need to be so hostile. I can explain everything, my friend is just very gifted and sometimes people experience that gift."

Ebondre raises his voice but not in a yelling tone. It's more like a stricter voice "I don't need your explanation, what I need is for you to get your bow and arrow ready." Ivorious says, "I see that your intentions are not just to win." "Damn right. Before it was to win, now it's to completely decimate everyone here including you and your friends."

"I really hope Ivorious wins, I can't stand it sitting here watching some guy who has a problem with me fighting my friends." Jabari says to the group worrying about Ivorious. Aziza tells him to calm down and don't worry, she says Ivorious will be fine reminding him that he and Azuro won their match. She then gives him a smile and Cornelia teases both when she makes a kissy face. "Now give him a kiss!" She said in a funny deep voice causing both the blush.

145

Let the battle begin. Both Ebondre and Ivorious stand at each in silence; you can literally feel the energy from both fighters. As they stand there the crowd sees a deep amount of dark energy swarming around Ebondre and a vast amount of light energy swarming around Ivorious. Both energies start to clash into one another the sound of them crossing each other like the crackle of electricity.

Torre comments "Oh man am I the only one who sees this. This just might be our most entertaining fight yet. I mean just look at those two storms of power emanating from both fighters. It would be better if one of them attacked already." As Torre uttered those words both Ebondre and Ivorious rushed towards each other and collided causing a massive explosion blinding the whole audience.

The crowd's murmurs can be heard throughout the arena "Oh my god. What just happened? Are they alright? This is getting crazy. Where do they find these people? " Jabari and the group stand up from their seats. Looking shocked Jabari's jaw drops "Woah! That was insane." He spoke. "You can say that again." Aziza added. Pitou says "I have never seen such great power clash like this before."

Galvan complains he "I can't see anything through that dust." And Blaine says the same thing. Azuro tells them both to be quiet, he sees something. Elon says, "Me too." It's Ivorious and Ebondre. As the dust settles from the attack, we see Ivorious and Ebondre with their weapons in post attack position. They're on opposite ends of where they started from. Their clothes and armor are torn and tattered. Both men are bruised and battered from the clash but the crowd wonders how they can have so much damage from one interaction with one another.

The crowd is very confused as to why both men have so many scrapes and bruises from one clash. Kirby pulls Jabari's arm telling him, "I saw it." Jabari replies saying, "Me too." Terri asks what they are talking about; he didn't see anything. Aziza tells Terri "No he saw it all that's why he said insane because he saw the whole thing. I only saw a little bit of it." Same here Cornelia said, "I saw parts of it but not all of it." She said with a stun look. "So, fast nobody saw it but us," said Elon. Azuro says he has never seen someone fight like that. Blaine looks at Galvan and tells him "After you and Jabari I'm going to fight that guy and Ivorious."

Terri looks at Pitou and tells him "I'm so lost right now." "Terri in that one second both Ivorious and Ebondre threw not one but twenty strikes at each other." Jabari said.

When the dust finally clears Ivorious falls to the ground defeated. Kirby screams no, and Galvan says, "Oh man". Ebondre walks to Ivorious, pulls him on his shoulder and carries him to the emergency medical tent. As he walks away, he looks directly in the crowd at Jabari.

Aziza looks at Jabari and says, "Jabari, I think he wants you next." He replies, "Well at the rate he's going to!" he replied with anger. Cornelia asks Jabari if he is okay, but he says no. "No, I'm not. This guy has pissed me off. The only reason he went all out on Ivorious is because he wants me. I'm not going to let my friends get hurt because of me."

Blaine tells Jabari that he likes that fire in him and Galvan says, "Hell yeah can't wait for that jerk to get what's coming to him." Kirby says he is going to check on Ivorious and Elon says we should all go.

Torre announces the next match. As the tournament continues, matches go by. They all sit in the room waiting for him to wake

147

up. While they wait the winners of each match have been announced. Ivorious wakes up and he sees everyone here, he asks how long he was out for. Jabari tells him he was out for about five hours and Aziza tells him he missed a couple of matches.

Ivorious drops his jaw repeating "Five Hours!" Galvan tells him he didn't miss much but a couple of matches. Yaza the axe guy vs Voltnus the lightning gun guy winner Yaza. Kirby tells him Brock won against Verica the pirate with his Hammer. The water gun girl Rachel won against Lizzie the fire witch. Aliyah the girl carrying a lightning spear beats the water sister Nakeya. Shyera, the girl who warned us about Dia, beat the chrome mage Nina. Apparently, she can use multiple blades of light to fight with. Pryce that ice guy beat Malina the fan dancing girl all he had to do was make it very cold she didn't wear that much clothing.

Cornelia then tells him the next matches that will begin. The rest matches are set to start in an hour. All that's left is Blaine, Warrick, Galvan, Wallace, Elon, Yamato, Lucinda, and Lunalana. "Really, I was out for that long?" Ivorious asks. Galvan replies "Yeah, it took long enough for them to get to me already." Ivorious begins to chuckle saying "I'm surprised you waited that long. Ow. Wow, guess that Ebondre really is as strong as he looks."

Kirby jumps on his bed and says to Ivorious "You were strong out there too." Jabari agrees with Kirby and adds "He's right most didn't see the whole fight and how fast you both were going." Blaine tells Ivorious he is an amazing fighter and says, "Hey Ivorious, after you get better and back to full strength, let's have a fight."

And everybody goes "Huh?" Galvan pulls Blaine to the side saying, "No fair I was going to ask first!" "Well too bad, you'll have to wait. So, what do you say?" Blaine said establishing that he was going to fight him first when he gets better. Cornelia jumps on both men saying "Really is that all you two can think about? Let the man heal first."

Blaine said, "I said when he's back to full strength." And this caused everyone to laugh.

As everyone is in a humorous mood the door opens and Ebondre walks in and the mood shifts to a tense atmosphere. Aziza jumps up and asks, "What are you doing here?" Ebondre tells everyone to calm down "I just came here to let the fire pit know his match is starting soon." Blaine looked at the clock and said, "Crap he's right I better get going and who are you calling the fire pit?!" Elon tells him to ignore Ebondre and Azuro asks "Is that it?" Ebondre response "No. I came here to apologize for taking my anger out on you because it wasn't for you but for your leader."

Jabari gets up and gets in Ebondre's face and says, "Alright I had enough of this, if you want to fight me ok then fight me! But if you want to fight me you have to win your next match." Bucking up to Jabari and he tells him "Trust me I will. And when it's our turn to fight I won't hold back because I promise you, I will take you down."

Ebondre says he looks forward to it then walks out. Kirby tells Jabari that it was so cool the way he got in his face. Galvan adds "Hell yeah the way you talked to him, that was insane. I like this side of you." Cornelia says she likes it too. "Even though male bravado is kind of annoying, I agree with him that it was pretty awesome." "Um guys should we get to the stands, so we can see the fight." Aziza said, reminding them.

Jabari said she's right, let's go. "What about Ivorious?" Kirby asks but Ivorious tells him, "I'll be fine, go on ahead and I will join you later. I promise." Jabari says, "Okay. If you say so."

As the rest of the group leaves to see the fight, Ivorious gets out of bed after they all leave. He walks towards the mirror in the room, lifts his shirt and sees a long scar across his lower abdomen that was caused by Ebondre. The nurse sewed up the wound, it seems to have closed but leaves a scar he touches it. And groans.

# Book One
# Chapter Ten
# The Flame Swordsman Vs the Flame Beast man and the Lightning Swordsman Vs the Lightning Tactician

Torre announces the next fight "Alright people are you ready for the next match let's welcome the next fighters Blaine the flame swordsman Vs Warrick the blazing beast. Will both fighters please step out."?

Blaine runs out and yells "Finally it's my turn!"

Elon says, "Well he seems very excited." Cornelia says, "That's an understatement."

Blaine then turns to the group in the stands and yells to him "Galvan!"

Then Galvan yelled "What?"

Blaine yells "You better be ready for when we fight! watch and learn!"

Galvan yells back "Don't need to cause I'm still going to kick your ass."

"He's already talking about his next match without finishing his first." Jabari said.

Warrick runs into the arena on all four he slides in on his two feet, his claws scraping the floor leaving marks. Warrick snarls and tells Blaine, "Don't underestimate Warrick. You hear and talk about the next fight but you have not even beat Warrick yet." Blaine looks at him and says, "Oh, sorry man it's just I've been meaning to fight that guy for a long time."

Warrick tells him, "You need to be Warrick 's first flame swordsman. But it won't be easy. Warrick's flaming claws will cut you down." Blaine tells Warrick that he likes his spirit and let's start this. Galvan cheers his friend on telling him he's got this, and the others join along with the cheering.

Warrick runs at Blaine as he swings his sword, Warrick leaps over him, grabs Blaine's shoulders while in the air and toss Blaine to the ground. He gets up then goes into a stance with

151

his sword holding both hands. As he does his sword starts to catch fire and he swings it. And a blade of fireflies from the sword, Warrick then crosses his arms and blocks the fire head on. When he lowers them, Blaine jumps at the chance and swings down with his sword Warrick then uses his claw to catch it.

When he does Blaine then kicks Warrick in the chest sending him flying across the field Warrick then digs his claw into the ground stopping himself from flying out of bounds. He then uses the momentum and flings himself back at Blaine. With his arms out wide, he then swings them down. And from that lets loose three large X shaped long ranged fire attacks. Blaine takes his sword and swings down canceling out the blast but is met with Warrick's claws afterwards. Warrick was able to claw off a piece of Blaine's armor exposing his chest and leaving a visible burning claw mark.

"My claws ability lets me leave burning open flesh wounds. Bleeding causes pain over time, so best to give up." Warrick says as Blaine holds his wounds. "No, that looks really bad." Kirby said. Galvan gets up and yells "Come on you can't lose damnit. We're supposed to fight!" Blaine tells him with a smile on his face. "You think this will stop then? You're wrong beasty. This is nothing!"

Blaine then ignites his sword then presses the flat side on the claw marks on his chest to cauterize the wound. He keeps a straight face the whole time. "You thought this was going to be a cakewalk, didn't you? I'm just getting started." Blaine told Warrick.

Blaine's body becomes engulfed in flames, fire covers him but doesn't burn him. Then using his fire, he then launches himself into the air. All fired up he then swings his sword down hurling a huge fireball towards Warrick. Warrick catches it with his bare hands but then hurls it because it was too powerful. Blaine then runs toward the direction Warrick tosses the fireball and uses his sword to hit it back in his direction. Warrick then extends his arms in front of him and tries to block it. But the momentum of the fireball is too much, and it sends Warrick flying out of the arena and he falls out from exhaustion.

Torre claims Blaine the winner of the match and the crowd cheers. "That's what I'm talking about." Jabari said, jumping up in excitement. Both Aziza and Cornelia jump and cheer "He did it." Elon told them he knew he would win. Galvan's excited because now he'll have to win to fight Blaine now. Azuro says he can't believe he cauterized his own wound in the middle of a fight. Torre, amazed by the match, says, "Amazing, spectacular, I am truly short of words to describe this fight. Taking care of an injury like that during a fight is so awesome."

Blaine then walks to Warrick as he begins to wake up, he reaches out his hand and offers help. Warrick looks at his hand for no more than a second and takes it and they both congratulate each other on a well fought match. Blaine tells Warrick that it was a good fight, he tells him that they need to do it again sometime. and Warrick says, "Warrick would like that." Blaine replies, chuckling , saying, "Blaine would too." then both begin to laugh.

"That's what I like to see folks good ole sportsmanship now time to get started with are next fighters Lucinda vs Lunalana! Lucinda the calm minded individual with the sharp wit and lightning-fast water strikes so watch out for that sword. Then we had Lunalana, the feisty spear woman with an unhealthy urge to stab people." Torre announced.

Lunalana bursts into the scene on to the arena, loud and yelling out Torre's name. "What did you just say?! I'll have you know that it's not an unhealthy urge to want to use your weapon as

153

much as possible. And it's not my fault me and my spear get along so well, we were made for each other."

Lucinda asks, "Can we please get on with this? I would like to win and leave while it's still daylight." The crowd goes "OOOOOH." Lunalana points her spear at Lucinda and says, "You're going to eat those words you bimbo, cause I'm going to shove them down your petite throat." "Bold words from a little girl." She tells Lunalana.

Torre instigates saying, "The smack talk ladies are not necessary but fun for the people. But now it's time to let your fist do the talking. Are you ready?" Lunalana is getting pumped and screams "Let's do this." Lucinda says, "Please you are not ready for this. Little Girl." "I'll show you. I'm starting out full force so be ready."

Lunalana begins to charge for a special already. "I'm shaking in the boots I don't have. Please tell me when you are ready to get serious." Lucinda said unbothered. Lunalana says she's sick and tired of her crap then Lucinda responds with this "Then go to the doctor and take a nap sweetie." Lunalana screams then charges full force at Lucinda. She's going so fast that she can't stop after Lucinda dodges it. She hurtles towards the wall and tunnels straight through it. "Alright I may have missed but your ass is mine." But she is interrupted by Torre. "Um, Lunalana." And she screams "What?" "You're out of bounds so the winner is Lucinda! That was shorter than I expected." Torre told her.

"NO. NO. NO." Lunalana screamed, and Lucinda told her "Yes baby doll you are out. Guess you are strong but I am just going off that move. Bye now." Lunalana lunges at her yelling "Bitch! I'll kill you!" Torre tells her "Calm down Lunalana you have yourself to blame." Lunalana screams and Torre calls security to come and get her. Security comes to escort Lunalana to the exit, but she is not going down without a fight. "Well, she was a very colorful character." Aziza said as Lunalana was dragged off.

"While the security handles her, we will continue with the next two competitors." Torre tells Galvan and Wallace their fight is next. Then asks will both fighters please step forward. Galvan says, "Alright I'll see you guys after I win." Cornelia tells him, "Hey you do know your opponent is right behind you." "It matters that I refuse to lose to this Neanderthal." Wallace scolded Galvan. "I have no idea what that is but I'm pretty sure that's an insult and I want to tolerate it. Get ready to have your ass handed to you with four eyes." Galvan told him. "If that's what you think, so be it, but I will give you a dose of reality and humility." He said, staring daggers.

Both Galvan and Wallace step into the arena and prepare for their fight. As they do, a hawk with a brown, and yellow feather pattern flies into the arena and lands on Wallace's shoulder. Galvan said, "Hey what's the big idea? Shoot the bird away so it doesn't interfere with the fight." Wallace says, "This is no ordinary bird, this is my trusted hawk Xerxes. He has always been by my side through thick and thin and by my side, he shall stay. I already had a talk with the officials and they said it was perfectly fine." Torre agreed, "It's true the bird is okay." Galvan tells him, "Okay but don't get mad if I hit him." "Trust me you won't." and with that, he commands Xerxes attack.

The hawk jets towards Galvan and tries to get in his face with his talons. Galvan flails trying to get the bird out of his face. "Get out of my face you overgrown chicken." Blaine tells Galvan to look out. Wallace runs up to Galvan and points his finger at him as lightning comes from the sky and strikes on top of Galvan's head. Wallace tells him, "See shouldn't count your chickens before they hatch. This battle is mine, you never really stood a chance." Galvan asks him, "Are you done talking yet?" Wallace stands there curious, "But how? How are you still standing? I hit you with a direct attack of lightning on your head."

Galvan tells him "You have literally no idea who you are up against do you? I stood in the rain with my sword and let the lightning strike me on purpose and for training. And sometimes just for the fun of it. Now if you're done warming up let's get serious!" Galvan's entire body starts to generate lightning. He takes his sword and then starts spinning it in his hand like a fan. He does it so fast that he starts hovering in the air then comes over and strikes the field. The blast sent debris all over, creating dust clouds. As the dust settles the crowd sees Galvan but Wallace is nowhere to be found.

Kirby says he doesn't see that guy Wallace anywhere! Terri yells "Dang Galvan you didn't have to kill him." Pitou says, "I do believe this is grounds for disqualification." Azuro says frantically "Really, you're worried about his status in the competition?!" Aziza said she had no idea Galvan was so brutal. Jabari says there is no way he's dead, then asks if he is. Blaine asks, "Is it weird I still want to fight him?" Elon looks at him and says, "Are you kidding me? No way you're fighting him."

Galvan starts looking through the rubble, "Oh crap I didn't kill him, did I? I didn't mean to; I swear it was an accident." Azuro tells Galvan to calm down and look up. Galvan looks above and sees Wallace being carried by his hawk Xerxes flying over his head. Galvan, looking stumped, asked Wallace, "How is that bird carrying him?" Wallace tells him, "Like I said Xerxes has helped me in more ways than you could ever imagine now Xerxes dive."

They dive toward him. Wallace takes his middle and index finger from both hands and generates power. Then collect them at his fingertips. He fires at Galvan knees trying to cripple him, but he is only able to dodge one. The second bolt gets him

156

on his leg, paralyzing him. Unable to move fast enough Wallace fires multiple bolts at him but Galvan deflects them with his sword.

Wallace taunts him "Come on where's all that talk from before? Or is that all you are just talking about? Do you know what they call me where I'm from? I am the Lightning Tactician. There is nothing I can't plan for even when it comes to a moron like you. There is nothing you can do that I won't have a plan for." Galvan starts to chuckle and ends up laughing at Wallace "You really think you can plan for something like me. You think calling me a moron is going to stop me or diminish my confidence you're wrong. All that does is encourage me to prove those people wrong. When I do the look on their face when they see an idiot triumph over them is the best feeling in the world. And you know what I can't wait to see your face."

Galvan gets up despite his knee not moving, he then jumps up and grabs a hold on to Wallace.

"I realize something each time you attack, the farther you are the stronger the attack, but the first time you got close you used a lot of power. You did it to see what I could handle so you kept your distance. But let's see how powerful it is when I'm squeezing you" Galvan said, figuring out his strategy. Wallace says, "Let me go." Galvan says, "Sure after this."

Galvan uses his body to force Wallace and Xerxes to the ground. Then he takes his sword and sends a power blast of lightning to the ground. Wallace takes it head on, but Galvan takes both his hands and claps. This sends a powerful thunder sound wave knocking Wallace out of bound.

Galvan tells him, "You may think you can make a plan for anything, but you will never plan for a reckless idiot like me with thunderclap to send you flying." Torre claims Galvan the winner and Wallace lies on the ground and says, "How is this possible?" "Hey, don't look so down. You know what you can do?" Galvan asks. Wallace looks at him and asks, "And what is that?" He tells Wallace, "Get up and smile because that was a good fight." Galvan grabs Wallace's arm and pulls him up and flashes a smile in his face. And Wallace shows one back.

Kirby says that this is the best day ever and he can't wait to see the last fight. He asks, "Who is it again?" Elon tells him, and Yamato tells me. Kirby mentions that they haven't seen him since the beginning of the tournament. Yamato tells them that he was just lying down. Aziza asks, "For the whole first part of the tournament?" Yamato says, "I just had a mild headache but I'm ready. Are you Elon?" Elon tells him, "Ready as I'll ever be." Torre says, "Now let's get to the final match of the first round, Elon Vs. Yamato."

## Book One
## Chapter Eleven
## Inner Demons

Both Elon and Yamato step on the field when they do there is an eerie silence. Then without warning, Elon raises his pike and Yamato takes out one of his swords. Both men jump in headfirst into battle. They are so fast the crowd barely sees them; all they can spot is the flash from the weapons clashing.

Kirby feels a disturbing presence, Aziza asks, "What's wrong?" Kirby says something doesn't feel right with Elon and Yamato. Aziza asks, "Is it because your friends are fighting each other?" Kirby says, "No it's not that." He looks at them and he starts breathing hard and Jabari asks what's going on. She tells him "Kirby, he says something's wrong." Jabari asks, "Kirby what is it?" Kirby, looking frightened, tells them, "There's just something not right."

Kirby was right more than he could have imagined. After the first 7 minutes both Yamato and Elon stop both are tired but not from fighting. Both were huffing and puffing, then Elon fell to his knees and screamed in agony. Blaine gets up and says, what the hell is wrong with Elon and Galvan says he wasn't even hit. Then Yamato falls to his knees and screams.

Cornelia, looking confused, looks at the others and asks, "Why are they screaming?" Jabari looks at Kirby and asks, "Kirby is this what you meant?" Kirby starts to sniffle, and whimper and

Jabari tells Kirby to look at him and tell him what's wrong. Kirby tells them all he feels something coming from both Elon and Yamato.

Both suddenly stop screaming. Then the eeriness from the battle blankets the entire stadium. A teal green aura and markings appear around Elon and a black and purple aura surrounds Yamato as well as marks on his body. In a deep distorted voice Elon and Yamato speak.

Yamato in the same demonic voice from before "My, for a second I thought I was the only one here. It seems you too have bonded with a human and to think I thought I would never see another demon weapon." Blaine being so confused he asked questions one after another, "What did he say? Demon Weapon? Bonded?"

Kirby with a scared look on his face says, "Yamato voice, it's the same as it was from before." "This isn't good if he's anything like before Elon is in trouble." Pitou said but Terri points out that there is something not right with Elon. Elon responded in a distorted voice, "I am nothing like you. You are a monster!"

Yamato gives a wicked smile and says, "You think you're any different from me? What's the difference from what we both are doing? Absolutely nothing." Elon replies, "I will end you Muramasa, prepare to vanish from this realm." Yamato unsheathes his sword "I would like to see you try Floracion."

Torre over the intercom says, "Okay I am officially freaking out why did their voices change. And why are they calling each other different names? What's going on? They're acting strange!" Kirby says, "It's just like before!" Blaine says, "Before? Before what? Kirby tells us." Kirby tells them what happened with Yamato and Aziza tells everyone to look at the field.

160

Aziza points towards Elon and Yamato, the aura around both starts to clash. Then they start going full on beast mode attacking each other, with each attack they destroy parts of the battlefield. Elon catches Yamato off guard then beats him relentlessly then slams him to the ground with the edge of his pike. It sends a shock wave through the whole field and the crowd starts to panic and evacuate the stadium.

This was getting out of hand; they were out of control and Kirby jumps up and says they need to stop this. But Jabari tells him it's too dangerous and tells him to stay back. Kirby yells, "No! They're my friends too!" Jabari then tells Terri and Pitou to get him out here. Terri grabs Kirby's back and picks him up and flies off.

Jabari tells Aziza and Cornelia to make sure people get out of here, but Aziza asks him what about him. Jabari tells her, Blaine and he will stay and try to break up the fight. Galvan and Azuro try to get some people out of the danger zone.

Kirby whines to put him down, but Terri tells, "I don't think so. Your brother told us to get you out of here."

Kirby says, "I need to help stop this."

Pitou tries to talk some sense into Kirby, "Don't you think your brother wants that too. He wants to stop this fight and save both Elon and Yamato. He wants to because he knows how much they mean to you, to him, and to the whole group."

Kirby tells them, "I can help. Elon was the first person who saved me when I came here so I want to do the same thing. I saved Yamato before, so maybe I can do it again to Yamato and Elon."

Terri and Pitou stop, they look at each other and think about what Kirby said. They let him go and Kirby runs off. Pitou looks at Terri and says, "Jabari's going to kill us." and Terri replies, "I know."

Jabari and Blaine get down to the field, he looks to Blaine and asks how to stop them. Ebondre steps in and says, "Simple we take them out." Ebondre said, walking towards them. Jabari gets in his face and tells him, "We are not killing my friends." Ebondre replies, "Your friends are destroying the place, so get your priorities in order." Blaine then runs up and grabs Ebondre's throats and throws him against the wall and says, "If you so much as touch Elon or Yamato I will break your neck!"

Ebondre in a choking voice says, "Get off me." Then Ivorious comes running to the arena and asks what' s going on. Along with Azuro, Galvan, Brock, Chrome, Winn, and Pryce right behind him. Jabari shocked to see him walking asks is he already okay. Ivorious says yes and asks again what's happening. Then Brock asked Jabari, "Why have your friends have gone crazy?"

Chrome corrects him "No they haven't gone crazy. They are being possessed by the demons of the weapons." Everyone looks at him and asks him to clarify. Chrome tells them that Muramasa and Floracion are demon weapons. He says he can feel the demonic energy leaking from their weapons. Jabari asked, "So what do you recommend we do?" Chrome tells them to knock the weapons out of their hands.

Winn tells them they will gladly help, and Pryce adds that they promise not to hurt them. Ebondre says, "You don't speak for me." "I swear to god if you hurt them." Blaine threatens him. Then Ebondre snaps at him and says, "You'll what?" And Blaine tightens his grip and tells him "Try it and you'll see." Jabari tells them enough! "We don't need to be fighting amongst ourselves, we need to save them, come on."

Meanwhile, Aziza and Cornelia meet up with Terri and Pitou as they run out of the stadium. Aziza notices that Kirby is not with them. "Pitou! Terri! Where's Kirby?" She asked frantically. Terri told them he's going to save Elon and Yamato. Cornelia asks how Pitou tells them he did it once before, so he thinks he can do it again. Terri adds that he made a very convincing argument. The girls run back to warn the others of Kirby's plan. Jabari plans out what to do with Elon and Yamato.

"Okay Blaine, Galvan, Azuro, Ivorious, and I will try to disarm Elon. And Ebondre, Chrome, Brock, Winn, and Pryce will disarm Yamato." Ivorious adds without cutting off their arms looking at Ebondre. They execute their plan and attack Elon and Yamato but after trying them they are overwhelmed by their power.

They try to talk Elon out of his rampage, they tell him, "Elon you need to stop this. Come on this isn't you. Come on, I know you're in there. Please think about what you're doing." Elon glares at them and in the distorted voice says, "Get away from him and stay out of this."

Elon commands a giant branch and knocks them all away. But Blaine dodges it and runs up to Elon, "I need you to snap out of it, come on." He said, trying to reach him. Elon screams for him to leave and Blaine is knocked away. The same thing happens to Ebondre 's group, they are knocked away by Yamato. Ebondre yells, "Dammit. He knocked us all back."

Aziza asks Cornelia, "Don't you know a little about demons, talk some sense to them." Cornelia tells her, "I can sense them but not talk to them. Besides, Floracion and Muramasa are no ordinary demons." He spoke. Winn suggests, "Let's offer them a drink, maybe that will calm them down." Pryce smells his breath, "Don't you dare tell me you're drunk." He scolds him and Winn responds "No."

Jabari's name can be heard from afar, it's Aziza running to him trying to warn him Kirby is still in the stadium. Jabari thinks, to himself dammit he never listens to me. While running towards danger Kirby tries to figure out a plan to save his friends. "Okay, I can do this, just like before, just show them my shield like last time. All I need to do is show them." Kirby said to himself.

Jabari sees him and scolds him from afar, "Kirby! What the hell do you think you're doing?" Kirby replies, "Saving my friends." Jabari tells him to get back here, it's too dangerous. Kirby yells no and Jabari says "Damn!" and says he is going after him.

Blaine sees some large debris and says, look out. Brock forms an earth wall to stop the flying debris. This is making it unable to move any further. But not for Kirby who uses his shield to block it. Ebondre tells Jabari, "Not to dump on you but you are horrible at keeping him out of trouble." Jabari tells Ebondre to shut up and ask Brock can you make this thing move up.

Brock tells him no it can only be placed in one spot, but I can expand it. Kirby moves forward even though he is pushed back little by little he keeps moving forward into the fray. "Elon! Yamato! Please stop this. You guys are nice people; you need to snap back to yourselves." Kirby screams trying to reach both.

Elon says, "Leave child, this is no place for you." Yamato says with a sinister smile, "No let him stay, I want to see the look on his face when I kill you." "Stop, neither of you are like this. Elon when I first came to this world you saved me from that monster that's the person you are. I want that Elon back please." Elon in his distorted voice tells Kirby, "You will see Elon again after this cut is wiped from existence." Yamato in his demonic voice says, "Took the words right out of mouth."

Both men jump at each other for the finishing blow, but Kirby jumps in the middle and yells stop. Just then a golden light explodes from Kirby's shield shining over Elon and Yamato. Jabari and the others even the rest of the spectators outside the stadium see it. It is so powerful the demonic aura disappears from Elon and Yamato completely. The light fades and Elon and Yamato lie on the ground groaning.

Elon gets up and he starts rubbing his head and he asks, "What happened here?" Yamato says, "I don't know everything is a blur. One minute we're fighting and then I can't remember." Kirby asks "Did it work? Are you back to normal?" Elon sees Kirby bruised and cut up, he crawls to him asking, "Kirby are you hurt?" Yamato asks, "Did we do this?" He says putting his hand on Kirby's shoulder. Kirby smiles saying, "You're back to normal. That's all that matters." With that he falls back to the ground.

Elon says he is confused, and Yamato says, "Same here." Jabari and others are seen running to them, Jabari asks Elon and Yamato if they are okay. Elon tells him "Other than my body being sore and head hurting I feel fine." Yamato tells him there is a little pain in my chest, but he's fine.

Ebondre tells him that he is about to feel a lot more than that. Ebondre takes his scythe and tries to slash Elon but Blaine intercepts him and blocks it. He then slams him into the wall and begins to punch him. Blaine, enraged , yells "I told you what would happen if you tried something I would..." But Jabari grabs him and tells him that he needs to calm down.

Elon looks at the scene unfolding and asks, "What's going on? What did I do?" Ebondre said it's not just him, it's Yamato too.

Yamato looks at Pitou and asks, "He came back, didn't he? Pitou tells him yeah and Yamato says, "This is all my fault." Jabari tells him that they can explain later right now let's get you both to the infirmary.

Jabari and the group take Elon and Yamato to the infirmary. Jabari helps Yamato and Blaine helps Elon. After a while they all sit in the infirmary with them for an explanation.

"Alright, we're all here so you guys want to tell us what was that all about out there?" Jabari said sitting. Blaine asks, "Why were you talking with those voices?" Azuro asks, "Why did you call each other Floracion and Muramasa?" Galvan asked, "What were those marks?" Ivorious tells them one at a time. While everyone wants answers, Terri is off to the side eating their biscuits that came with their lunch. And Pitou asks him if he is seriously eating right now, and Terri tells him that he is very stressed.

Yamato explains everything. "I'll explain, back in Japan I wondered about the country as a Ronin. I had no master, I wondered as I pleased with nothing to hold me back. I did a couple of jobs to earn some money but other than that I was a poor man. I did a job for a man, he wanted me to take care of some bandits who were harassing him. I confronted them and told them to let the man be, but they didn't listen. If I remember correctly there were fifteen of them, they all attacked me at once, but it was uncoordinated. "

"I was easily able to defeat them and to make sure they couldn't hurt anyone ever again I broke all their thumbs. This way they couldn't use swords or other weapons they could hold with their hands. Then after I defeated them the man rewarded me with a sword, the very same one I use now, Muramasa. I really didn't think I needed it because I already had one. When I left

, I came across a small village where there was an old blacksmith's workshop."

"I didn't really pay much attention to it because I was hungry. So, I stopped by to pick up something to eat. A small little shack selling dried meat was next to the blacksmith. The woman who worked there was the wife of the village blacksmith. They had two children, a boy and a girl. They complimented me on my sword and asked if they could hold it, but their mother said no. She was so nice, she offered me the food for free, she said it looked like I haven't eaten in days. Not only was she generous, but the blacksmith also offered to clean my sword, they offered me water and even a horse. "

"I got my stuff together and left thinking how happy they all look. And not just the family, all the villagers looked so happy with their lives, I couldn't help but be a little envious of them. I made it a good distance down the road until I started thinking about the family and turned my head to look back. I saw smoke coming from the village and rushed back there as fast as possible. But when I got there the village was destroyed homes, shops, people were burned to a crisp. And in the blaze, I saw the same group of bandits from before, they had followed me to get revenge."

"They killed everyone and set the place on fire. They were standing on the corpse of the family who helped me, the father, mother, son, and daughter dead. In that moment I felt darkness come over me. I heard a voice coming from the sword that said, "I can feel the anger, the hatred, let me out so we can shed their blood." I asked "who are you? Where are you?" He said not to worry about that then he said, 'Unsheathe me, release me, set me FREEEEEEEE!'"

"So, I did, then I saw blackness all around me and I started to see a little more until the blackness was gone. On the ground were the slain bodies on the bandit's every single last one of them. My whole body was covered in their blood underneath my clothes. I had markings all over. Then I heard the same voice say, "Wonderful now let's move on to the next slaughter fest" I said "No", But the voice said I have no other choice."

"I screamed at the top of my lungs and ran back to the house of the man who gave me the sword. I told him to tell me what this sword is. He could smell the dry blood and he saw the marks on my body. He told me that the sword he gave me was the sword of a demon named Muramasa, whose sole purpose was to kill. The sword could only be drawn by someone in great anger or an unbalanced state of emotions. He said that many had tried to tame it but could not and those people went insane."

"Once you have drawn the sword there is no turning back, this monster, this sword, chose me. Now I must bear the burden of the sword. When I was fighting, Elon Muramasa sensed Floracion. When we were fighting on the battlefield, they overpowered us.

Terri dropped his biscuit with shock. Aziza covers her mouth and says, "Oh my god." Ebondre, being impatient, says, "Finally, you're done, now it's your turn to be a green bean." Blaine turns to him and asks, "Why are you here?" Ebondre tells Blaine that he has just as much right to be here as him. Blaine tells him, "I swear I'm going to bash your head in."

Jabari tells them both to knock it off and tells Elon to explain.

Elon tells them. "It happened five years ago when my parents and I were on vacation at my grandparent's house. Strangers broke in one night and held my grandparents hostage. My father tried to stop them but ended up getting hurt. My mother and I ran and hid in the storage room where I saw Floracion. I heard one of the men coming so I grabbed it to defend myself and my mom. He had found us and came closer and closer until I yelled stay away. Then a vine from the floor shot up and knocked him down. "

"Like Yamato, I heard a voice come from the pike that wanted to help me. So, I took it and went to fight off the rest of the intruders. I ran to where they were, their weapons were out and ready to attack but Floracion told me to stab the floor. When I did, branches grabbed them and tangled them. Later, in the morning my parents told me that he was a demon my ancestor saved by sealing him in the pike. He thought I was in danger, but he knows now that Yamato is a friend."

Terri asks, "So wait he knows we're here?"

Elon tells him Yes.

"Well, that answers all our questions I guess." Jabari said, scratching his head. A knock is heard at the door and Torre walks are. Torre tells them that the stadium is fixed, and Cornelia looks at him and asks, "How?"

Torre tells her that they have several earth mancers who came and fixed it. He then tells them the matches will continue tomorrow. Pitou said with confusion "Will the tournament continue?" Torre answers "YEP" and he tells them to get some rest and leaves.

"He's too pumped after almost dying." Aziza said. "Good, I still plan on winning this. See you tomorrow at the fire pit." Ebondre said. Blaine tells him that he can't wait to beat him down. Torre comes back to tell Elon, "Elon I meant to tell you congratulations on your victory." Elon says, "Wait I won? But after all the damage I caused?" "Yeah, we reviewed the footage, and you were the last one to hit the ground so technically you won." Torre told him, and Elon said okay, unsure of how that even works. Torre says, "Okay bye now."

Kirby asks, "Can you even fight after that?" Elon tells him not to worry, he tells him that he heals faster when he's with Floracion so he should be fine. Kirby asks Elon, "So, he can hear us? Like right now?" Elon tells him yes, "She can hear everything we're saying right now." Kirby then asks if he can say hi and Elon tells him yeah, go ahead and speak.

"Hey, Floracion, I'm Kirby." Kirby asks, "What did she say, can't hear her." Elon tells him, "Don't worry she heard you and she says, 'Hi and it's nice to official meet you.'" Kirby's jaw drops, and Elon tells him, "Actually Kirby it was Floracion who realized you were in trouble and led me to you." Kirby says, "Thanks Floracion." Elon tells Kirby "She said thank you."

Jabari tells everyone that they should get some rest for tomorrow. It's going to be a big day. "Elon, Yamato you guys get some rest, and we'll see you tomorrow." He said as they all left the room except Blaine and he told them he can stay if they want. But they both tell him that's not necessary, "You can go back to the inn I'll be fine." Elon told him. Blaine is pulled by Cornelia telling him they'll be fine and let's go. She then tells Elon and Yamato, "Okay we'll be back to check on you guys first thing in the morning."

As everyone returns to their room at the hotel Jabari lectures Kirby on his actions today. "What is wrong with you? Why don't you ever listen to me? What were you thinking? Don't you understand I'm trying to keep you safe? Do my words go in one ear and out the other? Answer me."

Kirby responds. "Nothing's wrong with me. The only reason I didn't listen to you is because you didn't listen to me. I was trying to tell you, I stopped Yamato once before I could do it

170

again. And duh I know you're trying to keep me safe, but I was trying to tell you what you could have done to stop it but once again you didn't listen to me."

"Look I'm the oldest which means I look after you, I keep you safe, not the other way around. And what do you mean you stopped him before?"

"When I went off the boat."

"Wait, you said you got left behind!"

"Oh, I did say that, didn't I?"

"Look next time, do as I say, when I say it and don't do anything, I didn't tell you to do. Got it?"

Kirby then sticks his tongue out.

"Great comeback. Real mature."

"Fine, how about this? You suck!"

"Watch it!"

Kirby runs out the door.

Jabari runs after him, "Get back here Kirby, right now. I know you hear me."

Kirby replies, "No I can't."

As they run down the hall of the inn Aziza overhears them and asks, "Should we?" Cornelia stops her and tells her, "No this is between brothers, they can handle it themselves." And she replies. "If you say so."

While Kirby runs downstairs towards the mess hall you can hear someone rummaging through the kitchen. Three scruffy looking boys who seem to be a couple of years older than Kirby. Stanley is a little taller than Kirby and has medium-length black hair and bright red eyes with dark circles underneath. Walter, he has white skin with short white hair, sticking upwards on his head. His eyes are blue. August has brown skin, short brown hair and wears glasses and has green eyes.

"Come on Walter, pack as much food as you can." August told him, and Walter replied with a mouth stuffed with food "I'm trying."

Stanley scolds him "Not in your mouth you dummy."

Walter asks, "Then where is Stanley?"

Stanley tells him, "In the bag dummy!" And August shushes them. "Shhhh! I think I hear someone coming." And they duck down.

Jabari yells for Kirby, "Stop running and get back here.

Walter asks, "What is it?"

August looks over and tells them, "I don't know. Looks like someone trying to get ahold of their kid. Holy crap Stanley, Walter look!"

Walter looks and asks, "What are we looking at?"

August tells them, "That kids shield looks at it and it must be worth a fortune. Do you guys know what this means?"

"That kid is using a fortune to defend himself?" Walter told him.

August looks at him with a 'What face'. "What? No? It means if we get our hands on it, we can sell it and live the good life we deserve."

The chef walks in and catches them stealing his food. The chef pulls a knife and says, "HEY, what the hell are you doing? You steal from the Chef? You know what happens when you steal from the chef? You lose your hand!" August, Stanley, and Walter all scream and ask the chef not to cut off their hands. But the chef was not having any of it.

"You think apologizing will make up for you trying to steal my food?" He asks, waving his knife. "Yes." Simple Walter told him, the chef growls, and charges after them. August then yells for them to run!

The three boys run out screaming and Jabari carries a tired-out Kirby back to the room. Azuro peeks his head out the door and asks if everything is okay.

"Everything is fine, he just tired himself out." Jabari tells him. Jabari then asks Azuro if he is a bad brother.

Azuro responds by saying, "I don't think so. He's safe, not a scratch on him, and from what you've told me, you've been keeping him that way ever since you got here."

Jabari then says, "I know but he tried to tell me he could've stopped Yamato and Elon earlier. But I didn't listen because I was trying my best to protect him."

"Of course, you didn't, like you said earlier, you're the oldest which means you protect him. But sometimes it's okay to let it be the other way around."

Jabari looks at him and asks, "Wait. You heard me?" Galvan then pops his head out and says, "We all heard you." Everyone then pops their head out and says yes.

Terri tells him, "We were here in the room the whole time but just didn't say anything.

Pitou then adds, "We thought it would be best if you and Kirby talked it out."

Aziza asks Jabari, "So he just got tired and fell asleep?"

"Yeah, it was kind of strange though. When he ran outside and started to yawn then fell back. Just like that."

Aziza tells him it's best to just put him in the bed. Jabari looks at both Terri and Pitou and tells them that he'll have a talk with them later.

Terri then says, "The kid made a convincing argument."

Pitou tells him that wasn't helping the fact they let him go.

As everyone went to their separate rooms for the night and went to sleep a man was up and wide awake after the events that transpired over the day. And it was the same man that Lex had nodded to when he fought against Chrome. He is in a hotel room, in the dark with a lamp on. He's reviewing the footage from today of Kirby on a device he used to record it. The man with the white hair and bright yellow eyes goes by the name of Alabaster.

Lex walks in and says, "Master Alabaster."

Alabaster turns his head and asks, "What do you want Lex?"

Lex walks in with a tray, "I just wanted to see if you wanted something to eat master."

"No, come look at this Lex. Remember that boy, he caused that light, that light knocked both those two out of their demonic state. Do you know what this means?"

Lex answers, "No master I don't."

"It means that these three, the boy and the two demon weapon users are the perfect test subjects." Lex then tells him that he'll go retrieve them.

Alabaster stops him, "No, you idiot. We can't move on them now; their friends are watching them. Besides seeing the way, they fought whether I or you stand a chance alone."

"So, what do we do?"

Alabaster tells him, "Sit back and wait. But I am quite hungry. Yaku!"

"Yes, sir." He said with a depressed voice.

"Be a good servant and bring me that tray."

Yaku replies with yes master, Yaku has short brown hair and brown eyes, and he wears a black and purple checkered vest over a white shirt and black pants. He has an infamously large white scar that looks like a sword on the center of his face. It is situated in between his eyes, and it curves under his eyebrows and onto his cheeks.

Alabaster tells both, "We'll strike when the time is right Lex and Yaku cause what It's all about timing.

# Book One
# Chapter Twelve
# The Second Round Begins

The next day of the Tournament has begun. The crowd is bustling with even more spectators than before, even after the events yesterday.

Torre gets on the speaker to welcome everyone back. "Welcome back everyone so glad to see so many new faces. I guess words travel fast about what happened yesterday that you had to come and see it for yourself."

Aziza looks around and notices that the stadium is more packed than yesterday. "Wow, people must really want to see something like yesterday."

Cornelia says, "Yeah or have a death wish."

Terri says, "But you have to admit yesterday was entertaining until you know the whole demonic weapon taking over and trying to kill each other."

"I wonder if Elon will have the same problem." Jabari asks himself and Aziza tries to comfort him. "I don't think so. I mean no one else has a demon weapon but him and Yamato."

Cornelia steps in "That we know of. And remember the Floracion attack because he perceived Yamato as a threat. And if Elon goes against someone threatening there is no telling what would happen. But I'm pretty sure they'll be fine."

Pitou also tells them that they need to keep an eye on what someone will do. Referring to Ebondre. "Yeah. He was so determined to take out Elon and Yamato." Terri said.

Aziza thinks out loud "I wonder why Ebondre is like that. I mean sure I understand him being a little suspicious but willing to kill them without hesitation."

Torre on the speaker. "Now let's begin the first match of the second round. Here we have Galvan Vs Shyera." Both fighters step on to the field, but Galvan raises his hand. "Wait, I have a problem with this." Galvan tries to tell Torre and he asks, "What's the problem?" Galvan tells him with a blushing red face, feeling embarrassed, "I don't feel right hitting a woman."

"Aww. How cute he's embarrassed." Aziza said.

"Wow, didn't see that coming." Cornelia said surprised.

Azuro said thinking out loud. "Never thought about how he would approach a woman especially after the story he told us about his mother."

Shyera looks at him with an excuse me expression on her face. "What? Oh, come on. You shouldn't treat me differently from any other opponent you've faced. I am a warrior, a fighter, and a good one at that. I can hold my own against a man, so you shouldn't hold back."

Galvan tries to tell her his reason. "Looks it's not that I think you can't handle me, I mean I saw a fight in your last match. It ended quickly but what I saw was amazing. You took your opponent down like it was nothing, but I just don't think I can hit a girl."

Shyera tells him, "No Buts! If you think I'm an amazing fighter then don't disrespect me or yourself by denying you and I from this fight."

Torre through the speaker "Oh what a twist. Galvan, one of our most amped fighters, has a soft spot for the ladies."

Galvan is trying to get past it but can't. "No, I can't do it. I need to fight someone else."

Shyera throws her hands in the air then comes up with an idea. "Fine then, you want to fight a man, okay then. Pretend I'm a boy."

"What?"

Shyera takes her long white hair and wraps it around her lip forming a mustache and deepens her voice. Shyera tells him, "Pretend I'm a boy and fight me, this way it will feel like you're fighting a man."

179

Jabari says this should be interesting. Galvan gets hyped up and yells "If you think it will work. Let's do this!" Azuro puts his hand over his face in disbelief that this is happening. Torre then says, "Well if everything is settled let the first match begin."

Shyera takes two of her blades and rockets towards Galvan, she then tries to cross her blades and cut him down, but he narrowly escapes. "You hesitated!" Shyera said, keeping her voice and Galvan tells her, "Look, I'm trying to get used to it." Shyera then asks him, "Is it the breast because I don't think I can cover these up, so you are just going to have to deal with it."

Jabari said, "He seems good at first, but I think he still can't get around the fact that she is a girl." "Maybe it is the breast, some men have them, but they are just too big to hide." Aziza said. Cornelia shakes her head and says, "This is weird even by our standards."

"Come on and fight me already." she said in a deep voice.

Shyera pulls a blade out of light and now wields three of them. She holds two in her hands and the third one hovers above her. The blade that hovers follows the movement of the sword in her hand. She swings all of them Galvan doesn't hesitate this time and intercepts it.

He then grabs her and tosses her in the air, then gathers lightning in his hands then shoots it at her with full force. She summons a fourth blade and uses all four to block it. She then

180

crashes to the ground and speaks. "Finally, you're not holding back anymore. Now that you're getting serious, I won't hold back." Then Galvan teases her "You were holding back?" and Shyera responds "Hey don't mock me after I did you a favor!"

The two continue to fight, not holding back. Shyera then throws her four swords in the air and summons three more. One falls from the sky; she catches it and the other six come down. She holds one in her hand in a parry position and the other swords hover in a parry position.

Shyera then lunges at Galvan and winds her sword and all seven line up then she swings down. But Galvan takes his sword and can block all. She then takes all seven of them and forms a big blade of light. She aims and shoots a blast of light at him; it hits him in the middle of his chest. He takes damage but the side effect from getting hit with her sword is temporary blindness.

"How do you like my dazzlers affected when hit with a direct attack that could cause temporary blindness?" Galvan tells her "I don't like it. How can I fight and win if I can't see?" Shyera replies by saying "Wow, looks like your confidence is back. Besides the whole you not being able to see, sounds like a 'your problem.' And at first, you didn't want to fight me because you said it wouldn't feel right. So how is losing going to make you feel?"

"Okay I'll admit at first I didn't want to fight you. I didn't want to be that guy who won by beating up a girl. But now I don't want to be the blind guy who gets his ass kicked." Galvan said, swinging his sword to feel where he was. She tells him "Look I know you are much more capable than that. You are strong and that's okay when you're in a match to win. Think, if I was a killer would you not fight and defeat me to save your life?"

Galvan agreed with her, "Yeah I guess that makes sense." "So, are you still bothered by the fact that you're fighting a girl?" He turns her way still blind "Not as much as before." Shyera then says, "Good now I can finish this fight knowing I won on my strength."

Shyera then takes her seven blades and prepares to strike. But Galvan takes his sword, holds it longs ways and defends himself against her attack. Galvan smiles, "Hey I just figured something we both have in common." and Shyera asks "What's that?" "We're both really optimistic about winning and underestimating our opponents."

Shyera looks at him wondering what he's talking about. "Unless you notice, I have the upper hand, I have more weapons. You only have one weapon and you're using it to defend, and you're blind. Don't you think you should know when you're beaten?"

Galvan yells "I never know when I'm beaten!" Shyera looks at him, "What does that even mean? I don't know how to respond to that." Galvan's smile grows bigger, "What I'm saying is that knowing when you're beat means you accept defeat. That's when you run out of options, but I haven't." She gives him a chance to surrender. "How do you plan to get out of this? Just surrender already before I hurt you." Azuro in the crowd shakes his head "Big mistake telling him to get up."

Galvan takes his sword and strikes the ground sending a shock wave through it. This causes her to jump up and land on the ground. Because of this Galvan now knows where she is, and rushes at her. He knocks Shyera's sword out of her hand, this causes her to lose control of the other six.

He then wraps his arms around her and summons a lightning bolt. The strike is so powerful it stuns her making her unable to fight. "Oh, now who knows when they're beaten? Wait I don't think that makes sense" unable to speak she grunts. He then remembers that being paralyzed means she can't speak. The winner is Galvan, and the crowd goes wild.

Kirby jumps up and down "Yay he did." he said with a giant. Aziza jumps up and gives him a round of applause for his amazing win while he was blind. Jabari cheers for his friend congratulating him for his victory. "Awesome nice job Galvan!" Blaine says, "Yeah that's what I'm talking about buddy!"

"Impressive don't you think?" Elon asks Yamato to walk up to them in the stands. Blaine gets up and hugs both, "You guys are okay." and Kirby does the same and Cornelia tells them both to let them breathe.

Pitou looks at Azuro and asks what's wrong, and Azuro tells them "You know he's never going to stop bragging about it." Pitou pauses for a moment and says, "Yeah you're probably right." Yamato says that Galvan is very persistent even when the odds are against him. And congratulates him for that. Ivorious then says, "That's something most people wish they had."

Torre hopped in the booth, excited over the win. "What an amazing match at first Galvan was skeptical about fighting a woman. But now blind he emerges victorious after pushing through that skepticism. Let's give him a round of applause."

Galvan is escorted to the stand where his friends are and Shyera is taken to the infirmary where she could recover from the match.

Blaine rushes to him and puts his arm around him, "Come here that was amazing buddy. Even blind you still kick ass." Galvan says with a little cockiness "It's what I do best and I'm the best at what I do."

Elon congratulates him on his second victory. Azuro tells him "Yeah you really amazed us with how you won, while you were blind." Galvan says in the wrong direction towards no one, "I know right, I amazed myself when I actually grabbed her."

Terri whispers to Pitou, "Should we tell him that he is talking to the air?" Pitou tells him no and to let him just have this moment. They all tell him there was no doubt in their minds that he wouldn't win. But Cornelia pops up and says, "I did at first when she blinded. You thought you were done for."

Ivorious tells her, "You know something Cornelia no one can ever say you aren't honest." Galvan says that it's alright and that there is nothing that can be done to bring him down now.

Kirby runs to Galvan and jumps on his back, telling him he was awesome. Galvan tells Kirby, "Thanks kid, glad you enjoyed it. Anything for my number one fan." Azuro to Elon, "Told you he would let this go to his head." And Elon replies "Yeah but he kind of earned it."

Book One
Chapter Thirteen
Tale as Old as Time

"Now let's move on to our next match, which I'm pretty sure will be more entertaining than the last. Here are your next fighters, the flame swordsman Blaine vs the frost mage Pryce. Oh, yeah that's what I'm talking about: classic folks Fire Vs Ice. Will both fighters please approach the arena."?

"You got this." Elon told him as he walked down to the field Galvan says in the wrong direction, still blind from before, tells him to knock them dead. Jabari tells him he'll win hands down and Aziza says, "After you win, we will celebrate." Cornelia stops him, seeming to give words of advice but not really, "Don't set the place on fire, I need my eyebrows."

Pitou interrupts them. "Hey, I know you guys are encouraging him, but you realize Pryce is only a few inches away and heard everything you said." Pryce in a salty voice tells them, "I mean really you talk as if I'm not here and he already won. It's embarrassing and insulting." All of them say, "Whoops." Pryce storms off saying, "Let's just do this."

Torre commentates on the speaker "I hope you're ready for The next match folks we got a special treat. Of course, Blaine was cooler to watch Pryce, on the other hand. Pryce won his match easily last time, all he had to do was make the temperature drop against a girl who was wearing nothing but a crop top, sandals, and skirt. Now let the fight begin."

Blaine tells Pryce, "Hey let's give it our best okay?"

Pryce then says, "You know that would be great. If I didn't hear you talk about winning the match already before it even began."

"Come on, we were just being very optimistic." Blaine said to Pryce.

"Sounds more like you're full of yourself in my opinion." Pryce said, snapping at Blaine.

"I'm not cocky, I'm just an ambitious blaze." Blaine said.

"Allow me to put that blaze out." Pryce said.

Pryce blows his breaths as he does the temperature of the entire arena starts to go down and everyone feels the effect.

Kirby shivered as he said, "It's so cold." Aziza tells him, "It's ice magic. Frost breath. The user can exhale a chilling air from their mouth and lower the temperature around them. But it's more dangerous to be in front of it."

Cornelia asks her, "How do you know this much about Ice magic?" Aziza answers "When I was learning how to use mines, I stumbled upon some old books my parents had. Jabari then states that Blaine should be fine if he uses fire. "I'm not really worried about him as much, I'm worried about us and the audience. Look at them, they're just as cold as us." Jabari said point towards everyone.

Chrome brushes it off, "Please, this is nothing." he said, shaking the cold off. "It's 30 degrees, it's not that cold" but Pitou looks at him and asks, "How can you tell?" But before he could answer, Terri yells at him, "AND WHY ARE YOU NOT WEARING WARMER CLOTHES?" Chrome tells him he's wearing a vest and Terri yells "A VEST DOESN'T COUNT THEY ARE LITERALLY EXPOSING THEIR CHEST AND ARMS! "

Chrome tells him about how he traveled to Frostas, where he learned to tell temperature without looking at a thermostat. They don't have them because they are used to the cold and able to tell the temperature. "I can coat myself in metal and feel the sudden and slow changes in the air thus telling the temperature through the metal. Soon I learned how to do it with just my skin. And I'm not cold because where I'm from we learn to be like steel and not let the weather affect us."

"Yeah, like they said it's nothing." Galvan said, shivering vigorously while trying not to look cold. He is then scolded by Azuro, "YOU'RE TURNING BLUE GO PUT SOMETHING ON YOUR SLEEVES." He wondered what the hell was wrong with him. Galvan tells him not to insist that he can handle it but then changes his mind saying, "I can handle this. No, I can't, I'm going to need a jacket."

Blaine starts laughing and Pryce asks him, "What's so funny?" "I'll admit this is pretty cool! Seriously if I wasn't me, I would probably be in trouble. But what I can do will have your jaw dropping to the ground." Blaine focuses his flames on his sword, fire starts to swirl around it, all the way up to the tip. He then releases a heat wave that raises the temperature.

Aziza starts to fan herself, "Oh gods! It's so hot." "Can these assholes stop with the fire and ice tricks and fight? I didn't come dressed for this man." Cornelia said putting her hair up because of the heat.

A man walks through with water to sell to the spectators, "Get your Giovanni Water. So good the Gods approve it" Jabari gets some for the group he tells Kirby to drink some water. "Here, drink this." Jabari says to his little brother.

Blaine points his sword at Pryce shooting a flamethrower in his direction. Pryce pulls a whip from underneath his robe and cracks it in mid-air; it forms an ice wall that holds it off. Then he follows up with an ice beam. He cracked his whip and it froze while it was straight. Then a beam of ice fires at Blaine trapping his leg and keeps going to freeze his upper body then his head. Blaine is completely frozen in a block of ice. Pryce turns away thinking the match is won.

Pryce begins to walk towards the stands thinking he won, Pryce and Torre are about to call the match. "Well, I guess ice is the victor of the constant fight." Pryce said but then was mistaken. "But if it's constant how can you win?" Blaine asks with only his head not frozen.

Pryce demands he explains how he melted the ice and Blaine says, "Like this." He releases heat from his body, melting the ice and breaking free.

"Hey, can you explain how that whip and your ice manipulation works?" Blaine asks as the ice melts.

"Sure. I can create ice and channel that through the while like how you do fire and heat to your sword. When I crack my whip, it releases that cold energy and spreads it out like how I did with that wall. Also, I can freeze it and focus it in a concentrated way. Like how I froze it and shot my ice beam." Bryce explains.

"Ouu. Now that is cool. No pun intended." Blaine said, amazed by his power. He then takes his sword and swings it sending three blasts of fire one vertical, diagonal, then horizontal. Pryce can dodge the first two and cancel the last one out with his whip, but he still gets burned on his arm. "Damn it." He said getting burned. He then begins to freeze it to ease the pain.

"Sorry pal but that's the risk of fighting me. I don't hold back when fighting strong opponents.".

Blaine runs to Pryce, his hands-on fire which ignites his sword, Pryce then shortens and freezes his whip to be the same length as Blaine sword. He then charges with his whip giving off cold frosty air as both fighters clash with one another. As they do, a burst of fire and ice energy spills from the collision and the spectators feel the effects.

Terri is hopping from one side of the stand to the other "Oh. god, I'm hot, oh my god I'm cold, oh my god I am so conflicted." He said not being able to stand in one place.

Cornelia then says, "God I don't know if I should fan myself or shiver." Elon can be seen holding his mouth closed and then swallowing, Azuro asks him if he is okay and Elon tells him, "I can't stand it when things are too hot or too cold. It makes me physically ill."

They bounce back off each other from the first clash and they keep going. Parts of the arena are frozen or melted, people are sweating and shivering at the same time. The arena is filled with ice while parts are on fire.

Torre is up in the booth in his underclothes while wearing a jacket. "An amazing battle folks. A fight like this you can come out with several burns or frostbite. And not just for the fighters, audience members if you can't handle it please move towards the inside and watch from our indoor screens."

Kirby asks Galvan if he wants to go inside. Galvan says, "Why? I'm fine." he says. "One half of you is a little heated and the other IS BLUE!" Azuro said, scolding him.

Kirby points out an aura of fire and ice forming on the field. A smile can be seen on Blaine's face as he looks and apologizes for underestimating him.

"You're giving me a real run for my money. I mean when you froze me, I didn't think I could win for a moment, but I didn't want to go out like that. It would have been disrespectful to you and me." Pryce looks and says "Hmm. Continue." and Blaine does. "It would have been disrespectful to go out like that after boasting because you deserve a great opponent. Not some guy who talks a lot and doesn't back it up. So, how about we go out with one full on attack, the first one to fall loses."

Pryce grins and tells him, "Fine but don't complain about feeling numb because winter's coming." Both focus their energy Blaine shots out a powerful fire blast and Pryce fires a massive ice beam. When both attacks collide, they are caught in a
stalemate. The crowd murmurs with awe and excitement "Oh my they're evenly matched", "So that means this battle will be over when one gives out or the one overpowers the other."

Kirby asks Jabari if he thinks Blaine will win. "Honestly, I don't know, they're evenly matched, and it could go either way." As they look in suspense the ice beam seems to be weakening. Kirby looks and points out that Pryce is tiring out, so why is

Blaine still firing off so much? "I don't think he knows he's winning." Jabari said. Yelling at the top of their lungs to get his attention that he was about to roast Pryce. Blaine stops just as the flames are about to touch Pryce. Then Pryce falls to the ground.

"Thanks, I didn't think I was overpowering him." Blaine walks over and sees if Pryce's okay. He slaps his face telling him to get up, "Hey buddy you awake?" He asks him and Pryce responds, "Yes I'm awake." Blaine helps him up and gets him to the paramedics. Pryce tells him that he won the classic match, but Blaine reminds him that there is a constant battle between fire and ice.

Torre jumps with excitement in the booth over the match. "The winner is Blaine; amazing, just so amazing certain people never disappoint. Paramedics, please get Pryce and let's get ready for the next match." As the group cheer for their friend's victory August, Stanley, and Walter sit a couple of rows behind them.

Walter looks at August and asks, "Hey August, hey August, hey August, when are we going to steal the shield?" Stanley bops Walter's nose, "Quiet dummy you want them to hear us?" Then August bops Stanley. "Don't hit him. We're going to steal it from Walter but only when he's alone. And we're just stealing the shield, do not hurt the kid. We're thieves, not savages." Stanley eyes Kirby's shield, "Yeah we know. Just think when we get that shield and sell it, we'll be set for life."

Walter with a child-like disposition can't help but bug August, "Hey August." August is still looking at the shield thinking of ways to snatch but responds. "Yes Walter." Walter asks, "Why don't we steal the shield and the sword from the kid already?" August then tells him, "Because I'm sure the older brother and his friends will kill us the moment he realizes we're trying to steal the shield. And besides, we go for what we know we can get away with."

Walter says hey August again and August then says, "Yes Walter." Walter asks him in an innocent tone, "Will we all have our own beds to sleep in? No more sleeping in the streets, under bridges, and alley's?" August then looks at Walter, puts his hand on his shoulder, "Yeah Walter will all have our own beds, no more digging through dumpsters for food, and no more stealing clothes when ours get raggedy and holes in them."

In the row in the very far back Alabaster, Lex, and Yaku can be seen sitting. Alabaster's observing Elon, Yamato, and Kirby. Lex taps Alabaster's shoulder and asks, "Sir, when are we going to take the swordsman and spearman?"

Alabaster looks up from watching them and rolls his eyes, "When the time is right, like I said a hundred times before." He said, slapping the back of Lex's head. Yaku then asks, "Are you still going to get the kid too sir?" "Of course, we are but like I said last time, look at them, they're all one big group of bumbling friends. Don't you think they would take us down if

194

we tried to kidnap them?" He then ends with saying "So like I said, all in time. So right now, we will sit back and wait."

Here is the next match up: Jabari vs Chrome. "I hope you're able to live up to the last fight you had against Dia." Chrome told Jabari. Jabari walks down to the arena, his brother giving him the thumbs ups. When Chrome steps down to the arena he tells Jabari to listen up. "Look, I can tell from your last match that you really haven't gotten used to that sword of yours. But now I'm going to hold back."

"Thanks, I guess. But I think I'm getting better with it. I'm just not using it like you expect." Pitou asks Kirby and Aziza, "Is it me or has Jabari's attitude changed?" "What do you mean?" Aziza asks. Terri is pointing out that Jabari is smiling and looking forward to fighting and getting better with his sword. "I mean he still wants to get you and him home, but I think he is starting to like it here."

Torre announced for the next match to begin. Jabari closes his eyes; he remembers how hard Blaine and Galvan fight in their battles as he does the sword starts to shine with an aura of yellow and red. The sword is covered by a Fire and lightning layer.

With this, there are multiple reactions among the crowd from oohs, aww, and gasps. Jabari has stunned the crowd again with this display of power and Kirby turns to both Elon and Blaine. "It's like before when he was fighting that monster but more focused. He is able to concentrate."

195

Chrome smirks and says, "That's a nice party trick, but you got to do more than light show." Chrome charges at Jabari wielding his Maces and swings it down smashing the ground. Metal spikes start to rise towards him. Jabari just waves his sword horizontally across and the metal is electrified which then shocks Chrome.

This throws him off and as he tries to recover Jabari takes the back end of his sword and strikes Chrome on his side rather than his knee. Chrome lets out a yell and falls to the ground. The sword left a burn mark on his side from the electricity and fire.

"How? How did you learn to do all that? Before all you did was swing the damn thing and block it." He asked Jabari "I learned from watching Blaine and Galvan. Watching them in their fights gave me more tips on how to fight with my sword. My sword is an extension of me, and I need to learn not to just swing it but fight with it. And it's not just them. I learned something from Elon, Azuro, Ivorious, Yamato, and everyone else here in this tournament. So, I should be thanking you for the help."

"Well, I guess it's not just some parlor trick. Now let me teach you something else, my Mace can do so much more. Chrome smashes the ground, and the surface arena starts to turn into steel. Soon after, the top part of the arena is coated in metal. "It's a terrain effect magic. Without using my Mace, I can manipulate the arena and attack from any distance like this."

Using his arms and legs he moves the metal in the field and attacks Jabari. Large metal like ropes with small Maces attached to the end attack Jabari. Jabari dodges most of them but gets hit with a few bruising him. "It doesn't matter where you go, I'll be able to strike you. The only safe place is off the arena."

Torre speaks into the mic "OOOOh he's got Jabari on the run. Now I wonder how he plans on getting out of this one person." Cornelia asks in an unamused voice do you guys think she can still win. Aziza tells her the last match looked harder because she wanted to kill him so this match should be easier.

Jabari takes a firm stand on the field and stabs his sword into the ground. He then lifts himself and does a handstand while balancing the hilt of the sword. He focuses and the sword starts to heat off the metal, the heat then spreads across the field then reaches Chrome's feet. He jumps around because it's too hot. So, he forms a metal tentacle to lift himself up. But Jabari sends lightning through the metal. This forces him out of the ring making Jabari the winner.

Chrome lands on the ground falling back, he gets up and yells "Damn that was a good fight and you said you learned all that from me" Torre interjects himself, "I believe he said that about all the fighters." Aziza put her finger on her chin while looking up, appearing to be thin.

In her mind, she says to herself, "That terrain effect was interesting. I wonder if it only works with metal or all elements.

Would it work with my magic? I wonder what it would look like?" Cornelia notices and thinks "Wondering what she's thinking about. She looks like she's deep in thought and I won't bother her." Terri looks at both girls and thinks, "Wonder what they're thinking about. Who cares if I'm hungry?"

Kirby stands there proud of his big brother and calls him amazing. Jabari walks up and asks how he did that. "I think it just happened when I remembered Blaine and Galvan's fight. It happens once before, with fire and leaves."

Lex asks Alabaster, "Sir, how is it possible for some to use more than one element like that?" He responds, "It's not impossible but unusual. I'll have to keep an eye on that one too. I heard rumors that there are people who can learn more than elemental magic."

Blaine jumps on him cheering "I knew there was a swordsman in you I knew you had it in you." Jabari looked surprised and said "Really " and Blaine told him, "Of course from the moment I saw you. Your style is just different from what I'm used to seeing."

Azuro tells Jabari, "I notice you didn't try to harm him that much." Jabari says, "You're talking about hitting him with the back end and not the bladed edge." "Yeah. When you strike with the back side of your sword you show control. Not too hard that it would have shattered his knee and side but enough to bring him down. That restraint is true swordsmanship." Blaine said, praising him.

Galvan then rushes over, knocking Blaine out the way. "Alright now you and I have to fight Jabari either in this tournament or outside of it." Blaine told him to back off, that he gets the first fight with him. "Who?" Galvan said, getting in his face and Blaine replied "Tell me I met him first, so I will fight him first."

Ivorious says, "The second round isn't even finished yet." Azuro tells Ivorious, "There's no point if they've been wanting to fight him for a while." Elon then tells them "You should know by now how determined these two are."

Blaine tells Jabari to tell Galvan that he is going to fight him first. Before he could answer, Chrome walks up and congratulates him on his win. "Hey man Good job out there, really took me by surprise out there." Jabari then thanked him "Hey thanks, you were really great out there too. The whole turning the field metal and the metal tentacle Maces was cool." "Thanks, I just learned that a couple of weeks ago. I overheard your conversation, have you been a swordsman for long?" Wanting to know more about him.

Jabari tells him not with these kinds, he was using a fencing sword when he took the classes. Aziza asks him about his terrain effect magic. "Let me ask you a question. Is that terrain effect only for metal mancers or all elemental mancers?" Chrome says it can be used for all kinds of magic.

Cornelia asks what kind of terrain effect she would even have. Aziza imagines saying "I don't really know. Maybe a bunch of fairies would appear and help make friends with people." Cornelia says, "Naw. Just kick my ass."

Kirby pulls on Chrome clothes and asks how heavy his Mace is. He is told he doesn't know and asks Kirby if he wants to hold it. But Jabari stops Kirby saying it's too big for him, then Blaine rushes him and asks to fight him after the tournament. "Woah hold on, that's not fair. You can't fight both Jabari and Chrome first." Yamato tells them to let the man rest before you try to fight him. Chrome says, "Don't worry I'll be able to fight both of you after this is over."

Book One
Chapter Fourteen
Water Gun Girl

"Alright lets begin our next match Ebondre Vs Yaza. Oh well this should be over quickly." Torre said, realizing who's fighting. Yaza walks into the arena and Yaza speaks in a German like accent, "Haha yes this will end very quickly because I Yaza will win hands down." Yaza is a woodsman and a hunter from the Celadon nation. He lives in the woods away from society in a log cabin he made.

Ebondre walks down looking irritated, "Let's get this over with." Yaza laughs while saying "Yes let's." Torre says in the mic, "Like Ebondre said let's get this over with, because this is going to be the quickest fight ever." Yaza charges at Ebondre with his axe but Ebondre takes his spear and knocks it out of his hand. Ebondre then uppercuts Yaza and knocks him out cold. The whole crowd looks unmoved because they did not expect much from this.

Torre then says, "Man that was embarrassing to watch. Who's next? Oh, here we have some girl power. The Lightning spear Aliyah Vs Whirlpool pistol Rachel. With amazing names like that this will be way more entertaining folks I promise. Please step forward and someone get that bum out of the arena. Let the 5th match of the second round begin. Aliyah Vs Rachel."

Rachel is a 5.6 redhead with white tan skin wearing a sapphire cowgirl hat, long sleeve blooming white blouse, brown cowgirl vest with a blue trim, and brown cowgirl boots. Aliyah brown haired is a 5.7 girl wearing a pale-yellow, light armor to make it easier to move, it has bright yellow markings on it and pale white combat boots.

Rachel has a southern accent, "You ready for some fun hon?" Aliyah scoffs at her, telling her that they are here to fight, not play games. Rachel asks, "We can't do both Sunshine? How about we get ice cream afterwards?" Aliyah smirks and says, "Sure we'll go for ice cream after I win." Rachel makes a pouty face saying, "Ya so sweet Hun. But my guns go out in a wave of glory." Aliyah tries to correct her, "Don't you mean a blaze of glory?" But she replies, "Nope I mean a wave." Aliyah brushes her comment to the side "Bet you'll run out of bullets before I run out of spear."

Rachel opens with a barrage of bullets Aliyah can deflect with her spear with ease. She feels some little drops of water. She sees that Rachel bullets are just water. Aliyah looks confused when she asks, "Did you really bring water guns to a fight?"

Rachel gasps and clutches her shirt collar and says she is offended. "These are not just water guns; they are high pressure water pistols. I can unleash as much water as I want if there is moisture in the air. Let me give you a demonstration."

Rachel shoots a powerful stream of water at Aliyah but she puts up her spear and deflects to streams with the blade end. The blast goes off into the crowd and hit's Torre in the commentator's booth. "See, I told you that these were more than just water guns. Now let's get crazy." She said the rapid fire increased.

Rachel points her guns in the air then starts shooting bullets after bullets of water in the sky. They start to rain down all over Aliyah causing physical damage. Because when the water falls and hurts like rocks. "Oh yeah, I'm making it rain sugar. How do you like my water guns now sugar?" Aliyah runs around trying to avoid rain drops. "Ow okay. Maybe I underestimated you at first and those are more than just water guns. But now let's add a little lightning to this storm."

Aliyah leaps into the air and hovers for a moment before letting loose a discharge of electricity. Rachel starts shooting in the center of the field and water starts to flood, this flood almost knocks Aliyah out, but she stabs the ground with her spear dispersing the water. Rachel then slaps her guns together and forms a bigger one and fires a hydro pump and knocks Aliyah out of the arena against the wall. As she falls, she spits out water and the field begins to dry.

Aliyah gets up from the ground, she puts her hands on her knees and she coughs up water and groans "Oh god" she said trying to catch her breath. "And that pumpkin is how you win a fight with water guns." And with that, the crowd gives it up for Rachel for her amazing win. She then waves to the crowd thanking them for their applause. "Thank you Thank you" She then pulls up Aliyah and tells her "Hey sweetie you promised ice cream afterwards, so you need to stick to your word and pay."

Torre speaks into the mic without thinking, "Such a bubbly girl I'm glad she won." And Aliyah looks to the booth and yells, "Hey what happened to being non-bias?" Then he tries to correct himself by congratulating her too. "Nice Job Amy." She yelled back, "It's Aliyah!" But she brushes it off and he moves on to the next match.

# Book One
# Chapter Fifteen
# Heaven and Earth

"Sure, now let's move on and Aliyah remembers to buy her some ice cream. Here we have Winn, someone taking that bottle away from Brock. Begin the match when you're ready."

Winn steps in the rings stumbling like before with his speech again slurred. "Hey, can I hold my bottle? I need someone to hold my drink."

Brock looks frustrated with Winn's actions "Don't you dare disrespect me with your foolishness!"

"What are you talking about Kwan?"

"My name is Brock! You'll address me with respect, but I shouldn't expect much from a filthy drunk."

"Hey why are you being so mean, buddy? I don't have a drinking problem. I just like to relax, and this helps me."

"No, the fact that you don't take this seriously and show up drunk is disrespectful. But I will teach you some manners."

"Hey, calm down." Winn said while his speech was still slurred. But then it changes to an intimidating voice. "Just because I'm a little drunk doesn't mean I can't kick the shit out of you."

Winn's tone of voice and demeanor changes from drunk and silly to intimidating and serious. His facial expression changes from a happy smile to a sinister grin.

Torre jumped out of his seat out of shock "Oh my" He said. "Where did this guy come from? Is it just me or did it just get serious?" Torre said, speaking into the mic and Winn answered. "Like a heart attack and now the gloves are off."

Kirby looks confused at this and says, "But neither of them are wearing gloves." Pitou puts his paw over his face and tells Kirby it's a figure of speech. It's uncanny and kind of scary how he got so serious. His attitude changed in that split second.

"Oh, so you can be serious just not sober at the same time?" Brock asked.

"Yeah, it's just that when people talk down to me like they're better than me because I drink. I can't help but get a little angry."

"Well, I can't help but get angry when an intoxicated dumbass doesn't have enough respect to come to a fight sober."

"You know something that reminds you of me when I was younger. Hate the sight of someone drinking all the time whenever you see them. I know how it feels but when I kick your ass, I'm going to have a celebratory drink over your unconscious body."

"Let's hope you don't stumble over."

Winn takes his Boomerang and opens his fans from both ends and starts spinning it. The spinning creates a wind tunnel, and he fires it at Brock. But Brock puts up an earth wall to block the attack but when the wind tunnel hits the wall it is strong enough to leave a crack. Winn then leaps into the air and fans a gust to knock Brock off balance.

It does little to no use, because being of the earth nation they are not so easily moved by the wind. With that plan failing Winn then proceeds to stir up mini twisters but Brock firmly plants his feet in the ground and uses rocks to hold him down preventing him from being moved.

Brock stares with a look of disappointment, thinking for a moment Winn was putting up a challenge. Winn, as nimble and agile as he is, glides in and starts to throw jabs at Brock. But his opponent isn't as slow as the rocks he fights with and is able to catch each one with his bare hand. Winn can land a direct hit to Brock's face, but this doesn't faze him one bit. As Winn continues to punch Brock and the face, Brock asks with an unfazed look.

"Are you done yet? I will admit being an Aeromancer has its advantages but to me those are weak punches. Like your attacks before, it will do no damage to me. I see why you fought that Dion guy the way you did. You use the air because you're physically incapable of fighting with your fist. Well at least against me. Don't get me wrong, your punches are strong on a normal person."

"But trying to blow me out of the ring, uplift me and I let myself get hit just so I can see how weak you are. I can see why most crimes in Cyan involve stealing. No one would ever confront someone."

As Brock continues to talk about Winn and the airmen's crime, Winn is visibly furious.

"SHUT UP! DON'T YOU STAND HERE AND TALK DOWN TO ME LIKE YOU KNOW ME!" He said charging at Brock, Winn lashes out at Brock swinging his fan left and right sending blast after blast of air. Winn begins to tear up with anger as Brock dodges all his attacks. Brock even backhanded one of the air blasts hitting it to the commentator's booth. Torre ducks down and asks in the mic, "Please don't break this, I have to pay for damages."

In the frenzy, Winn can't control himself, Brock gets close and grabs his Boomerang. Then Brock proceeds to encase Winn's hands in rock so he can't attack and throws him out of bounds and walks away.

"Hey let me go! This is not over! Get back here and fight me!" Screamed as Brock kept his head turned away from him.

"With the way you're acting now you don't deserve to fight me. Come back when you have control over and aren't just waving your weapon like an idiot."

"Oh yes. Um, Winn is unable to continue so the winner in Brock!"

Brock looks at Winn, dead in his eyes, "Winn was it? You are truly pathetic."

Jabari looks confused and asks, "Hey, do any of you know what just happened?"

Ivorious explains what happened, "I think I can explain what just happened. You see, Winn is from the Cyan nation also known as the air nation. Airmancer are very agile, light footed, and nimble making them the best for undercover missions and sneaking around. That's why they have the best espionage service out of all other nations."

"But this ability of theirs makes them amazing thieves. There is one city called Cloud city where crime is rampant and no authorities whatsoever. You can't open a business anywhere in the city because you'll get robbed and your business will go under. The city was so bad that the city's council built a wall around it. Then used tight air currents to keep people from flying over it and out of it."

"Why doesn't the national government or royal family step in?" Jabari asked.

"Cloud city was closed off from the rest of the country before the wall. It's in the northern part of the continent so they really just gave up on it." Ivorious tells him,

"That so sad," Kirby said, hearing how the city Cornelia adds, "Not just sad that's wrong, Cyan forsaken the people of Cloud City." Galvan asked, "Can they do that?" Ivorious tells him, "They can. And when a country does something like that the Conglomerate will have to step in if it violates human rights."

"Who?" Pitou asks. As Pryce pops up and explains. "The Conglomerate is a group of elected officials from each of the continents to create a better global community. There is a representative from each state in the nation. Those representatives speak for their ruler. They report what's going on to their Monarch and then report to the Conglomerate what the Monarch said." "So why don't you step in?" Chrome asks. And the answer is very blunt. "Every country has their problems. Cloud City is just one of many problems in Cyan." Pryce says.

While they were explaining the whole time, Kirby ran off with Pitou and Terri following right behind him. Pitou jumps on his shoulders and asks him, "Where are you going and why is there such a rush?" Kirby tells him that he's going to check on Winn because he looked sad and wanted to see if he was okay.

Terri asks, "Why? You don't even know him." Pitou tells Terri that just because Kirby doesn't know him doesn't mean he can't care. While running Kirby tripped but he is caught by the back of his shirt, he looks up and sees Brock. Brock then holds him up by the back of his shirt to his face.

"Thanks, Mr. Brock." He said laughing nervously.

"Why are you running in the halls boy." He asks in a stern tone and Kirby tells him he's trying to find Winn.

"Why in the world would you be looking for that drunk?"

"To make sure he's okay, he looked really sad after your fight." The boy said in an empathetic voice.

"Look. What was it? Kirby. You seem like a nice kid, you worry about people you don't even know, but don't let that get you in trouble. Look, that guy is a drunk, so he will never be worth worrying about, okay. They never are. Just a little advice." Brock then walks away leaving Kirby with a worried look.

Then after that August, Stanley, and Walter pop out from the corner. Pitou screams because they scared him "Oh crap! Where'd you guys come from?" And Terri adds "And why do you look so scruffy?"

"Who are you calling scruffy, rabbit?!" Stanley said, raising his fist at the rabbit. Then he is pushed out the way by Walter who ogles over Pitou and Terri. "Aw look at the puppy and bunny! They're so cute. Is it okay if I pet them?" Kirby told him, sure Pitou and Terri won't mind. Then Terri pulls Kirby to his face and tells him, "Um I am not your pet to hand out."

Walter grabs them both and pets both Pitou and Terri with excitement. "Oh, you two are so soft and fluffy and cute." Pitou says it's not too bad and Terri responds with, "Yeah whatever. Behind the ear, please." August then steps in and introduces himself, "Hello my name is August me and my friends here wanted to ask you about your shield."

"My shield? Why?"

"So, we can see how much it's worth." Stanley said out loud causing August to try to reword what Stanley said. "He means how much value it has, to you, in price, because we are going to appraise it." He tried not to draw suspicion away from what Stanley said. "Oh, that's okay I don't plan on selling it." Kirby sees Winn and darts off, August tries to tell him to wait but Kirby says, "Sorry we got to go." Pitou tells them bye and Terri says, "See you later scruffy kids." August smacks Stanley in the head.

"What was that for?" Stanley asks, rubbing his head.

August told him, "You almost ruined our cover."

Stanley tells him he was taking too long. "August! August! August!" Walter said three times in a row. "Yes, what is

Walter?" Walter asks, "Can we get a puppy like that?" August tells him yes and Stanley then scolds Walter. "You dummy! Why did you stop to pet the dog and rabbit?" Walter then tells him because it was a puppy and a bunny. Then Stanley proceeds to call him a dummy then slaps him in the back of his head. Then Augusts slaps Stanley, August then tells him "Don't hit him. Besides, it was just wrong timing."

They catch up to Winn as he walks in a bar Kirby calls out for him. "Winn waits!" Winn is still sniffing from the fight "Um Hey. Wait, you're that kid brother of one of the other fighters. Jabari's name and your name are Zuri."

"No Kirby."

"Oh sorry. Is there something I can help you with?"

"No, we were just seeing if you were okay. We saw you tear up a bit."

"A bit? He was crying after he lost the fight. Sorry." Terri said, and Pitou asked him, " Do you not have a filter when you talk or do you say the first thing that comes to your head?"

"I'm fine, but that guy was right. I'm nothing but a drunk just like my old man. I guess it runs in the family. I have been drinking for the last 5 years when I was 14 years old. My dad was a horrible drunk and chased my mom away, left me behind and I followed right after him."

213

Kirby tells him, "Well that's not your fault kids are impressionable." trying to make him feel better.

"Well, I ain't a kid no more. I asked my dad why he drank so much. He said, "Because it helps him escape reality". Hell, I was trying to escape but never found a way out." He spoke.

"Well, I think we all need a dose of reality occasionally. I get it sometimes the real world is boring and awful. You want to leave it for a while. I do that with my fort back home, no bad things are allowed. But when you leave reality don't you leave the ones you love behind like family and friends and you always have them." Kirby said, trying to make him see his point and feel better.

"Hey kid listen aint nobody going to want to be friends with a drink like me. When you're like me, people don't want to be around you." Winn told him and just like that Kirby grabs his arms and tells him.

"I can be your friend. We all can."

Terri asks him, "What do you think you're doing?"

"Come on you guys, you heard that he needs a friend so he can join us. Jabari already had a vision of him, so he must become a friend eventually. Come on."

Winn asks him why he is doing this, and Kirby responds, "I don't know because you need a friend and it's nice."

Winn smiles and tells him he'd be happy to have him as his friend and Kirby takes away his beer. And says "Good you don't need this. Let's go!"

He walks to the group and says, "Guys. I'm back and I got a new friend." Winn says, "Hey there."

Jabari asks Kirby "Hey. Kirby, where did you go?" Kirby tells them they went to check on Winn and explains their situation.

Kirby tells them he saw how sad he was after the match and wanted to go check on him. Aziza and Cornelia both at the same time say, "Aw so sweet." Kirby then says, "I explained everything to him so after the tournament, he's coming with us." Elon looks at Winn and asks, "Wait, he told you everything?" Winn tells him yep everything he made sure to explain everything the best he could, but I got most of it and I'd be happy to help. Jabari tells him it's nice to have him onboard with us.

Torre says, alright now that the break is over let's get to the next match. Keyon vs Lucinda. Lucinda walks in and tells Keyon, "Well I can't wait to duel with you." and Keyon replies with, "Whatever." "I guess I start us off. Let me begin with a showstopper." She said Lucinda performs a very promiscuous dance with water circling around her. "Get ready for… what the." Keyon comes for her, places his palm against her chest and knocks her back out of the ring.

"What the hell?" She said trying to recollect what just happened. and Torre says, "Well that was anticlimactic." Lucinda looking confused can't accept the fact she lost so quickly, "No it can be over that quickly. I demand a rematch." Lunalana heckles Lucinda from the stands, "Aw what's wrong? Can't handle losing? At least I was able to show off a little, but you didn't show anything at all. Ha." Lucinda shouts at her saying, "Shut it, bimbo!"

Kirby asks, "So was that the last match of the day?"

Terri said, "I think so."

Aziza tells them no because Elon or Azuro haven't gone yet.

Cornelia then says, "Well who's all left to fight?"

Jabari tells them that Elon and Azuro are the only ones left. Elon said It was bound to happen when two of us had to fight each other. Azuro then says, "Out of all of us I thought Blaine and Galvan would fight each other first." Blaine asks, "You knew you two were going to fight?"

Elon tells him no but when it was coming close to the end, he knew it was a possibility. Kirby says, "Wait so who do we root for when both are friends are fighting." Then Jabari told him "We should just watch and see the outcome of the fight." and Aziza agreed saying "That's the best thing to do."

Blaine pulls Elon over to the side and asks him if he is okay to fight after the whole him and Yamato freaking out. "Hey, I know it's been a while since your last fight, but do you think you'll be able to fight without..." and Elon jumps in to finish "Going all demon weapons crazy? I'll be fine Floracion and I already had this talk not going overboard like last time. I'll be fine." Blaine then says if you say so.

Both steps down into the arena. Elon says, "Let's give it our best, Azuro." He responds, "Wouldn't have it any other way." Elon takes his pike and stabs the ground with it, half of the field starts to bloom with flowers. Grass blankets the ground, and a giant tree sprouts.

Azuro does the same with his saber and when he stabs the ground water floods the other half of the arena. Water sprouts form, whirlpools appear, and the water fountain is created from the water. The whole field is covered with water and grass, then in the middle where they meet it form a marsh like terrain. The energy of Elon and Azuro have Terraformed the field just by impaling the ground! Amazing!

Both jet towards each other. Elon leaves behind a slipstream of grass from his feet and Azuro leaves behind a slipstream of water both men clash on the field sending shockwaves on both the water and grass. Azuro then takes his sword and slashes down and knocks Elon into the patch of grass then sends a tidal wave at him but Elon puts up vines to cancel the attack.

Elon then sends a mass of razor leaves toward Azuro, but he surrounds himself with rings of water to block some but gets scratched by a couple. A large tree hand then reaches from the ground and grabs Azuro then proceeds to throw him out the ring, but an arm of water catches him. Both fighters are not holding back despite being friends. The fight continues for fifteen minutes.

Aziza says, "Just sitting here waiting for one friend to lose it feels weird." "It's conflicting." Yamato said, watching closely. Blaine asks him can sense anything; he tells him no and that Elon is fine. Kirby says, "I don't want to choose one over the other."

Ebondre gives his input saying, "I can. I rather the aqua-mancer wins than the one who can't control his own weapons." Blaine jumps up and says, "I'm sick of your shit." Ivorious tells Blaine to calm down. Ebondre says to him "Your friend is right. Remember how bad he looked when he fought me? You'll get your chance to fight me, just sit and wait." Pitou tells them to look at Elon and Azuro.

Azuro huffing and puffing tells Elon, "When it's just you, you're more coordinated but I don't plan on losing." Elon told him, "Well one of us has to. And I'm afraid you don't have much of a choice. Now Floracion!" Four vines swoop up and grab Azuro causing him to drop his sword unable to escape he is thrown out of the ring and loses the match.

"And the winner is Elon. This concludes the second round of the tournament and now we will honor our winners. Blaine, Galvan, Jabari, Brock, Ebondre, Rachel, Elon, and Keyon. We will continue tomorrow." Torre concluded the second round of the tournament.

Elon tells him he did a good job. Azuro tells him thanks and lets him know he is an amazing fighter. Torre says, "That this tournament is all about folks making bonds, testing your skill, and winning that prize money."

The scene cuts to Jabari and the others talking to Chrome, Winn, and Pryce. "You want to come with us?" Jabari asks with a surprised voice and Chrome replies, "Yeah. Your brother came and explained everything to Pryce and me after he explained everything to Winn. So, we both decided to help you get home."

Winn explained, "After our match and a little convincing from Kirby the choice wasn't hard. Your visions must mean something. The fact that you started having these visions the day we were all in the same place. And that we're all able to see it, it means something, like we're connected." Pryce asks him if he has had any more lately.

Jabari tells them not really and Aziza says, "So eight down two to go" and Cornelia looks at her and says, "What?" Pitou tells Cornelia, "She's right in the vision there were ten of them. So that would leave Brock and Ebondre." "Yeah, love to see how you get those two to join. They seem like the lone wolf guys that don't go along with everyone." Cornelia said, letting out a little laugh. Jabari then tells them to worry about that later. Until then he suggests that they all get some dinner to celebrate.

As the group leaves for dinner Alabaster and August groups are coming up from different directions and are discussing their plans. Walter taps August on his shoulders, "When are we going to get the shield huh?" August then shushes him, so he doesn't speak loudly telling him when the time is right. Stanley asks aggressively in a whisper voice but not whispering "Well when is the time right?" And August tells him when it's time now to shut up.

In another part of the stadium, Alabaster and his lackeys are walking towards their hotel and Lex asks Alabaster, "Sir where do you think the demon weapon users got them from?" He responds by telling him, "I don't know but we can find that out later but for now we'll just focus on capturing them and their weapons. But honestly, I can't wait, Yaku will go back to my suite and prepare dinner." Yaku replied, "Yes sir." Alabaster tells Yaku, "Because you've been a good little servant you can eat the dinner too and not just my scraps. But outside on the patio." Yaku then responds, "Okay Thank you?"

The group is having dinner at the Inn. They talk about the day's events, they laugh, finish and head to their rooms. The morning comes, and the third round of the tournament starts.

Book One
Chapter Sixteen
The Third Round Begins

Torre screams excitedly telling the stadium, "Good morning everybody! Who's ready for the third day of action pack fights, determined warriors and Giovanni purified water so good the gods approve of it. Not to mention Giovanni's new clothing line coming next month to shops, markets, and bazaars." Cornelia shaking her head says, "Shameless advertising." Torre then responds by saying "It's called making a living!" And Cornelia turns and asks, "How did he hear me?"

The first match of the third round starts off with Keyon vs Rachel. Aziza then turns to everyone and points out, "Has anybody really been paying attention to this Keyon guy. He has been beating his opponents with little to no effort." And Cornelia agrees and tells her, "Yeah, I notice but with everything else going on it slipped my mind."

Rachel walks on the field with some pep in her step, "How ya doing sweetie?" Keyon looks at her and asks, "Do you always call people by confections?" Rachel puts her finger on her lip and says, "Good question sugar. I think I do. I don't know what confections are. Does it make you mad pumpkin?"

Keyon grins and tells her no; he says to her it's kind of cute. Rachel giggles and tells him, " Ya sweet hon! But flattering will only get you so far with me." Keyon then asks her, "I wonder how far? Guess I'll have to find out."

Lucinda in the crowd is visibly pissed from her loss yesterday. "Oh yeah flirt with the country hick." She said with a salty attitude. Lunalana then injects herself in the conversation, "Stop being a hater." "On whom? And who are you calling a hater? If I remember correctly, I beat you without doing anything but moving out the way while you got yourself out!"

Lunalana rebuttals, "Yeah but I took my loss with grace." Lucinda then yells back "You fought the guards."

Rachel tells him to let this party start. Starting off Rachel tries to flood like last time. Hoping to win quickly but Keyon is nothing like Aliyah. He appears in front of her , grabs her and picks her up by her waist and carries her in his arms and then places her outside the ring.

Rachel asks what just happened Keyon tells her, "You lose pumpkin." She throws her hands in the air, "Aw shucks! But hey I got you wet a little." Keyon tells her, "Yes you did." Torre daydreaming about Rachel says, "Huh it's over already? Did Rachel win? No, oh man, good job Keyon I guess." He said unhappy, then announced the next match.

"Now the next match is Jabari Vs Brock." Jabari and Brock step onto the field, Jabari tells him, "Hey I want to talk to you about something." Brock looks at him uninterested and says to him, "If it's about your visions and your little crew. No thanks. I notice that Chrome, Pryce, and the Drunk are sitting next to your friends. You were all together last night at the Inn. You want me to join you because of your vision."

Jabari smiles and says, "Yes, I'm glad you get that. So, what do you say? Will you join us?" And he tells him with a straight face no and Jabari asks him why. "You and your friends appear from out of nowhere, during this whole tournament every time something happens that involves you or your friends, I'm somehow dragged into it." Jabari asks, "Like how?" and Brock explains "The visions, your friend's little demon weapon malfunction, and your last match against Chrome. How were you able to do what you did?"

"Which would make you more upset I don't know, or I haven't figured it out yet?" Jabari asks him. Brock says, "You're trying to piss me off now. No more talking." Jabari sees that he is serious, "Fine if I win you have to listen and come with us. Deal?" Brock replied, "Fine I agree to the terms and if I win, I want nothing to do with you." Brock then uses his hands to cut into the ground and lift a large cube of rock and hurls it at Jabari.

Jabari dodges it but that was just testing his reflexes. Brock creates a giant wall and presses his palm against it. And on the side facing Jabari small pieces of the wall start shooting off like small little bullets. He lifts his sword to guard his face, the rocks cut him up all over. Jabari thinks to himself "Elon's razor leaf attack would be helpful. I did that one thing with fire and lightning. Maybe I can."

Jabari then takes his sword and imagines razor leaves when Elon did it. Then he points his sword towards the earth wall and a giant tree sprouts up from behind. The leaves are sent flying towards the walls; the leaves cut it up until it crumbles. And Torre commentates saying, "You know I still haven't figured it out. Is Jabari a pyromancer, Floramancer, or Electromancer. Maybe this Virginia place teaches someone all types of elemental magic."

Brock then calls him out, "And that right there. How are you able to manipulate all these elements if you're not from any of the ten elemental nations? Are you from one of the other four? Nothing about you makes any sense."

Jabari then tells him, "If you just come with us and let me explain you'll understand why you need to come with us. And maybe we'll find answers to the multiple element thing. "

Brock then tries to explain to him what he just told him, "I need to come with you to understand why I need to come with you? And maybe we'll find answers."

Jabari then looks up thinking and says, "Yes? If it makes sense." Brock then reminds him that he needs to beat him first.

Brock covers himself in a hard rock like shell and charges at Jabari. Brock is moving fast so Jabari takes the hit, then Brock circles around with the rock shell and constantly tackles him.

Jabari yells at him, "Dammit, come on, get out of the shell." Jabari's eyes begin to shine. He puts his hand towards Brock and lowers his hand and the shell of rocks begins to fall apart. Standing there looking at him, "How did you do that?" He asks him. Jabari then covers his hand in rocks and punches Brock in the gut. Then hits the ground causing a mini quake. It throws him off balance Jabari summons a massive earth hand, grabs Brock and tosses him out and he hits the wall.

"Well, I guess this means you're coming with us then." he said walking towards him and Brock sucked his teeth and said, fine. Torre commentates saying, "Yeah my second favorite won! If you haven't figured it out, my first favorite was Rachel. Congrats to Jabari." Jabari then walks up to him and asks, "Now will you listen to me?" Brock tells him yes and he'll go with him as we agreed.

Torre tells the next match "Up next is Blaine Vs. Galvan. This should be fun, both fighters have given us a good show. Can't wait to see how they do against each other." When the fight was announced, the whole group responded with several reactions.

Elon and Azuro both said simultaneously "Oh god no."

Ivorious said he's been dreading this fight ever since he met these two.

"For the love of god why did those two have to fight? These idiots will probably destroy the whole arena." Terri said, hiding behind his ears in fear of the upcoming battle. Pitou jumps behind Terri's ear, "For once Terri I agree with you. This is something I've been wanting to avoid. I'm afraid this will bring the house down."

Aziza asks Cornelia if they are overreacting, Cornelia tells her, "I don't think they're overreacting. Look at those two."

Blaine's face shows a big smile, and he tells Galvan, "Looks like we will finally have our battle. Our long-awaited fight." Galvan smiles right back at him saying, "It's about time we settled this. Who's the best swordsman, Fire or Lightning."

Chrome said, "They are really excited about this."

Pryce asks nervously, "What gave it away how hard they're smiling at each other or them cracking their knuckles."

Winn adds, "Their bodies are oozing magical power, I can tell this fight was a long time coming, they seem like great rivals yet friends."

Blaine and Galvan are fired up, both jump from the stands to the field, Blaine tells him to let's do this and he is not going to hold back one bit. Then Galvan tells him he would have it any other way.

"Both fighters please step oh, there already there. Now let's begin the next match."

Jabari pulls Kirby to him telling him, "This is going to make Kirby stand by me." Kirby asks, "Would it be better to stand near the exit?"

Both Blaine and Galvan stand facing each other with the look of determinations in their eyes. Without hesitation, they both draw their swords, Blaine lights up with flames all around his body while Galvan's body is circled by electricity. Both dash towards each other and clash and an explosion of fire and lightning bursts out.

Both at a stalemate Blaine shoots a massive flamethrower by jumping back and pointing his sword towards Galvan. But Galvan had summoned a lightning bolt to cancel it out and both men clashed away with their swords. The crowd was amazed and scared at this fight; they couldn't decide if they wanted to stay and watch or leave.

The ground begins to crack underneath their feet and the heat and electricity circulate through the whole arena. The sounds of their battle like a roaring beast with every clash of their swords. Flares of fire and lightning shoot out and people begin to move inside to watch the rest of the fight. But the group stays, and they feel the effects of the fight.

Terri looks at Jabari and asks, "Hey Jabari and Kirby, what's up with your hair? It's all puffy." Jabari told him, "It's called an afro, the humidity and the electricity caused it." Terri points out the same thing with everyone else and Aziza tells him that her hair has always been like this. Pitou then tells them to listen because Blaine and Galvan are laughing.

He was right laughing can be heard from the field and all you could see was nothing but smiles on their faces. Their final clash resulted in both knocking each other's swords from their hands. Both swords flew out of bounds. Blaine looks up to the commentator's booth and he yells, "Hey can we get our swords?"

Torre tells him, "Sorry the moment any of you leave the ring the match is over. And frankly, you two are less of a threat now." Galvan asks, "So what do you want to do? How are we going to see who's best now?"

Kirby says, "Oh no both their swords are out of bounds how are they going to fight now?" Elon jokes that they could start punching each other. Azuro says, "Do you really think they would resort to ... never mind." Then they did exactly what Elon thought. Covering his fist with flames and the other with lightning both just started punching each other left and right. Azuro asks, "What happens when you see who's the best swordsman?" Elon tells him, "You know something, I think they already came to that conclusion and they're just having fun."

And how right he was, both had concluded that they were both equally great swordsmen at this moment in time. With that they would train to get stronger to surpass the other but until then they decided to just have fun with it. You see smiles, hear laughter as they punch each other. They go for two hours until Blaine punches Galvan out and wins.

Torre's snoring can be heard over the loudspeaker until Blaine tells him to wake up. "Huh. Is it over? Finally." Cornelia says, "Who are you telling? Wake up everyone, it's over." Jabari asks "Who won? Torre congratulates Blaine and yawns.

"You two sure look like you were having fun." Azuro told them in a tired voice. Both look beaten and battered. They have black eyes, cuts, scrapes, bloody noses, and clothes are torn and tattered. Elon asks, "Are you guys okay?" and Blaine tells them they're good. Kirby asks, "Are you sure? You guys look awful." Galvan tells him, "Wrong kid, we look awesome."

"Hey Elon Azuro, come over here." Blaine tells them, and Elon asks why, and Blaine says, "Because I can't hold him and myself up anymore." Both fall, Elon catches Blaine and Azuro catches Galvan but Azuro falls on Cornelia. Cornelia says "Oh god! Really?"

# Book One
# Chapter Seventeen
# Moon Over the Forest

Kirby then pulls Elon's arms and Elon asks what's wrong and Kirby tells him. "I just realized your next and the only person left is..." and everyone finishes by saying Ebondre. Ebondre then walks over to Elon, he tells him, "Let me make this clear, the fact that you can't control your weapon is what concerns me. You could put innocent people in harm's way."

Jabari jumps up and says, "You got to be kidding me. Elon would never do something like that." "Maybe not him but who's to say his weapon won't. You're a disaster waiting to happen and if necessary, during the fight I'll... well you know. Let me clarify my problem is with the fact you can't control your weapon." Ivorious tells, "He controlled it in his last fight." But that doesn't sway Ebondre's concern.

"But what's to say it won't happen again." Ebondre asks Elon directly to his face.

"It won't." Elon tells him.

Ebondre asks him again, "Can he be sure?"

Elon stands there silent and Ebondre tells him, "Exactly. I won't try to kill you but ..." Elon interrupts him saying "I get it."

Ebondre walks off and towards the ring. "He's right, if I lose control, I'm a threat to everyone, even you guys. I would never want to hurt my friends." Elon said, doubting his abilities. Aziza tries to convince him he's wrong about his doubt, "The only reason that happened last time is because Floracion didn't know you and Yamato were friends. Then in the battle with Azuro you kept it under control and won."

Jabari tells him, "Yeah going against Ebondre doesn't change the fact that you can keep control." Pitou then adds "But he and Ebondre aren't friends." Elon still doubts himself, "I don't think I can. That guy just makes me feel on edge. I should just drop out."

Blaine wakes up and grabs Elon's shirt and pulls himself up. "What did you just say? Are you insane? Don't you ever say that! Giving up is never an option especially when you haven't even tried! So, you're going to fight, you're going to keep it together, and you're going to win! Got it?" Then Blaine passes out again. "Did he wake up just to tell you that?" Terri asks.

Ivorious tries to play devil's advocate, "Maybe Ebondre isn't that bad. He did say he didn't want to kill you." Cornelia says in a sympathetic voice, "Maybe he is not as much of an asshole as we thought and just wants to keep people safe." Terri asks, "You think so?" Cornelia and Terri answer "Nah he's still an asshole."

Elon walks down to the field where Ebondre was waiting "Took you long enough. Are you ready?" Ebondre asks him. Elon replies, "As he'll ever be, and Torre tells them to let the last match of the third round begin. Elon inhales then exhales he takes his pike and ready himself for this fight. Ebondre did the same with his scythe both waited for the other to move.

"What are they waiting for?" Chrome asks wanting something to happen and Pryce tells him that's the point. "They're waiting for the other to make a move, because the first one to make a mistake loses." In a split-second Elon leaps forward in the air and swings his pike at Ebondre. Sharp pine needles fly at Ebondre, a green slipstream follows behind them. Ebondre doesn't do anything until the last second. A shield formed from the aura of darkness to block the attack.

"What the hell, well okay that's new, " Ebondre said, "Surprised? I don't bring my shield out often but for this fight, I don't think I have much of a choice. Never know when you're going to snap."

Elon replies "That's not me, I'm not a monster."

233

Ebondre then tells him, "You're right you're not a monster but you fight with one and you lose control. I've seen people fall under the pressure of demon weapons where I'm from."

Jabari then asks, "Hey guys where is he from?"

Aziza recalls from the beginning of the tournament "I think he's from the Ebony nation. Actually, he and Lex were the only ones from the Ebony nation."

Kirby asks, "What's it's like?"

Ivorious tells all that he knows "The Ebony nation is one of the most powerful nations. They are ruled by a King who has several kids by different women. The economy of Ebony is really booming and that's all I know."

Brock then tells the group, "But there are dark rumors surrounding a city in the nation. The city is Taupe. It's on the outskirts of the kingdom to the capital." With curious ears, they all lean in and Brock continues "Rumor has that the city is clear of all homeless."

Winn looks at him and asks, "But isn't that a good thing?" But Brock continues, "You would think so drunk, but no rumor says that there is a man, a researcher who works with science and magic, who abducts homeless people and experiments on them."

Aziza gasps upon this "Oh my is that true?" She can't believe this can be real.

Brock continues, "A lot of people have said the same thing Taupe isn't that safe for tourists either; they have been known to go missing in the city. That's why people tend to avoid that city."

Ivorious scratches his head and says, "Weird the same thing used to happen in a city in the Ivory nation."

Elon and Ebondre have been fighting for 20 minutes. Ebondre points his scythe towards and sends a blast of dark energy from the tip of the spear. The blast knocks Elon down and sends him sliding across the floor. Ebondre notices Elon's eyes.

Elon huffing and puffing and thinking to himself, "I don't think I can keep this up any longer."

Then he hears Floracion's voice in his head, "Let me take over, I can help you." Elon tells him, "No I don't need your help I can do this with turning."

Ebondre looks at him and tells him, "Hey, get up. What's wrong with you?"

Elon tells him in the distorted voice from before "I'm fine. It's **nothing.**"

"You're turning, aren't you?"

"No, I'm not."

Kirby, looking concerned, runs to the bottom of the stadium, Pitou goes down there with him and says, "He doesn't look so good."

Azuro asks Yamato if he feels anything, Yamato tells him, "Not fully but he's slowly rising."

"'See this is what I was worried about, you can't control it. I don't want to, but I will…."

"QUIET! You think you're so mighty because you don't use a demon weapon. You don't know anything about him. So, don't you stand there and judge him." Floracion said through Elon's mouth.

Yamato says, "Now he's almost consumed."

"Elon lunges at Ebondre with his pike, Ebondre dodges but Elon forms a tree and shoots bullet seeds. Ebondre uses his shield to block it but one seed hits his eye and temporarily blinds him then Elon charges and tries to kill Ebondre."

Jabari yells for Elon to stop before it's too late but he doesn't hear him. Just as the possessed Elon tries to finish off Ebondre but Blaine jumps in and blocks his attack sending Elon back. Then Blaine punches Elon in the face and Elon gets back in control.

Blaine yells and scolds him, "What the hell is wrong with you? You almost killed him!"

Elon says, "Blaine?"

"You could have gotten disqualified! Are you stupid."?

Everyone looks stumped and falls over in their seats. Jabari gets up and screams, "That's why he stopped him?!" And Aziza adds on, "Not for almost killing a guy but for almost disqualifying himself."

Blaine tells, "You need to keep better control of that pike man, you can't let it control you. You needed that punch to the face because you were about to lose it again." Elon looks at him and tells him thank you.

Torre then gets on the mic and tells them, "I don't know why you're thanking him. Look at your feet, he blocked your attack which sent you back, then the punch put you out of the ring."

Blaine says, "Whoops."

Torre tells them, "Even though he was trying to help his friend, he ended up helping him lose. The winner is Ebondre." Blaine tells him his bad and apologizes to Elon. "It's okay you snapped me out of it thank you." Jabari says that was very unfortunate and Cornelia asks him "Unfortunate or stupid?"

Book One
Chapter Eighteen
Moonlight

"Now please clear the field for the first match for the fourth round. Ebondre vs Jabari. Then Blaine vs Keyon. Then after these two fights, we will have our final round. But first there will be a small break."

Ebondre interrupts him and tells him "No, I want to fight him now." And Torre asked him if he's sure about that and he said yes. Jabari says it's fine with him and begins to walk down to the field. Aziza tells him "Be careful okay. Because I think Ebondre might not hold back."

Kirby asks, "What do you mean? He didn't try to kill Elon. Well, at least not for the first few minutes."

"Well yeah, but he really doesn't like Jabari for some reason." Terri gives his opinion, "I mean if someone was having visions about me without permission I'd be upset too."

Pitou puts his paw on Terri's mouth and says, "Will the writer please shut you up?" Kirby tells him, "I know you're going to win. You want to use my shield?" Jabari tells them thanks.

Jabari takes the shield and walks down the ring. And the match begins. Both with a weapon and shield in their hands both men charge and clash with the sword and scythe. Ebondre unleashes a fury of stabbing attacks, with each trust it launches a dark energy. Jabari can barely block them even with his sword and shield.

"I'll admit you're good with a sword but a sword and a shield you're just awful. You can't even block right." Ebondre tells him.

Jabari tells him, "Hey let's take a time out from insulting me and listen. Look, I know that me and my friends are not your favorite people, but you have to come with us."

"Excuse me."

"We're trying to get me, and my brother home and you need to come with us. I don't know why but you just have to. Maybe you play a part in us getting home."

239

"And what part might that be?" Ebondre asks.

"I don't know yet. Right now, I'm on my way to Rangi City because my brother. He had a vision of Zanatar's Valley, a boat on a dock and it read Ran on it. And we've been literally going off on that."

"Enough of this nonsense! Now shut up and fight me!"

"Just listen!"

Both raise their weapons collide with one another and this triggers another vision. Jabari, Kirby, and the other eyes start to glow but this time their bodies start to glow with their corresponding hues. Blaine's whole body starts to glow red, Elon green, Galvan yellow, Azuro blue, Ebondre black, Ivorious white, Chrome gray, Pryce Icey blue, Winn sky blue, and Brock brown. Jabari and Kirby glow gold and silver.

The series of visions shows money from both worlds, clothing, and water bottles. A row of people in uniforms red, white and grey hold gun-like weapons. Jabari, Kirby, Blaine, Elon, Galvan, Azuro, Ebondre, Ivorious, Chrome, Pryce, Winn, and Brock see it. The scene cuts back to the fight, all of them are still glowing. The crowd is stunned by what they are seeing. Everyone is in shock and awe.

Aziza says, "I don't believe what I'm seeing on the field" and Cornelia asks and points out "What about right next to you?" Pitou asks Kirby if he is okay and Terri panics saying, "He's not responding!" Yamato looks at them and none of them are responding, they won't answer anything. Stanley goes wow and Walter calls for August, then August tells him he sees.

Yaku stares in awe, Lex asks, "Master, are you seeing this?" Alabaster responds, "I see. Boys, we're no longer going after just the demon weapon users, we're going after every single one of them." Rachel and Amy drop the ice cream, Lunalana yells, "Holy Sh*t." The vision stops when Ebondre looks at Jabari and walks out the arena, surrendering the match to him.

Torre nervously says, "I'm literally speechless, this has been the freakiest group of fighters ever. What was that? I've never seen anything like this before. What are these people?"

"So, I guess I'm going with you. But now this means you better not lose to the next person."

"Let's move on to the next match, Keyon Vs Blaine."

Both Jabari and Ebondre walk up to everyone who is still in a daze.

Aziza tells him, "So, you want to tell us what you saw, because me, Cornelia, Yamato, Pitou, and Terri couldn't see what you saw."

"I saw an army bottle, water, clothes and money."

241

Aziza and the others look at him in confusion, Jabari tells them he doesn't know what it could mean. Terrie tries to get their attention, but Cornelia shushes him.

"Not now. So, this must have been really important because you were all glowing like fireworks." Cornelia says.

Terri calls for them again, "Guys!"

Brock smashes his face saying, "Quiet rabbit."

Pitou then yells, "People." Everyone then says, "What?" And Pitou tells everyone that Kirby's eyes are still glowing. Terri adds, "That's what I was trying to tell them!" Jabari grabs Kirby and tries to shake him out of it telling him to wake up. Cornelia suggests, "Should we take him to the medic?" Terri asks her with criticism, "And tell them what?"

Kirby wakes up yawning "What happened?" Jabari tells them they all had a vision. Jabari asks him if he is okay and Kirby says he's tired then falls asleep right there. "Come on, rest up. The vision must have taken a lot of him. I'll hold him until my next match." Jabari said.

"Will Blaine and Keyon please step down."

"Okay, Jabari after I win it'll be you versus me. Alright, you ready Keyon?" Blaine said ready for the fight. Keyon tells him, "Yeah I'm ready to have a talk with Jabari so I'll be quick."

242

Keyon lunges at Blaine, he tries to jab at him with his sais towards, Blaine parries it and swings his sword down creating a vertical flame. Then he stabs his sword in the ground and shoots fire in the ground. The flames begin to shoot out from the cracks in the arena.

"I see you're not going to be that easy to take out. You might be the first person to make me use my magic." Said Keyon. He then leaps into the air and dives down on Blaine who sends a powerful fire ball his way, but it has no effect.
Keyon has covered his body in a thick layer of shell-like armor.

Keyon, still covered in the shell, burst out with tail wings and talons while still maintaining a human-like appearance. He grabs Blaine by his shoulders and throws him out of the arena. The whole arena is shocked and left speechless after what they just saw. Their faces are left blank.

"WHAT THE HELL JUST HAPPENED? How did he make a shell, then grow wings and talons?" Blaine said, trying to figure out how he lost so fast.

Aziza asks, "What just happened?"

"I literally have nothing to say. I just don't." Terri said.

"And I thought me turning into a demon was the most bizarre part of this whole thing." Elon.

"Alright explain what the hell was that?" Blaine questions Keyon.

"I don't know the exact name for it, but I call my body manipulation ability "Life Form". I can manipulate my body to a cellular level and gain the traits of all live organisms." Keyon explains.

Blaine looks at him with a blank expression on his face. "What?"

Keyon then takes his hands and rubs his temples trying to find a way to dumb down his explanation. "I can turn my body into animal parts."

"WHAT?!" Blaine yells still confused.

"Have any of you ever heard of this ability?" Pitou asked.

"I've never heard of something like that." Aziza says.

"I studied a lot of spells and powers but never anything like that." Cornelia says.


Book One
Chapter Nineteen
People Like Us

"Now that I have recovered from the anxiety. Let's begin the final battle of the Tone Town Tournament. Jabari vs Keyon! The battle will begin in five minutes." Torre said.

Aziza asks Jabari "Are you ready for this? This is a lot of pressure. But you need to focus. Be ready! You got this! I can't hear you!"

"I didn't say anything but thanks, Aziza, for the pep talk." He was surprised by her enthusiasm. He then asks her to hold Kirby.

Torre announces for both the final contestants to please step down. The crowd is rooting for their favorite fighter, we can clearly see who the fan favorite is.

Keyon looks into the crowd at Jabari's friends and looks back at Jabari and says, "I don't know what it is but something about you is so off. But at the same time… never mind forget what I said. But before we begin, I have one question. How are you able to manipulate multiple elements? I only ever heard of people being able to manipulate one and with training that element's sub capabilities."

"I've been meaning to ask the same question from the beginning. How is he able to do that?" Torre asks. As he did the whole crowd began to question it too. Along with his companions.

"Hey before I came along: Did you guys know he could do that? Or did he just get the ability or…" Winn asked.

"He was able to do it once when we first encountered a monster before we met Galvan." Elon said.

"Oh, that's right. He was able to shoot razor leaves at the monster and set them on fire. I just assumed it was some rare kind of magic but with everything that has happened up to now I really don't know what it is." Blaine.

"And I don't even know what it is." Said Azuro.

"How much do you want to bet he's going to lie and tell everyone it's some super rare magic?" Cornelia asks.

Ebondre looks at her and says, "You think you know everything don't you?"

"Oh, it's a super rare magic that you can only learn through intense training. You can use multiple elemental magic. Yeah, that's what it is. I can't manipulate the elements." Jabari told him, trying his best to convince him.

"Told you so." Cornelia said mockingly.

"Hmm. Let's just get this started. I won't hold back, not because you're powerful but because you're powerful and inexperienced." Keyon said, preparing for battle.

Keyon then springs forward in the blink of an eye. He swings his sais down and Jabari blocks it with his sword. Keyon then turns around and back kicks the blade. The kick sends Jabari back but not out of the ring.

"Damn! What the hell? This guy must never skip leg day or something. How the hell does he have that much power?" Jabari said to himself. He then looks at Keyon's legs and sees the leg he jumped forward with looks like a rabbit's foot and the leg he used to kick with is the leg of a horse.

"This fight has already gotten off to a bizarre start. Keyon leaps forward with a rabbit's foot and delivers a massive high horse kick with the other when the first attack fails." Torre said giving a play by play of fight.

Keyon tries the same attack again but when he leaps towards him, Jabari swings his sword at him and fires off a powerful stream of water. This causes Keyon to use his rabbit legs to jump in the air, he changes from rabbit legs to horse legs and plans to smash down on Jabari.

Jabari seeing this he bawls his hand to make a fist and swings it up to send a rock pillar at Keyon in mid-air. Keyon then grows massive wings and dodges the attack. He then dives down with talons out ready to strike. Jabari parries it with his sword but is struck with a whip-like object; it is a thin tail.

"Damn!" Jabari said in frustration.

"If you're upset about that then you'll hate this." Keyon said right before his tail sprouted quills and he started to assault Jabari from close and mid-range. Jabari is on the defense going back and forth between the tail and sword.

Jabari then stabs his sword in the ground. He punches the floor causing pillars of rock to shoot up. The pillars are arranged in 8x8 checkered formation. He closes all but one of the openings. The formation reaches from one end of the field to another.

"Now this will cause him to only go in a few directions. There are only so many choices. He can choose to come from that one path, or he'll grow wings and fly over."

"What the hell is taking him so long? Is he waiting for me like I'm waiting for him?"

Jabari stands waiting for Keyon's next attack until he feels a disturbance in the ground.

"What the hell? I can feel something moving through the ground. But what is it? Shit!" Jabari says as he jumps from the space he was in right before Keyon jumps from underground with mole claws.

"You're a smart fellow. I didn't think you would pick up on what I was doing so fast. But still, you're not using your full power. You're holding back, but the question is why."

"Nobody here is holding me, I'm just not trying to..."

"To what win? Go all out? You think I'm not worthy of seeing your strength?"

"No! I'm not holding back but I don't want to hurt you. (Thinking) because right now I'm just winging it. Besides, aren't you the one who said I was powerful but have no control?"

"Let me take that back. What I meant was you were afraid of going full force. I watched your matches carefully ever since you got here because I knew there was something off. You have this power, you seem to have some grasp. But you hold back out of fear of hurting people like you did with Dia but when you go full out you do it out of fear of not beating them like with Chrome or Brock. You are being guided by fear, which is natural, fear is key to survival, but you need to know when to let it guide you." Keyon told him.

"Um thanks? But why are you telling me this?" Jabari asks.

"You should take some lessons from this loss." Keyon said as he grows massive wings and covers this with a razor shell covering them.

He soars in the air and then dives down while spinning and right before he hits him, he closes himself in his wings and tackles Jabari head on.

The crowd jumps up to see what happened to Jabari.

"Oh no Jabari!" Aziza cried out of fear.

This causes Kirby to wake up. "What's going on?"

"Jabari!" His friends shout from the stand.

As the dust settles Keyon looks to see the aftermath of the match. But to his surprise Jabari is still standing. Jabari coated his body in rocks to protect himself. The blast blew away most of the rocks and part of his shirt.

"Damn idk what's crazier that attack or me blocking. I'm serious because I thought oh, he's trying to kill me. But now it's my turn. So, hold still."

Jabari takes the rock armor and wraps it around Keyon so he can't move. He then uses the air to leap in the sky, takes his sword and summons leaves and water. He then swings his sword downwards in front of him. This causes the water and leaves to violently circle him. He then dives and strikes Keyon. Keyon tries to brace for impact but to no avail the attack breaks through his shell. After the attack Jabari gets up, clothes torn and tattered. He stands a couple of feet away from Keyon. The attack weakens Keyon to the point where he can barely stand. He stands in a crater made from the attack that went all the way through the ground.

"Okay it's clear to see that you adapt fast under pressure. You were able to think of that on your feet and then improvise an attack like mine. But now we are both on the verge of collapse but who will fall first." Keyon said huffing and puffing.

"Um you because technically you left the arena because you're touching the ground." Jabari said pointing it out.

"Well, it appears I am. Well do me a favor and carry my body to the infirmary...oh" Keyon said right before he passed out.

"Only if I don't pass out after you." Jabari said, falling to the ground, sighing.

Torre screams in the mic "OH YEAH THAT WAS THE MOST AMAZING FIGHT I'VE EVER SEEN!" The whole crowd cheered for Jabari. "Let's give a round of applause so loud the gods can hear it!" Torre said, and the crowd does just that.

"Now let's congratulate our champion of this year's Tone town tournament. I am honored to reward you with this prize money for your well-earned victory. Here is your reward: 500,000 Hueleons. So, what are you going to do with your winnings if you don't mind me asking?"

Jabari tells him, "We are about to roll up out of here and head home let's go."

Torre repeats after him, "Roll up out of here?"

Kirby tells him it means about to leave, and Torre asks, "Is that speech well used in Virginia" Kirby says yes. Both brothers wave goodbye and leave with the group following behind them Torre and the crowd waves goodbye and he tells them, "Okay well you be safe wherever you go and come back again." Kirby screams we will. "Well, that concludes the tournament."

"This is great now that we got the money, we can get a bigger cart and head towards the next town." Blaine said, patting Jabari on his back. "I had no idea you learned so much about how to sword fight in the time you were here." Blaine Continued.

He tells them that they deserve some credit too, he watched and learned from all of them and Aziza grabs his arm. "I think we should celebrate tonight and leave in the morning." She said, and everyone agreed.

Cornelia gets in his face and says, "You okay? You don't look so excited for someone who won the tournament."

"I'm just a little surprised that I won. That guy is stronger than he looks" Jabari tells her, trying not to think about the match.

"I'll say, you were holding back during all your other matches, but you really went full on with this one." Cornelia tells him.

Blaine then tells him with an ecstatic attitude, "Listen we gotta fight before you go back home, we just have to." Jabari tells him he promises but for now, let's celebrate.

Walter, August, and Stanley are watching them from afar. Walter calls August name and responds by saying, yes Walter and Walter ask August "Can we go to the dinner party?"

Stanley then jumps on Walter and scolds him "Didn't he say we'll take the shield when the time is right."

Walter says, "I know but I'm hungry I meant to get food." Stanley and August can hear Walter's stomach. August then tells him not to worry they will eat but Walter asks him how.

Stanley then bops August on his head and asks him, "Hey has August ever let you starve? Has he ever said he was gonna do something and didn't do it?"

Walter answers, "No and no." Stanley tells him to stop worrying. "He said we're going to eat so we're going to eat." August tells them that they will sneak in.

As the celebration party started all contestants were invited to join in. There are mountains of food and music playing to lighten the mood. Having so much fun people started dancing, you could see Rachel grabbing Aliyah's hand to dance, and Dia dancing all by herself. God that girl is creepy.

Shyera tells Jabari, "You were amazing out there, I never knew someone who lacked swordsman skills could be that great in a fight."

Jabari replies, "Who said I lack skills?" "The rabbit did." She answered, with that Jabari looks at Terri with dagger eyes.

"What I had to make people bet against you, I got people to bet 50 hueleon each." Terri said, explaining his actions.

Then overhearing him Yaza gets in his face and says, "50? You charged me $100."

Dia walks up to Jabari, "Hey Jabari congrats on you win." "Thank you, Dia." He said not remembering how crazy. she was.

"It's amazing, after a fight like that you have no scratches or any bruises. What a shame I wanted to see blood. So, let's make this happen." She said pulling a knife.

Aziza tells her, "Girl you are crazy." And she says to Aziza, "Be careful now, flattering will get you so far with me."

Shyera then says, "Of course you would find that flattering."

Dia tells her, "You're lucky there's security here."

Jabari thinks to himself, "I haven't seen Keyon, maybe he left. What did he mean?"

Aziza sees him staring off and asks him what's wrong, he tells her he's fine. Aziza says to him, "I haven't known you for long, but I can tell when something's wrong. You don't look fine. Is there something you want to talk about? You know you can talk to me."

Jabari tells her, "I know. Thank you. You're sweet and I promise everything is fine." She grabs his hand and pulls him and says, "Let's dance."

August and his group sneak into the party unnoticed and he tells them to go and eat.

As the night went on there were laughs, jokes, and other festive activities. Later in the night when everyone went to their rooms Jabari talks to Kirby about what happened when Pitou and Terri fell asleep. He told him when they get home, they'll try to figure everything out. In the morning, the group went to purchase a cart big enough for 14 but before they did a friend had to depart from their journey.

Book One
Chapter Twenty
Man in The Road

"What? What do you mean you can't come with us Yamato?" Kirby said in a loud disappointed voice.

Yamato tells him, "After what happened here, it showed me that I still need better control of Muramasa. Until then I must bid you farewell, I hope you make it home safe, I will never forget you Jabari and Kirby."

"But wait you're from Earth so why not come?" Jabari asks.

Yamato tells him, "Because this Zanatar's Valley may lead you to your home but not to mine. We are not of the same time. But I have learned to like this place. I've been here for a while."

Kirby yells, "Aw man!" And Yamato tells Kirby, "Don't feel sad. The friendship we have transcends time and space, nothing can break that."

Jabari tells him, "Well we wish you the best of luck wherever you go."

Yamato tells him thank you. But Alabaster and his group watch from the shadows. "Master the demon weapon user is separating from the main group. What do we do?" Lex asks.

Yaku said, "So is this when we get him. Right Sir." Alabaster thinks and tells them, "I want to watch some more and then take him when he's alone." Yaku tells them others are coming and Alabaster tells them to hide.

Shyera comes running to the cart before they leave and right behind her are Zeke, Warrick, and Wallace. Shyera tells them to wait, "Before you, I want to apologize to you Jabari." She said, and Jabari asks for what.

She tells them why she wanted to say sorry, "For saying that you couldn't handle Dia and saying you should give up. You proved me wrong and won. So, I'm sorry."

Jabari tells her, "It's okay , you're cool."

"Cool but I don't feel cold." She spoke.

Jabari tells her, "No I mean I'm not mad, I forgive you."

"Oh. This language you speak from Virginia is very different from where I'm from." Shyera said.

"That's right you're not from this world either or our time in our world." He says remembering Shyera's story. Shyera tells him it's okay because she has come to terms with it.

Wallace then tells Galvan, "I just came to say it was an honor to battle you Galvan and I hope we'll meet again soon. I would like to come up with new strategy plans and we can have a rematch."

"You got it and maybe you can teach me some of those tactics." Galvan said, putting his arm around Wallace laughing.

257

Terri then says, "He is a tactician, not a miracle working." Galvan then grabs Terri's ears and tells him to shut up.

Warrick tells Blaine that he wants another fight with him, and Blaine agrees and tells him they'll have their rematch. Warrick starts sniffing around Kirby and Kirby asks, "What do I stink? I took a shower." Then Warrick starts sniffing through his pockets.

Jabari asks, "What's in your pocket?"

He looks nervous and says, "Uh nothing." When Warrick reaches in, he pulls out meatballs. Jabari scolds him, "What did dad and I say about stuffing your pockets with food?"

"That's how you get ants, but in this case man beasts. Here you can have one if you want." Kirby said, offering Warrick some and he started eating.

"And now he's eating it out of your hand, even if I don't do that, now he's licking your face." Terri said, shaking his head. Zeke tells him down boy and apologizes for it, Kirby tells them It's fine Pitou does it. Pitou whispers, "Don't tell them that."

The main group said their goodbyes to their new friends. Aziza marvels at the new cart they bought saying she's surprised they had carts this big.

Brock asks Jabari, "So where are we off to now?" And he asks who has the map and Azuro reads the next location is Dye city.

Chrome then asks, "How are we supposed to get there, where is their horse?" Pitou gets in front of the cart as Ebondre and the newcomers look really confused. Pitou transforms into his wild fang form and gets hooked up to the cart. The newcomer's jaws drop, and Kirby tells them the same thing happened to them the first time.

Jabari says, let's go and down they jet to Dye City. Pitou tells everyone to hold on, he has to grow bigger because there are more of them, so he'll be going faster. As they take off August, and the others hide in the bushes waiting to swipe the shield.

"Get ready, here they come, he's in front so pounce at the right time." August said to them.

Stanley calls Walter making sure he hears them, "Ok you hear that Walter? Walter? What are you doing? Get out of the road."

August looks confused, "What!? What are you doing?" He asks.

Walter is seen trying to move a small lizard out of the cart's direction. "Come on, move out the way little lizard. I'm getting the lizard to move out of the way."

August tells him they are closing in; Stanley pushes Walter out the way but gets run over by Pitou. Kirby asks Pitou, "What was the bump in the road" and Jabari asks Pitou if he hit something. Pitou said he doesn't know, and Terri told him that there was nothing in the road he saw. They ride out and Stanley lays flat on the ground moaning.

August runs to Stanley and asks if he's ok, Stanley lashes at him, "I'm no not! I just got run over!"

August asks, "Why are you crying?" and Stanley says, "I'm not crying!" August goes, "Not you Walter." August asks, "Why are you crying, Walter." Stanley snaps at both August and Walter, "What the hell is he crying for?" Walter told them crying, "That rabbit called Stanley nothing and that wasn't nice." August tells Walter, "It's okay Walter I'm pretty sure he didn't mean anything by it." Stanley shakes his head "Why is he crying? I'm the one who got run over."

The scene cuts to the group on the road and tired from doing nothing, Terri asks how long until they get there.

"I don't know. Where's the map?" Jabari asks, and Aziza tells him it's right here and she says they should be there in five hours. To kill some time Pryce asks Jabari to tell them about their world and what it's like.

"Well looking at yours and mine it's really not that different from yours. Like how people here have powers. We have people in our world who can be born with them. This professor Luther Tate and Arturo Vasquez research the gene that gives them their powers. But there's a lot of people who don't like them because of that." Jabari tells them.

Cornelia then says, "But they can help that they were born with it."

Jabari tells them, "A lot of people feel that way, but a lot of people are scared because one person has all that power."

"That's how some people are in this world about mancers." Brock tells him.

Kirby goes, "What? I thought everyone could do or at least use some magic."

Brock tells Kirby, "Not everyone is born with the ability to manipulate the elements or other types of magic. They are born regular and some people see them as inferior. It's a problem all over the world."

Jabari said, "But there were people in Tone town who couldn't use the elements." Aziza tells him, "Tone town is one of many places where mancers and non-mancers get along."

They turn down a path through an open trail with some bushes and trees down the way. They look and see someone in the middle of the road. The group comes across a man bloody and bruised laying on the road. They stop to check on him as they do several of the blue shadow beast come running from the side. They group jumps out to fight them off.

Cornelia and Aziza go for the man, when they get to him they are surrounded by the shadows. Aziza uses her magic to fire spears into their heads. But when a monster comes from behind her, Cornelia punches the shadow with her hands. Aziza turns her head to see Cornelia's hands glowing with circles on them.

"Cornelia, since when can you do that?" Aziza asks.

"Long stories tell you later, look out right behind you."

Kirby and the others watch from the cart until two shadow beasts charge towards them. Terri screams for someone to do something! Kirby takes the shield and charges back and knocks the monster back into the other. He then throws the shield which ricochets off both knocking them both down.

Kirby picks up his shield with excitement and asks, "That was so cool Terri, did you see that?" Terri has a scared look on his face and in a soft voice tells Kirby, "Behind you." Not being able to hear him Kirby asks him, "What did you say?" Terri screams with a terrified tone, "Behind you! One of the monsters is behind you!" Kirby looks behind him and there stood the monster just looking at him. The monster grabs him and leaps into the air, growing wings and taking off.

Pitou tries to grab the monster but is too slow, Kirby screams, "Someone get this thing off of me." Terri jets off with his ears, "I'll go get him" he said as he flies after the beast. He catches up and tells the monster to drop Kirby and says, "I know you hear me." While flying forward he spins with his ears out like a top knocking the monster in his back. The monster loses his grip on Kirby and Terri catches him and retreats to the others.

262

"Thanks Terri." Terri told him, "No problem but THAT THING'S NOT GIVING UP! HELP!"

Jabari looks to the skies trying to find them and Aziza says she sees them. "Terri's flying and he's got him, but they got company." Jabari tells Ebondre to give him a lift, Ebondre summons his shield Jabari runs and jumps on Ebondre's shield. He tosses Jabari up to cut the beast down. The shadow beast falls gasping trying to speak, "Kirr" then kills over.

They all look at the monster, thinking to themselves what that was about. Jabari asks Kirby if he is hurt, and he tells him he's fine. But Kirby tells him what happened right before the monster took him. He tells him how it just sat there and stared at him. Pitou walks over to Terri and tells him good job.

"No problem. But we should probably ask why the shadows were chasing that guy."

Blaine lifts the man up and slaps his face, "Wake up old man." The man wakes up dazed, "What? What's going on? Where am I? Who are you, people?"

Terri gasps and tells the man "You people?! I'll have you know I am a rabbit, sir." Galvan tells him they found him in the middle of the road and lets him know he was about to be attacked by monsters.

Aziza asks, "Sir can you tell us who you are and why were those things after you?"

The man introduces himself as Ruben, "My name's Ruben. I was running away from blue shadow monsters who kidnapped me and others. Where are they?"

Elon tells him he's the only one they saw. The man tells them there were others who escaped like he did; they all ran in separate directions. The man then coughs up blood. Aziza looks at all his wounds and tells them this isn't good, that they need to get him to a doctor. She then asks how long till Dye City now. They look at the map and tell her an hour, Elon said he can use some herbs that will help with infections and heal his cuts. Pryce can heal him with ice if that helps. It can numb the pain and heal broken skin and bones.

Jabari tells them that they will have to wait until then, so they get him in the cart. Come on let's go he said as they all hop in the cart and race to Dye city. Ivorious pulls Jabari over and tells him about what he saw with the monster. He saw how that thing looked at Kirby; it looked like it was angry at him. So, Jabari asks him what he thinks he wants with him. Ivorious suggested maybe the shadow wanted to take Kirby to wherever they had this man and wanted to take him.

Kirby overhears what was said and he looks at the man. They arrive in Dye City and rush to find a hospital for the man. The man was kept alive by Elon and Pryce performing healing magic on the man. Aziza asks a woman to carry a bag of food for help.

Book One
Chapter Twenty-One
Female Archer's Determination.

"Hey, excuse me, do you know where a hospital is?"

The woman responds "Sure it's over there past the food market... (Gasp) Ruben oh my gods! What happened to you? Where did you find him?"

Cornelia tells her, "We found him on the side of the road and that's what we're trying to figure out. How do you know him?" The woman tells them he's her husband. They all go to the hospital and get him in. While they wait for him to wake up, the woman explains what has been going on lately.

"My name is Beth, my husband and a group of other men went to look for missing teens from our village. And now you're telling me the men are missing too."

"From what he told us, that's what we think. What exactly took the kids?" Jabari asks.

Beth tells them, "Three people saw it but two were attacked and didn't make it. The one who lived said it was a blue shadow creature. Several of them attacked and kidnapped several teens, 9 to be exact."

"This is getting bad. These things are killing people!" Ivorious said, looking at Jabari.

Kirby sits there thinking phasing everyone out, "I wonder where that thing was going to take me. He might know." He gets up and walks over to Ruben. Kirby tries to wake him up, Ruben then places his hand on his head. His eyes start to glow then he sees a mountain. He sees several other men are being carried by the shadow beast. Then they break free from its grip, then they all run in separate directions. Kirby is then pulled off Ruben by Jabari.

"What do you think you're doing Kirby? I am so sorry Beth."

"I saw them!"

"Them who?" Jabari asked.

"The man who she was talking about I saw in my head. While from his head. It's like I saw what he saw when I touched him. They were being carried by the shadow beasts on a path towards some mountain. They all broke apart from it. There was a guy with red hair and a piece of bread. Then a man with brown and black hair. And a guy with black skin and brown hair." Kirby said.

Beth gasps and covers her mouth then says the names of the three men Kirby describes, "Luger, Febrix, and Tobyo. They went with Ruben and went after the monsters. And the mountain."

Jabari asks her, "Do you know the mountain?"

"Mount Nakure."

"A woman with copper skin, glasses, black hair who looks around Jabari's age and a little shorter than Aziza burst into the room."

"Mom, is dad back?"

"Shiba! He's here but needs to rest."

Shiba makes her way to her father. She starts to tear up at the site of his wounds.

She screams, "Who did this to him?"

Kirby pulls her arm and tells her, "Shadow beast and the others are still out there."

"Mom, who are these people?"

Beth explains, "These people found your father in the middle of the road, they saved his life from those beasts. They were taking them to Mount Nakure."

Jabari asks Beth, "Can you tell us where this mountain is?"

Beth tells them, "Right before you enter the city the mountain path is a mile away."

"We'll go there and see if we can find them." Jabari tells her but Shiba grabs his arm telling him she's coming too.

Beth pulls her back and accosts her, "Shiba?! Are you crazy? Look at what that thing did to your dad. He was a wreck before they healed him."

"I'm going mom! I want to kill this thing with my bare hands for what it did to dad. I'm going, and I will be back."

Aziza tells her, "We'll stay here with your mother, Cornelia and I will keep her safe while you guys go find the others."

"Looks like we get to bash some shadow beast again." Kirby says, grabbing his shield, but his brother stops him. "Not you,

you're staying here with Aziza and Cornelia." His big brother said.

He drops his shield and groans, "Aw but why?"

"That thing grabbed you and almost flew away. We were lucky enough Terri was able to catch that thing and get you back. Here you'll be safe." He tells his little brother.

"But I was helping in the fight too. Didn't you see me throw the shield? And how it bounces off not one but two of them."

"I did, and you can use that to help protect the people here. Okay?" Jabari said.

Jabari asks Shiba if there is something she needs to get before they head out. Shiba says she already brought everything she needs. She shows them her bow and arrow, she and the rest are ready to go. Leaving behind Aziza, Cornelia, Terri, Pitou, and Kirby. Aziza asks Beth if she can tell us about the teens who went missing.

"Well, it happened over the course of three weeks. Three the first, five the second week, and the last week nine I mentioned earlier. But it's not just them, other villages, towns, and cities children and teenagers have been going missing. Nobody knows where they are, who's taking them, and I'm afraid my daughter is next."

"And all of them have been taken by the shadow beasts?" Cornelia asks Beth she then replies, "Is that what people have been calling them."

Kirby is seen walking outside with Pitou and Terri. Kirby looks around and sees all the boarded-up house people hiding in their homes. Even though the town isn't empty, they are still given the feeling the town has been abandoned. Kirby looks at all these houses and sees a pair of eyes of a little kid. Kirby waves but the boy is pulled away from his window by his dad.

"These shadow beasts have really thrown this whole town in quite a scare. It's the middle of the day and not a person is on site." Pitou said.

Kirby says, "I wonder where the last attack happened."

Pitou asks him, "Didn't she say two witnesses died?"

Terri stops them, "Yeah and I think we found it." Terri said as he pointed to a scene where blood is spilled on the ground and two chalk outlines.

"Whoa." Kirby said walking closer to the scene, Pitou stops him saying he thinks it's best if they get back with the others. A trash can gets knocked over around the corner, Terri jumps behind Kirby.

"What was that?" Terri said, shaking behind Kirby.

Pitou said, "It came from behind that corner."

Kirby says he's got this, he then throws the shield towards a pole it bounces behind the corner hitting Stanley. Stanley then falls over rubbing his head.

"Ow, what the heck kid that hurt." Stanley said then August came from around the corner.

August said, "I said 'Duck'".

Stanley told him, "No he didn't!"

"I'm pretty sure he did." Walter told him.

Stanley tells Walter to shut up, then August tells him "Don't talk to him like that!"

"Hey, look, it's the scruffy kids from before." Terri said.

Kirby asks them, "What are you guys doing here?"

August comes up with some excuse for their being there to hide the true intention. "We're here on vacation."

Kirby tilts his head in confusion, "Really? You guys sure picked a bad place to go on vacation. People in this town are being kidnapped and killed."

"We're traveling around Hue." August replied.

271

Kirby doesn't question them anymore and tells them it's not safe out here.

Stanley then says, "Yeah I bet. Little kids throwing shields around hitting people. "

Walter runs to Pitou and Terri calling them doggy and bunny. "My name is Pitou. But since you're so innocent, doggy is fine." Walter then asks if he can pet the doggy, Pitou tells him fine.

"But no, we're serious monsters who have been kidnapping teenagers." Kirby said.

"Why are you worried you're nine." Stanley said.

"I'm ten I'm just short, come on let's get back to the hospital."

Back on Earth Ishtarel calls friends over the door.

"Where are they?" Ishtarel said pacing back and forth and Tazama told him, "Calm down, they'll be here... now." Three men and two women swoop down from the sky and appear in front of his house. One of the women, Una , has long black dreadlocks that cross over her chest. And Yuriel the other woman has dark skin with long black hair with silver tips at the end. Jushura is a dark black skin man with a grey hair afro, Kashi another brown skin with long black hair and finally Asharo a light skin man with short natural brown hair.

Una smiles and says, "Long time no see everyone."

Yuriel ignores her, "Yeah. Can you tell us why you called an emergency meeting?"

Jushura tells him, "Yes you sounded distraught."

Kashi says while burping a bit, "Yeah, I had to have another drink because you sounded so stressed out."

Asharo looks at him, "I doubt that to be the real reason you got another drink."

"Hey, guys listen." Tazama said.

"Jabari and Kirby were pulled through the door into Palette." They all gasp with panicked looks on their face.

"Oh no." Una said as she covered her mouth.

Yuriel asks, "How is that even possible?"

"I thought the door was sealed." Jushura said.

Ishtarel tells them, "It was but someone opened it. I don't know who, what, how, or why but somehow the door was open. Whoever opened it, made sure I wasn't there to stop whatever it was that came out and took my kids."

Asharo asked, "What are our next steps?"

"And what can we do to help?" Kashi asks.

"I don't know but Tazama saw into the future and saw them finding their way back. But I called you here to warn you to be careful. If they were able to break the seal on the door, they just might be able to open a new one."

Back in Palette, we see Jabari and the others approaching the mountain.

"So, this is Mount Nakure?" Jabari asks, staring at the trail leading to the mountain."

Shiba rushes her way to the front, "Yes this is the mountain your brother saw. This is where they were taking them?"

Galvan says, "It doesn't make much sense."

"What do you mean?" Blaine asked him.

Galvan explains, "Think about it. If I wanted to kidnap someone, why take them to a place close to where you took them from?"

Elon tells them, "Maybe to hide them in plain sight."

"Good idea. If those monsters brought them here and hid them well enough and the search party missed them, they would be in the clear. I mean the best place to hide something is somewhere someone has already looked." Jabari said.

Shiba runs and looks to the ground, "Look! Footprints! They were here, and a struggle happened, look at the dragging marks."

Ivorious points out that there are footprints from the shadow beast as well. The group pushes forward towards the mountain following the footprints. Meanwhile the others back in Dye City talk about the missing teens. Aziza asks Beth how long this has been going.

"Like I said it's been three weeks for missing teens here but altogether 6 months from all over."

Cornelia asks her, "How come there has been no news about it?"

Beth tells them, "We tried telling authorities, but they did nothing. We went to Hue city and Tone Town to put up posters and tell people. But they were overshadowed by the tournament. I think I've seen your friends before, didn't they participate? Your boyfriend won."

Aziza blushes and stutters trying to correct her, "My boyfriend? No, he's not my boyfriend. We're just close friends."

Beth then tells Aziza that she reminds her of herself when she was her age.

Aziza tries to guess what she means by saying, "Young and optimistic?"

Cornelia says in a snarky tone, "Powder puff and bubbly?"

Beth tells both they are right, and Kirby walks in saying they're back. Aziza looks and whispers to Cornelia. "Did you know he was gone?" Cornelia responds, "Didn't even notice and who are those scruffy kids? "

Stanley's irritation shows when he says, "Why does everyone call us scruffy?"

"They're my friends from Tone Town." Kirby tells her.

"See aren't you glad you stayed behind? You met up with your friends and got them inside before those things got them." Aziza told him.

Kirby said they went walking and they saw the whole scene. Beth said she wishes they would clean that up. Beth asks Kirby if he and his friends would like something to eat. She tells them that she can ask the nurse to bring them some food.

Stanley tells her that's nice but before he rejects her offer Walter says that's awesome thanks her. August whispers to Stanley to let him eat. They haven't had a meal since the banquet. They thank her for her kindness.

Aziza remembers from before and asks Cornelia, "So, Cornelia do you want to tell me about your hands now?"

Cornelia tells her bluntly, "Oh that's right, I never told you did I. I'm a witch."

She looks at her and says, "Oh so, is that why you're a little bitter sometimes?"

Back with Jabari and the others, they are going further and further to the mountain. Until Jabari tells them to stop, Shiba asks him what's the hold up.

"Look. This is where they must have escaped and scattered. We found your dad on the road, so he must have gone northeast and these must be the footprints of the other men." Jabari said.

Ebondre says to them, "They all scattered but all of them didn't get away." He then points to where they were recaptured and drugged. Two of the men got away, but the monster got the other two.

"The monster got them and took them to wherever the children were. The dragging marks lead towards the top of the mountain." Ivorious said.

The group walks towards the trail where it leads into the mountain. As they approach the cave, Shiba turns and points her arrow at Chrome. Chrome screams what the hell and she tells him to duck. Shiba launches three glowing orange arrows that strike down two of the shadow beasts that were hiding. A third one tries to counter and slashes Shiba leg. She then takes her bow and stabs the beast in its face.

Chrome tells her, "Next time say duck first before you scare me. " Shiba tells him she's sorry.

Elon looks at her leg and tells her to let him look, Shiba tells him she's fine saying it's just a little scratch. Azuro says it's three scratches and they aren't little; Elon tells her he can help. But she says she's fine.

Jabari puts his hand on her arm and tells her, "Hey look I know you want to find your dad's friends. Get back at those things for what they did to your dad. But you can't if you're hurt and won't get help. Let Elon heal you then we'll keep moving." Shiba reluctantly says okay and lets Elon heal her.

"Nice job talking some sense into her." Blaine told Jabari.

Jabari tells him she is just very protective of her dad and just wants to stop those things from hurting people. They follow the path that leads to the cave of the mountain. Back at the hospital Beth and Aziza trade thoughts on Jabari.

# Book One
## Chapter Twenty-Two
### Kind of a Kaiju Attack

Pitou looks out the window at the houses that are boarded up, "Why would these shadow beasts kidnap people?" He asked out loud to himself, Kirby tells him, "Because they're bad."

"No. Think about it. They pull you, your brother and I into this world. Then we find an atlas and they follow our every move wherever we go. Then they start kidnapping teens and men. Doesn't really add up."

Walter said, stuffing the food in his mouth. "Maybe they're following because they want something from you. I mean that's what we do when we see someone who looks rich."

"What did you just say?" Terri said, looking at him, raising his eyebrow.

Stanley covers his mouth saying, "Nothing! He just likes to talk." He then whispers to Walter, "Are you trying to get us caught?"

Walter mumbles with Stanley's hand on his mouth, then Stanley moves his hand. "Hey, I think I just saw something. outside." Walter said.

Aziza and Beth stop talking and look at the window and Cornelia asks "Where?"

 August tells him he's probably just seeing things and tells him to keep eating.

"You might be right. What are they trying to get? You think it's Zanatar's Valley." Kirby asks Pitou.

"Maybe but how would they even know, when you didn't know until you got here?" Pitou asks.

Back at the mountain, the group travels down the tunnel. They walk down the path and see trails of blood. Dragging marks where it looks like people were clawing at the ground to escape. They discover a door.

Jabari says, "This is not good. I don't like the looks of this, and I got a bad feeling about what's on the other side of this door."

Winn asks, "Do you think it's someone waiting on a fight?"

"Or the result of a slaughter." Ebondre said, this causes Shiba to shutter. Blaine then elbows him, letting him know that he's making her nervous. Ebondre then says, "I don't sugar coat anything for anyone."

The group enters the door and stubbles upon the bodies of the search group torn and tattered. The men were beaten to death for reasons unknown and there was no sign of the teens. Shiba falls to her knees and lets out a painful cry.

"NOOOO! Luger! Febrix! Oh god!"

Jabari places his hand on her shoulder to console her. The others look around the cave but no one else is here.

"It looks like no one else is here." Winn tells him.

"He's right. I see where the teens would be, but they are not here now. Look at something written on the wall near Febrix." Pryce points out.

This causes Shiba to get up and look for herself, "What did he write? 'Blue eyes? Red eyes?' What does that even mean?" She said, holding back the tears in her eyes.

"Come on Shiba! You need to be strong, okay. Your dad is back there waiting on you."

Blaine asks "Why did they bring them up here just to kill them? It makes no sense."

Elon thinks about the note and says, "Maybe they saw something they shouldn't have when they came to the mountain."

Blaine then says, "Wait if these things killed the search group then..." Before he could finish Shiba jumps up and says dad fearing the monsters will go to finish the job. Jabari tells them let's go and they jet out of the cave into a group of red shadow beasts.

"Aw crap more of these things." Chrome said.

"But they're Red this time? Jabari, have you fought these kinds before?" Pryce asked him.

Jabari looks at the monsters he's seen before but never this color, "No, we haven't. Not these before."

They are then charged by the beasts, this time they are more relentless. The scene cuts back to the others in Dye City and a growl can be heard from outside.

Walter then hears the same sound again and the others hear it too. He asks everyone while still eating, "Now do you guys believe me? There is something out there." He spoke.

Aziza gets up, "Beth gets behind me with your husband. Cornelia gets over here, Pitou, Terri, and Kirby get behind Cornelia, you too scruffy kids."

The whole room goes silent. They can hear a low growling sound, then a shadow beast leaps through the window. But this one is different from the others before. A light Red shadow but instead of heading for Ruben it sets its sight on Kirby and jumps for him.

"Cornelia, Kirby looks out." Aziza said.

The monster smacks Cornelia away, then Cornelia yells for him to use his shield to protect him and the others.

"On it, you three get behind me." Kirby takes his shield to protect him and the others. The monster bounces off, but the beast rebounds and then disarms him by knocking his shield away.

"Well, that hurt my self-confidence." Kirby said looking as his The shield slides to the other side of the room.

Walter looks and asks Kirby, "Are you new at this whole fighting thing cause if you are it's okay. "

August interjects and says, "But maybe not at this moment in time."

The monster then grabs Kirby, and Pitou rushes the monster yelling to put him down. The beast then grabs Pitou and throws him out the window. Terri throws Kirby his shield and bashes the monster's head without any effort. Then Pitou takes down the beast and bites at his neck causing him to let go of Kirby. Aziza then fires a powerful blast knocking the monster down and Pitou does a rapid front spin. The monster flies out the window.

"Woah, that was cool. How come the dog is fighting better than you?" Stanley asked.

Aziza rushes over and asks Kirby if he is okay, Kirby tells her he's fine. Kirby tells Terri to give him some air, Cornelia tells the three scruffy kids to watch Beth. Aziza tells Pitou to move the monster away from the hospital. Aziza shoots mini bullets and Pitou then front flips into a spin to sweep across the shadow beast legs. But the shadow grabs Aziza and Pitou then throws them into a bakery shop. Then the shadow grows over 20 ft. Tall.

"Oh, that hurt. You okay?" Pitou asks Aziza.

Aziza says, "Yeah. Thanks for breaking my fall."

The bakery owner hides behind the counter saying, "Take what you want but just don't hurt me."

Kirby takes his shield and throws it at the monster, "Hey! It is not nice to throw people and damage others property. Leave the townsfolk out of it. Terri flies to an open area."

"Like where?"

Beth tells them that there is a park, it's huge and that thing will cause less damage. Kirby tells Terri to let's go, they fly to the park. Cornelia chants an incantation, "Witches of the north give me strength." Cornelia's hands start to glow with a swirl symbol on them.

She then enchants her feet so she can leap into the air and lands on the head. She tries stomping him down, but the shadow quickly recovers and knocks her off. Then she enchants her hands to land a powerful punch to the monster's face. But like before the monster quickly recovers from it and chases after Kirby, who leads it to the park. People see the beast coming and are evacuated by Cornelia and Aziza.

Aziza tries to get everybody out of the park, but Cornelia sees that they aren't moving fast enough. "What are you people deaf? Get your kids and get out while you can."

"Terri lands on Pitou. This thing is slow and with the three of us, we should be able to come up with a plan. Pitou lands on him. What are we going to do? This thing has it out for me and it's not like the one from before that snatched me from the cart. It wants to hurt me, and I didn't even do anything." Kirby said.

"Maybe they're mad about you hitting them with your shield." Terri suggests.

Pitou tells him, "No, Kirby is right, this red one is not like the ones we faced before. The energy, the aura, it's different, more malicious like it's holding a grudge against Kirby." Kirby tells Pitou to go to Aziza and Cornelia, he has an idea on how to stop the monster. Pitou says okay unsure of what Kirby has in mind. He then zooms and grabs them.

"Why is that thing so determined to hurt you?" Aziza asks.

"I don't know but I have an idea. Do you see that statue in the middle of the park, the one with the sharp point on top?" They look and see it and say yeah.

"Let's see if we can knock him on it. If we combine attacks that should be enough to knock him over on it." Kirby said.

Cornelia tells him, "Great idea but I don't think that thing will fall for it that easily. We need a distraction."

Terri tells them he's got an idea, "I know the perfect distraction. I'll be back." Terri flies off back in the direction of the hospital and the scene cuts back to August, Stanley, and Walter.

August sits down and says out loud, "Well that was...I don't even know how to describe that thing."

"I think we're in over our heads man. Maybe this shield isn't worth all the trouble." Stanley said, trying to convince August.

"I think you're right, let's just leave."

Terri pops up, "Hey you three we need your help. We need distractions to help beat that thing." He said to them,

Stanley yells at him, "Are you crazy? We're not going anywhere near that monster!"

Terri looks at Walter and gets another idea, "Hey Walter if you help us Doggy said you could pet his bushy tail."

Walter's eyes open wide and he asks, "Really bunny?" Terri tells him yes and Walter tells him he'll gladly help. Terri says good then tells him to hold on and flies off. August tells Terri to put Walter down and Terri tells him if he wants Walter back, they must follow. Terri takes Walter and flies off with him, Stanley and August chase after him.

Kirby, Cornelia, and Aziza are hiding and waiting on Terri. "Where is that rabbit? I bet he bailed on us." Said Cornelia.

287

Aziza looks up and sees him, "Here he comes and is carrying one of those scruffy kids."

Terri flies in with Walter, "Now listen Walter, see that big monster over there? Get its attention, say your Kirby's best friend, and try to get it to chase you towards that statue."

"Okay and then I get to pet the doggy's tail, right?"

Terri rolls his eyes, "Sure kid. Whatever."

"Yay. Hey, monster see that kid, I'm one of his best friends. So, what are you going to do about it."? Walter said getting in front of the monster.

Walter goes towards the monster and does exactly what Terri told him to do. The shadow begins to chase him, Stanley and August catch up to him. August tells Walter to get back here and Stanley says look out, now all three are being chased.

Pitou asks, "Terri, did you mean for all three to be chased?"

"No, but hey they're all running in the same direction so it's good."

Kirby tells them, "Now guys they're in front of the statue!"

Aziza fires a beam of magic and Cornelia uses a blast from an incantation both to hit the beast in his face. Pitou slams into

288

the monster but the beast grabs him and throws him at both Cornelia and Aziza knocking them down.

Terri panics and asks, "AHHH! Kirby, what are we going to do?"

Kirby thinks to himself, "Come on there has to be something, I wish I could do more with this shield then throw it. Aw man I wish Jabari was here he could light his sword on fire and end this already."

Just as Kirby said fire the shield starts to blaze with a pyre, his eyes start to glow, then Kirby calls Terri.

"Terri picks me up, flies me far enough and then charges at full speed into its head."

"Um okay."

While the monster is still recovering from the triple attack Terri takes Kirby and flies him as far as possible. He then jets towards the monster; the speed causes the fire to spread creating a fireball like appearance. At top speed, Kirby slams his shield into the monster knocking it over. It lands on the statue destroying it, as the monster fades Kirby can sense something from the beast.

"Kirby you did it! Hey, why are you crying we won?" Terri asks while looking at Kirby. Kirby's eyes started watering uncontrollably but he wasn't crying.

"I don't know. I don't feel sad, but I can't stop crying."

Aziza then pulls herself from under the rubble after getting him by Pitou. "Oh, my head." She said rubbing it.

"Your head? My back! Get off me Pitou you weigh a ton like this." Cornelia said, trying to get from underneath him.

"I'll have you know I was much bigger than this so be grateful I lost the weight."

Aziza praises Kirby for his plan, "Kirby your plan worked, you stop the monster!"

"No, we wouldn't have been able to stop the monster if you guys didn't blind him. I need to sit down for a minute, I'm a little tired."

"Hey, what about us? We were the distractions." August said.

Terri corrects him, "Walter was the distraction, you guys didn't even want to help."

Stanley scolds Walter, "You idiot!" Stanley hits Walter upside his head. "Why did you go off flying like that? We could have been killed because of you!"

Walter starts to cry, "August, Stanley hit me!"

"What the hell is wrong with you?! I told you, you can hit him like that." August said as Walter ran behind him.

"August, don't let him come near me." Walter said.

"It's okay Walter he didn't mean it." August tells him.

Walter says, "Yes, he did!"

August tries to calm him down, "No, he didn't I promise. Did you?"

Stanley reluctantly says, "No."

"Now apologize!" August said.

Stanley walks to Walter and says he's sorry. Walter then stops crying and says, "I forgive you." Walter then hugs Stanley.

Cornelia looks and says, "Okay I'm so over them, they went from scruffy to just weird."

Stanley shouts, "We ain't scruffy, we took baths!"

Terri asks, "Where exactly?"

August tells them they used the sink in the bathroom and Cornelia gets up and dusts herself off.

"Come on, let 's check on Rufus and Bonnie." Cornelia said.

Aziza corrects her, "You mean Ruben and Beth."

"Yeah, sure whatever. They won't even show up until the next book."

As the group got to the hospital Beth and Ruben were moved to a different room. They go to check on them, soon after the others return. Jabari and the others walk through the door and Shiba rushes her way through to see her dad up and well.

Shiba asks him, "Dad are you okay?"

"I'm fine Shiba, thanks to these wonderful people, they were able to kill that nasty shadow beast."

Shiba turns to them and gives Kirby, Aziza, Cornelia, Pitou, and Terri a hug saying, "Thank you. Thank you all so much."

Aziza tells her that they couldn't have done it without Kirby. Cornelia says that he came up with an amazing plan and it worked like a charm.

Blaine tussles Kirby's hair, "You did a really good job kid."

Elon says, "Wish we were here to see it."

Kirby says, "I couldn't have done it by myself, it was me, Pitou, Terri, Aziza, Cornelia, Walter, August, and Stanley."

Galvan has a stumped face and asks, "Who are the last three?"

"They were the scruffy kids but they're clean now kind of. Kirby met them back in Tone town and they were a distraction." Cornelia said.

Azuro asks, "So what else happened while we were gone?"

"When you guys were gone, a shadow came and attacked us and the weirdest thing was after me for some reason. Like I did something to it, the thing is I've never seen a red shadow before." Kirby said.

"Strangely, we saw some on the mountain." Ivorious tells them.

Beth then says, "The mountain! Did you find the teens? Are they safe?" Beth asks.

"What about my friends, are they okay?" Ruben asks.

The boys go quiet and with a look of anguish on her face, Shiba tells her father.

"Dad Luger and Febrix they're dead."

"What?" Ruben asks with his jaw dropping in disbelief.

"We found a hidden path in the mountains and followed it. We found a cellar where their bodies were. We rushed back here because we thought they were coming for you." Shiba told him.

Ruben asks, "Why? Why did they kill them?"

"We don't know." Jabari said.

"Can you tell us anything from before that might have given them a reason to kill them?" Elon asks Ruben.

"I headed down the mountain and right before I got out of hearing distance, I heard one of them yell. 'What are you two doing here? Get your brother out of here.' then I heard a scream." Ruben said.

"Who were the other two?" Aziza asks.

Ruben tells her, "I don't know. I didn't see any of them."

"The two people he saw could be the ones behind the killings and the kidnappings? Red eyes and Blue eyes." Pryce asks the group.

Brock then says, "Possibly. These two could have something to do with it."

Ebondre then says, "Not only that but if these guys are controlling the shadow beast." Then Jabari finishes for him by saying, "Then they could have been responsible for bringing me and Kirby here in the first place."

While that thought sinks into everyone's head, they explain the message they found in the cellar. The red eyes and blue eyes are written in blood.

In the far distance, in the shadows two Silhouettes can be seen. It shows their backs with a tall and short figure. The tall one is wearing a blue mask and the smaller one is wearing a red mask. Both their hair has locks, the blue mask locks are longer.

"You were reckless! Why did you attack him?" Blue told and asked him.

"Cause I'm angry at him, just like you're angry at the other. They deserve everything they get." Red said.

"I know you're angry, but we cannot let that get in the way of our goal. We need to tell him. He will have to handle it from here. The children are his problem, not ours." Said Blue.

"Are you sure it's a good idea to let him keep kidnapping them, he's just an incompetent human." Red asks.

"I know but like I said that has nothing to do with us. Unless we need a reason for them to come back." Blue tells him.

"Those stupid townsmen, we should have dealt with him sooner. Now they know what we look like." Red said.

"Calm down. The only thing they know is that there are two of us and the color of our eyes. Besides, they are going to know who we are when we make our debut." Blue told him.
They both have a mask that covers everything but their mouths. The scene cuts back to the group getting ready to leave.

# Book One
## Chapter Twenty-Three
## We Do It to Survive

"Alright, we got everything we need. So, let's hit the road to Wawa Town, right?" Jabari asks.

"Yeah, that's it." Aziza tells him.

Shiba comes running to them screaming and waiting and Terri says, "How much you bet she wants to come along?"

Pitou says, "20 Hueleons."

Shiba does exactly what Terri said, telling the group, "I'm coming too."

"Ha, pay me." Terri said.

"Sorry I broke the next bet against someone who has money and also not against a dog."

Aziza asks, "Why don't you want to stay here with your parents?"

"They're staying with another family in the next town over. Besides, if these things are still around, others will die. And teens will be kidnapped to who knows where. And besides, I know all about Jabari and his brother being otherworldly."

Jabari asks "How?"

"Well, you weren't very discreet with it, when you said it aloud in the hospital." Shiba said.

Jabari shrugs his shoulders saying, "Okay, I guess. I see you won't take no for an answer."

"Not trying to be that girl but I'm pretty sure you're breaking cart laws. I mean this isn't a high occupancy vehicle but yeah." Cornelia says.

Jabari tells Shiba to come on if she's sure. Pitou says, "Great more weight to carry." Kirby tells Pitou, "It's okay Pitou the merrier." "Sure Kirby." Pitou said.

To Wawa town, Kirby said. In the Shadows the two from earlier watched them.

"I hate him." Said Red as he watches them.

"Calm yourself. We'll see them soon enough. And then when the time is right, we'll make them suffer."

August and his friends follow behind Jabari and the others in a stolen cart.

"Why are we still following them? I mean these guys are literally attracting danger." Stanley asks, speaking to August. "But do you know where they're going? To Wawa town. What does Wawa have?" Augusts ask them with a grin on his face. Stanley answers, "I don't know. People?"

Walter answers, "Restaurants that we can afford? Cleaner streets to sleep on since we can't afford a hotel?"

August tells them, "All this is true but no. What did the kid have that we don't?"

Walter says, "A positive attitude?"

August tells them, "No weapons and Wawa town has a Weapons market."

Stanley and Walter both say at the same time, "Weapons Market?"

"Correct and what happened here might happen there. If it does, we can loot those weapons and sell them. Forget that shield. When we get to Wawa Town we'll be able to steal from right under their noses. They'll probably be handling those monsters and that will cause a distraction giving a window of opportunity."

Stanley smiles and tells him nice thoughts. Walter asks, "But what if those monsters don't come?" August tells them that he overheard them earlier saying, these things are popping up wherever they go. The scene cuts to the team on their way to Wawa.

"This cart is amazing it fit's so many of us." Terri said, sitting on top of Cornelia's head. "Oh please. You're so small you don't take any room."

"It's okay Cornelia since I'm riding on Pitou there is more space." Kirby said.

Jabari asks, "Kirby when I say be careful do you hear me do something reckless?"

Kirby tells him "No, I don't think so and besides I've been riding for 20 minutes and have fallen yet."

"Key word yet." Jabari says.

"Stop treating me like a baby." Kirby said.

Brock says, "He has a point, at that age I was dropped in the wilderness for two weeks and I did perfectly fine."

"See there is no need to worry." Kirby said.

Jabari tells him, "No, cause when you say no need to worry that's when I worry the most."

"Hey, icy look at the map and tell us how long it's going to take." Chrome tells Pryce.

"Pryce. My name is Pryce, and we should get there in less than half an hour."

Aziza notices Kirby staring off into space, "Kirby is something wrong?"

Brock tells him, "You've been staring out in space for a while."

"Kirby what's wrong?" Jabari asks him.

Kirby tells them what happened after the monster was defeated. "When we beat the red shadow, it felt like I was hurting on the inside and I don't know why."

Blaine says to him, "Maybe it's just you're not used to knowing how to end your opponents."

Elon says, "Blaine he's a child, of course he's not used to it."

Ebondre scoffs, telling them, "When I was his age I was hunting, fighting and killing monsters."

"That alone should be reason enough. Look how you turned out." Ivorious said.

Aziza points to the horizon, "Look I can see it. Wawa town." The group arrives in the Suburban town of Wawa home to some of the country's fine resorts and getaways.

Jabari tells everyone, "Remember we're just riding through, we're not stopping."

"But I gotta pee." Said Kirby.

"Can't you hold it Kirby?" Jabari asks.

Aziza interrupts him, "Um Jabari."

"Yeah, Aziza?"

"I have to pee too." Aziza says and Cornelia says her too. Jabari asks if anyone else has to pee and everyone raises their hand.

"Okay, bathroom break and back on the road."

They pull into town and find a restroom, Aziza returns first. While everyone is using the restroom, she notices a shop and wonders about it. Cornelia walks out and follows her.

"Where are you going?" Jabari asks Aziza.

"To the little stand, just to look around."

Cornelia goes with her, "Yeah it beats waiting near the bathroom." She speaks.

Kirby walks out and says, "I'm finished."

"Okay, now we just wait for the others." Aziza pulls his arm towards the stand. "Jabari came here. Look at these clothes, they would look great on you. Come and try them on." Jabari says okay.

"It won't take long just try some on and they even have some for Kirby."

Cornelia pumps Kirby up saying, "Yeah kid you'll be going home in style with some new clothes."

"Awesome! New clothes! Let's go Jabari!"

"Do you think they'll have anything in our size?" Ask Terri. "I doubt they carry a size rabbit and oh wait never mind I actually see something in your size and me too." Pitou said.

The six of them walk towards the stands to browse at the clothes. The others come out one by one, soon then August and his group arrives exhausted.

August scolds Stanley, "Finally, damn it we made it here in one piece, we stole a cart, but you couldn't find a horse."

Stanley yells back, "The mules were the only thing there! Come on Walter!"

"I'm tired! August can we please get some water?" Walter asks.

August tells him, "Soon Walter we'll get all the water you want. When those monsters come, we'll rob the weapons market blind, sell them and rack up."

"Even Giovanni's Water?" Walter asks, and August tells him yes.

"I was thinking about something." Stanley asks.

"Like what?"

"This place has more than just a weapons market. There are clothes, jewelry, and so much more. I think when these monsters come, we rob everyone. I'm talking about clothes, jewels, weapons, and food."

"Now let's not bite off more than we can chew." August tells him.

"Like you said everyone will be so busy trying to stop those monsters. We'll be able to swoop in and take what we want." Stanley said.

Walter gets excited, "Let's do it August! I know we can get away with it."

Meanwhile, Shiba and the others are browsing the weapons section of the stands. Shiba spots Jabari and walks his way. Shiba taps her foot, and asks Jabari, "How long are we planning on being here? Unless you forgot, we need to find those missing kids."

"I know but after everything, I think we all need to relax and have some fun. Don't you think? I mean especially you, so I think you could use this." Jabari said.

"I guess so but..."

"Hey look, we'll look around for an hour or two and leave. Hey, come with us and do some shopping or just look around." Said Jabari trying to reassure her.

"I guess you're right."

"Hey, guys, come look at the outfit I picked out." Aziza said.

The scene cuts to August and the others waiting for the monsters to show up. An hour goes by.

Stanley grows impatient and asks August "Damn it! What the hell is taking these monsters so long?" Walter says, "Maybe they took the day off?"

"Shut up dummy!" Stanley said.

August tells them to give it time, "Something will happen sooner or later." Walter then whines saying, "But it's been an hour and they look like they're about to leave."

Book One
Chapter Twenty-Four
She's a Brick House

As they watch waiting for the monsters to show up, a medium tall, thick, brown skin woman with long black hair and bangs covering her eyes walks up to them. The woman then takes out a piece of paper and speaks.

"Excuse me, I'm handing out these flyers to bring awareness to the recent kidnappings of young people. If you happen to see anything suspicious, please let the authorities know." She said handing them a flyer.

August looks and takes the flyer, "Um okay. We will be sure to let you know what we see."

"Thank you, I appreciate your help."

"Hey, August, look at all these kids who are around our age." Walter said.

"Hey, guys! How ya been?" Kirby said, popping up behind them.

Stanley screams, "OH CRAP!"

"Oh, hello there Kirby. We're great, how have you been?" August said.

"Awesome. We're on our way to Rangi City after this, then home. What's that paper?" Kirby said.

August has an idea to make Kirby and his friends stay a little longer, so the monsters are sure to show up. August tells him in a worried voice, "Oh, it's a flyer for those poor missing children. Haven't you heard? More teens are going missing. That woman has been handing out these flyers, trying to get people's attention, but no one seems to care."

"Oh no that's so sad."

August plays the role a little more, "It is sad and if only they could find someone who cares."

"My brother and our friends could help. We may be on our way home, but we can still try to help."

"Bless you." August said as Kirby runs off to tell his brother. Kirby says to them, "I'll go get them, I'll take the paper."

As Kirby runs off to tell the others Stanley asks, "What was the point of that act?"

August tells him, "Now they'll feel compelled to help and stay longer. Which means now those monsters now have a better chance of showing up."

"Wow, you sure are smart to come up with that plan on the spot." Walter tells him.

"Please, I could have thought of that." Stanley said.

August brushes him off, "Sure, whatever. Now we wait."

The scene cuts back the group getting ready to leave.

Jabari looks around, "Okay we're all here but Kirby."

Kirby runs yelling, "Wait, look what I got."

Ivorious asked, "What is it?"

He takes the flyer, "It's a flyer with a bunch of missing kids and all of them look around the same age, like the ones from Dye City."

Jabari asks Kirby where he got this from, and he tells them he got it from August and his friends. Galvan asks who and Azuro reminds him of the scruffy kids. Kirby tells them a woman was handing these out. Aziza looks and sees a woman passing out papers and asks if it was her. Kirby says maybe and walks over there.

"Kirby you can't just walk up to random people like that." His brother told him.

Pryce tells him, "Can't be mad, children his age just want to help out but still you shouldn't let your brother run off to strangers."

"Unless you realize we are all kinds of strangers." Winn said.

Kirby starts talking fast, "Hey Miss I got your flyer, and I came to tell you me and my friends are having the same problem. Shiba's village also had teens go missing so we think we can help you out."

"I am sorry I did not understand a word you just said." Rashida said.

Kirby is huffing and puffing, "Oh man, what I said was." And before he could finish Chrome and Brock put their hands over his mouth. Chrome tells him, "Stop before you pass out."

Shiba walks up to her, "Excuse me miss but I think you and I have a similar problem."

Rashida asks, "How is that so?"

Shiba tells her, "Teenagers, children from my village have gone missing like the ones here. And my friends and I are trying to track down where they could be. So, I think we can help each other."

Rashida stares at her.

Shiba says, "Well?"

"I would greatly appreciate your help. My name is Rashida."

"My name is Shiba. Nice to meet you and these are my friends Jabari, his brother Kirby, their dog, and rabbit Pitou and Terri. Then their comrades Blaine, Elon, Galvan, Azuro, Ebondre, Ivorious, Chrome, Pryce, Brock, Winn, and Cornelia. And I almost forgot Aziza Jabari's girlfriend."

Jabari and Aziza both say, "What?" at the same time and Jabari asks who told her that. Shiba says, Terri and Jabari glares at the rabbit and Kirby tells Aziza her face is blushing.

310

Cornelia asks Rashida, "When did this whole thing start?"

Rashida tells her, "About a week ago, it just happened here but it's been happening all over the countryside."

The scruffy trio sits behind a kiosk and Stanley says, "All they're doing is talking."

"August when will the monster show up?" Walter asks.

"Give it time! Geez, these things didn't have a problem before why now." August said getting upset.

"I'm so bored right now I can scream." Stanley said.

Just as he said that a terrified woman's scream. Walter says, "Geez Stanley it's not that bad."

August says that wasn't him. The scene cuts to a woman screaming and people running from stands flying in the air. A new shadow beast has appeared, it takes on the shape of a giant golem.

"Finally, now just like we planned to jack the stands with the weapons, jewels, and other stuff. Stanley goes ahead and leads the monster there."

Stanley tells him, "Hell no! Walter, you go do it."

Walter says okay then runs out in front of the monster to get its attention. But it pays him no mind whatsoever.

Walter turns around and yells it's not working. As he does the monster then begins to swing at him, but it is intercepted by Rashida who uses her arm to knock the monster back.

Kirby's jaw drops as he says, "Wow."

Cornelia suggests, "How about we let her handle this?"

Shiba asked, "Are you serious?"

"She might need a little help; those things might be a problem." Aziza said as giant balls that are as tall as they are start rolling towards them.

Jabari gives them a plan, "Okay let's go help her out. We need to take out these rollers and the big one. Kirby, Pitou, and Terri get these people out, so they don't get hurt."

Kirby nods his head, "Okay. Let's start with our scruffy friends."

"Agreed!" Pitou said.

"Save the scruffy kids." Terri said.

"Come on we'll attack from three points five on both sides and four of us will strike the front. Aziza, Cornelia, Shiba and I will attack the front of the Golem. Blaine, Ebondre, Galvan, Brock and Chrome the left and the rest on the right, to keep the smaller ones from getting any further." Jabari said.

Rashida tries to hold the giant golem, then she knocks it down with her fist. Cornelia asks, "This chick, what kinds of magic is that she's using?"

Aziza says, "I don't recognize any kind of magic coming from her."

Pryce suggests, "Maybe she's not human."

Azuro says, "Maybe a demon."

"No Floracion would sense something." Said Elon.

"I don't care what she is, she's kicking ass and I like it." Blaine said.

Shiba asked, "Was it like this before I came along?"

Ebondre says, "I think so."

"Yep, every time but on the upside, we always meet strong people every time we run into these things." Galvan said.

While the others hold back the shadow golem Kirby, Pitou and Terri are getting people to safety. Kirby tells the citizens, "You need to keep running, get out of here." Pitou guides people telling them to go this way, "Come on people let's move those tails. "

"Come on, people move it. Run like you want to see tomorrow. Kirby the scruffy kids, where are they?" Terri said and asked.

"I think they got out of the danger zone."

The scene cuts to August and his companions looting the stores.

Stanley is smiling and says, "Told you guys this was a good idea." Walter then corrects him by saying "No you didn't, this was August's idea" and Stanley tells him, "Shut up." August tells them both, "Both of you keep quiet and keep looting, get as much stuff as you can."

Walter then asks August, "How are we going to carry this stuff?" Stanley says he got an idea. Stanley leaves and pulls up in an automobile that resembles an early 2000 convertible with four doors.

August asks, "Where did you get a Hooptie from?"

"Found it at the cart shops. This thing cost more than that prize money of 500,000 Hueleons. Load it up! We're cleaning this place out." Stanley said.

Terri flies over and spots them, "Hey there you guys are. What are you doing here?"

August stares at him with a blank look on his face, "We are um... looking for stragglers."

"Okay, well Kirby was just worried, just stay over here while we clear everyone out."

"Can do rabbit." Stanley said.

The scene cuts back to the group fighting off the shadow golems. They are exhausted and the golems don't seem to be backing down.

"This is ridiculous, these things aren't getting tired at all." Ivorious said.

"How do you think the others are held up?" Pryce asks.

"Blaine, Galvan, Ebondre, Chrome, and Brock the five of them vs all those other golems. I'm pretty sure they'll be fine." Elon said.

Meanwhile, With the battle against the giant golem, both Aziza and Cornelia are knocked back into a stand.

"DAMN IT THAT HURT!" Cornelia said.

"This thing, is it as strong as the others you've fought?" Aziza asks Jabari.

"No, they were smaller and went down with one hit." Jabari tells her.

"My arrows are having little effect. Its skin is too hard to penetrate. The only one doing any real damage is Rashida." Shiba said.

"I still don't think this chick is human." Cornelia says.

Aziza tells her we can focus on that later. Rashida is going toe to toe with the golem taking all its blows like it's nothing. Cornelia says, "I don't think we can get physical with those things like she can."

Jabari remembers what Shiba said about the skin being too thick to penetrate. But he then notices that the whole body of the golem is covered in thick skin, except the joints on his elbow and knees.

"You're right Cornelia, we can't get physical with it. Which is why we won't, we'll just provide support." Jabari said.

"Like what?" Shiba asks.

"When they're in the middle of their clash we'll attack the golems' knees and elbows." He tells the ladies.

"Because there are only parts not covered." Aziza said, realizing Jabari's Plan.

"Why though?" Cornelia asks.

"Because when designing armor, they leave parts uncovered for better movement." Shiba said.

"Come on. Rashida, keep it busy." Jabari said.

"Ok, I heard everything I got." Rashida told him.

The golem goes in for a punch, but Rashida then grabs its arm and wraps her leg around it trying to hold him down. And she holds it down so the others can strike. Jabari gives the order for them to attack.

All four attack the weak points, Jabari and Shiba take the arms while Aziza and Cornelia take out the legs. Both arms and legs are out of commission, but the golem is relentless. It then begins to break off its own arms and legs after they are rendered useless. It begins to roll like a ball, Rashida moves out the way and the rest follow.

"Are you kidding me?" Jabari said.

"It just broke them off like it was nothing." Aziza said.

"Of course, they're dead weight now. Shit!" Cornelia said.

"Any more ideas?" Shiba asks.

Jabari tells them he's thinking, and Rashida tells him in a calm voice. "Might want to think a little faster because it's coming back."

Meanwhile, Kirby's group has evacuated the last bit of civilians out of the area.

"Okay, I think that's everyone from this area. What about you two?" Kirby said and asked.

"Clear on my end." Pitou said.

"Good over here. Do you think we should check on the scruffy kids?" Terri asks.

"Where are they?" Kirby asks.

"They were helping people near the shops over there." Terri told him.

"Then they should be fine, they are out of the danger zone." Pitou said.

Meanwhile, the scruffy kids load all the goods into the hooptie.

"Is that everything you guys could find?" August asks.

"Yeah, now let's get out of here. Walter, come on!" Stanley said.

"Coming. Look, I got these cool hats." Walter said.

"Walter, those are for women." August said.

"You couldn't find one for men? And why hats in the first place?" Stanley asks.

"I just like them. Hey, look over there." Said Walter.

They turn to see a group of 5 kids somewhere around their age 13 or 14. They are trying to find their way out.

"Crap. Stanley watches the hooptie. What are you guys doing here? This place is too dangerous for kids." August said.

"You look the same age as us and we're trying to get out of here. But what are you rats doing here?" Kid 1 said.

"That's not a nice thing to say." Walter told them.

"Keeping people safe that's what we're doing!" August told them.

Stanley tries to get August's attention, and this causes August to ask. "What is it now? I told you to watch Hooptie."

"Those little round things are back."

August pulls both Stanley and Walter out of sight but the five kids are spotted by the little golems. The golems roll up on them, take them, and roll off. Their cries for help can be heard as they are carried off.

"What the hell was that?" Stanley asks.

August looks like the monsters carry the teens away, "I don't know but let's scream before they come back."

"August. Those things, they just took those kids." Walter said.

"I know Walter, I saw but the most important thing is that none of those kids were you, Stanley or me."

The scene cuts back to Jabari and the others.

"This is so annoying; I didn't tag along just to get crushed to death!" Cornelia said.

"I have another idea." Jabari said.

"A good one this time I hope." Shiba said.

"And it doesn't involve you being a smartass. Listen, we'll all attack in one area. Rashida and I will take it from there. The moment he stays still strikes the center of his chest. Now!" Jabari said.

They all strike the same spot Cornelia starts off with a Hex blast, Aziza with her fairy magic, then Shiba with his arrows. Rashida follows with a mega punch and Jabari takes his sword and comes down on it. With their combined strength they can shatter the armor.

"It works! We broke through." Aziza said.

"Yeah, but like only that one spot, what about the rest?" Cornelia asks.

"Don't worry, Rashida stands right there in the direction of the rolling golem." Rashida says, "Okay." Shiba asks "What are you doing Jabari?" He tells her to just watch and he's going to need to get some air.

Jabari's eye begins to glow, a mighty gust of wind picks up the massive golem. You can see the strain it's putting on Jabari. He lifts the golem as high as he can, to about ten stories, then he drops it. The golem begins to fall, and Rashida catches on to the plan. She holds her fist up, the spot where they shattered the armor is where her fist hit's. With that blow it kills the Shadow Golem. Jabari falls to his knees in exhaustion.

"That was amazing," said Shiba.

"Yeah, I guess it was." Cornelia said.

Aziza walks to him and tells him, "That was a pretty good plan of yours."

"Thanks." He said blushing.

"Hey, lovebirds hurry up. Let's meet up with the others." Cornelia yelled at them.

Meanwhile with Blaine and the others they are trying to defeat the mini golems.

"I have an idea." Said Winn.

"What' that's? Drink them into submission." Brock insulted Winn.

"No, and actually I need you, Azuro and Galvan."

"What do you need us to do?" Azuro asks.

He tells them to follow his lead. Winn starts off by opening fans from both ends of his Boomerang. He starts to spin it rapidly creating a tornado. Winn then tells Azuro and Brock that he needs some water and rocks. Azuro shoots water into the vortex along with Brock adding some very large rocks. Then Winn instructs the others to start knocking mini golems into the vortex of water and rocks.

"Start knocking them in!" Winn yelled.

Chrome asks why and Pryce says to just do it. Blaine says he doesn't see where Winn is going with this, but he says ok and does it. Winn then instructs Galvan to now strike the vortex with lightning. Galvan smiles now seeing where this is going. With full force, Galvan brings down his sword with a lightning bolt. The blast was strong enough to render them all immobilized.

"Ha ha ha. That was awesome." Chrome screams with excitement.

Kirby appears from the sky with Terri and lands, "We're back, all the citizens are safe."

"And we took care of the Smaller golems. Thanks to Winn over here not only is he good at handling the bottle. But coming up with a good plan." Blaine said.

Jabari appears with the girls, "Hey you guys. Good you're all ok we took care of the giant shadow golem."

Walter comes running to them and August and Stanley are behind him.

"Walter, you guys are okay." Kirby said.

"We need your help." Said Walter.

"What is it?" Shiba asks.

"We saw a bunch of kids get snatched from them by those big golem things!" Walter said.

"When? Where?" Rashida asks.

"While we were looking for civilians to help, we came across a group of teens. But then those things came out of nowhere and took them." August told them.

Aziza asks, "Which way did they go?"

"East."

Blaine asks, "What's to the east?"

Elon tells him, "The Port. Rangi City."

"Isn't that the last stop before... what's that place again?" Galvan said.

"Zanatar's valley." Azuro said.

Ebondre gets in front of Walter to ask, "Why didn't you try to fight those things off?"

"Ebondre really?" Ivorious asks.

"What? If they were helping look for people, they should have been able to fight then." Ebondre said.

"I was too scared to move." Walter said.

"And you were supposed to get them to safety?" Brock asks.

Walter shows a guilty face. He looks to the ground with disappointment at himself for not helping those kids and lying about it.

"Give him a break! Okay! It was only the three of us and five of those things! So, back off!" August said defending Walter.

"Calm down. It's nothing to get worked up about." Pryce said.

"Yeah, you guys tried to help, sure it didn't end well but we'll get them back." Winn said.

Chrome walks to Walter and puts his hand on his shoulder, "You got a good heart to try and help people you don't know. That right there is a great quality. You just work on fighting and no one will stand in your way! Okay?"

Walter looks up with a shocked face and says, "Okay."

"We need to leave for Rangi City." Rashida said.

"Well, there's no way we're getting back in that cart, it got thrashed in the fight. Money gone to waste." Terri said.

"We won't have to, we can take a Hooptie." Rashida said.

"They have those here?" Jabari asked.

"Do they have them on earth?" Shiba asked.

"Yeah, but they're like old cars." Jabari said.

"What's a car?" Blaine asked.

"The Hoopties are over here." Rashida said.

"Okay, four to a car and let's go." Jabari said.

"Thank gods no more carts." Cornelia said.

"No more pulling a cart." Pitou said.

Book One
Chapter Twenty-Five
To Rangi

They get in and drive off. It's Jabari, Kirby, Pitou, Terri, Blaine, and Elon in the first. Then in the second is Aziza, Cornelia, Shiba and Rashida, the third car contains Galvan, Azuro, Ebondre, Ivorious and in the last Brock, Chrome, Winn, and Pryce. as they drive off August and his group drive off in another direction.

Walter, still thinking about what happened, calls August's name, "Hey August."

"Yes, Walter?"

"I have a question."

"Yes?"

"When those things came, why didn't you pull those other kids to hide too?"

Stanley scolds him, "Don't ask stupid questions Walter! You know why."

August stops Stanley, "No, it's okay I'll tell him. Because Walter none of those kids were you or Stanley. We three need to stick together because no one in our lives looks out for us. So, we do look out for each other. There's only so many people I can give a damn about. And I choose you two."

Walter can be heard sniffling, "But what those guys said. We lied about helping and they tried to cheer me up, but we didn't do anything but lie."

"Hey, think about it like this, those rich kids probably never had to struggle. So, this could be good for them. And don't forget they called you a rat." Stanley said, trying to cheer him up.

The scene cuts to the others driving down the road with Jabari's group first.

"Elon, do you have the map?" Jabari asks.

"Yes, it's right here. With Rangi being a seaport city, it does some of the most trading and one of the wealthiest cities. Just right behind Wawa and Hue." Elon said.

"So, what do we do when we get there, all Kirby saw was the valley and the port?" Said Blaine.

"I think we'll find out when we get there." Said Kirby.

"I don't think it would be that simple." Said Jabari.

"I'm just being optimistic." He said to his big brother.

Jabari's Comtrix starts to ring.

"Hey, so what is the plan when we get to Rangi?" Aziza asks.

"I guess find the port that Kirby saw and go on from there." Jabari says.

"Okay." Aziza said.

"I'll tell the others." Jabari said.

She responds with an okay then the Comtrix cuts off.

"Now that he's gone let me ask you a question." Cornelia said.

"What is it?" Aziza said.

"Really Aziza?"

"What? What is Cornelia?"

"What is it that made you come along?" Cornelia asks Aziza.

"Because I wanted to help my friends after they helped me." Aziza tells her.

"But you didn't know that until you came to Tone town to 'watch and observe the other fighters.'"

"What are you getting at?"

"You came because Jabari caught your attention."

"I mean yeah, he caught my attention because he helped me and my parents in our time of need."

"So, no feelings whatsoever?"

"A little but is it that obvious why I came along?" Aziza asks.

"Yep." Cornelia said.

"Yes." Shiba said cosigning Cornelia.

"I just joined the group, and I don't know you at all, but I would have to concur with your friends." Rashidi says.

"Well, what's your reason? Since you want to know mine." Aziza asks Cornelia.

"Bored with nothing else to do." Cornelia said.

"Really that's your reason?" Shiba asks.

"Well arrow, what's your reason?" Cornelia asks.

"Don't call me an arrow. He's going to help me find the people responsible for kidnappings and the death of my dad's friends. You were there. Him and his brother being here obviously have something to do with it. And when we get to Rangi we'll find our answers and those kids, I hope. But I own him."

"I agree with Shiba, he can help us find those kids but also, we probably wouldn't have beat that thing if it wasn't for his thinking." Rashida said.

"Hey, there's no need to feel embarrassed. He's a great guy and I even see him blush around you. Even though you can barely tell by his skin complexion." Said Cornelia.

"I agree. About him being a great person. The fact that he offered to help me in my time of need and lend me words of advice was truly kind of him." Said Shiba.

"And the confidence he has. He's able to place that confidence in us on a whim. It truly is inspirational to have many companions come and help him." Rashidi said.

"Yeah, and to top it all off, he didn't even know us. He could have just stopped, freshen up and rode on by when he came to my town. But he chose to stay and fight, encouraging me to fight. And when this is all over, he and his brother will go back to their world and we'll probably never see them again." Aziza said.

The scene cuts to Galvan's Hooptie.

"Can you keep this thing steady?" Azuro asks Galvan who's driving the Hooptie.

"I never drove one of these before." Galvan said.

"I have a question for you three. It's clear that you two in the front have known Jabari and Kirby for longer than I have. So, why did you decide to help him?" Ebondre said.

"I first tagged along so I could fight him and Blaine. The fights became more intense. I wanted to see who we would go against next. I thought the opponents would get stronger and they did." Galvan told Ebondre.

"So, you decided to come because you wanted to fight monsters that took people from another world." Azuro said.

"And because they're my friends and I wanted to help them. And you Azuro?" Galvan asks.

"One of those shadow things attacked my friend's village, she was hurt. I found out it came from a cargo ship from Hue. I came to find out where these things are coming from and end them. And like you said we became friends." Azuro said.

"What happens if he goes back to his world before you find out?" Ebondre asks.

"I can't ask someone who was taken from their home to stay. So, if that happens, I'll accept it and venture onwards." Azuro said.

"By yourself?" Galvan asks.

"Who else would come?" Azuro asks.

"Hey if it means fighting those things again, I'll come. Great stories to tell back home." Galvan said.

"Really?" Azuro asks.

"And what about you?" Ebondre asks.

"I wanted to see them get back home safely. If I were to leave after meeting them, I would never know and be worried. It's what I was taught growing up, to help others when needed." Ivorious said.

"Well, what's your reason?" Azuro asks.

"To find out more about this guy. You believe him out of nowhere and just go along with it. He might be more trouble than he is worth. And besides, I want to see this other world he came from for myself." Ebondre said.

"Why would he go through all of this if he wasn't telling the truth?" Ivorious asks.

"Just call it healthy curiosity." Ebondre said.

Meanwhile, in Chrome car, Winn confronts Brock's attitude towards him.

"Hey, I have to ask, what's your problem with me? You keep getting on me because I drink a little. What's your deal?" Winn asks to confront him.

"My deal is people like you ruin your own lives and are somehow able to drag others down with you." Brock told him.

"People like me?" Winn asks.

"Drunks like you, can't control your actions, don't care who you hurt and you're always so reckless." Brock said.

"When?" Winn asks.

"During the Tournament, you blasted a gust of wind into the commentator booth. You lack discipline."

"How about we change the topic?  Like what do we do when we get them back to their world? " Pryce suggested.

"What do you mean?" Chrome asks.

"Do we go our separate ways? I mean there has to be some reason we're connected to each other." Pryce said.

"What?"

"Back at the tournament we all had the same vision caused by him. So, what does that mean?"

"Guess we'll get our answer when we get to Rangi."

They get the message from Jabari about going straight to the port and the scene cuts to them riding into the city. They get out with the map and proceed east to the port.

"Okay, the map says it's on the east side of the city. Let's go."
Jabari said.

"So, when we get there what do we do?" Aziza asks him.

"I guess when we're near it my and Kirby's eyes will start to
glow like last time." Jabari said.

"So, will you be joining us or staying on this side Terri?" Pitou
asks.

"Why do you ask?" Terri asks.

"Just curious." Pitou said.

"Hey, Aziza, are you okay?" Jabari asks.

"I'm fine." Aziza said.

"Are you sure? It's just, ever since we got out the Hoopties and
started walking you've been really quiet." Jabari said, worrying
about her.

"I'm just a little tired." Aziza said.

"Um okay." Jabari said, confused.

Cornelia pulls her to the side.

"Hey what's with you?" Cornelia asks.

"Once we get them back to earth, we'll never see them again. I'll never see him again. So, I'm just preparing for it." Aziza said with disappointment.

"By what? Acting distance? Hey, you don't know that maybe he'll be able to come back. Maybe." Cornelia said.

"Yeah maybe."

"Maybe you could ask him to stay?" Cornelia suggested.

"I can't! What kind of person would I be if I asked someone to give up their life and move here? And what about his brother?" Aziza asks.

"Then go there with him." Cornelia suggests.

"You think I should just go?" Aziza asks.

"Or maybe you should just accept the fact that you won't see him again."

"I don't know what to do."

"Tell him before he goes. I think that's your only option." Cornelia said.

Book One
Chapter Twenty-Six
Hard to Say Goodbye

As they continue through the town, they spot the pier. "Hey, look, it's the dock." Elon said.

"Is this the one you saw Kirby?" Blaine asks.

"Yeah, this is the one." Kirby said with a sad voice.

As they approach the dock Elon can tell something is wrong with Kirby.

"Hey, Elon, what's wrong with the kid?" Blaine asks.

"I don't know he was quiet most of the trip here." Elon said.

"Hey Jabari. You might want to check on Kirby." Blaine said.

"Kirby what's wrong?" Jabari asks.

"What is it?" Pitou asks.

"I don't want to go!" Kirby said as he started to cry at the thought of leaving.

"Hey, calm down, it's ok." Jabari said, trying to cheer him up.

"No, it's not! I don't want to say goodbye to our friends! Once we go back, we'll never see them again!" Kirby cried.

"Hey, that's not true. We might see them again." Jabari told him.

"Really? Will we be able to come back?" Kirby asks.

"Um... I promise if there is a way to come back and forth, we will."

"You don't even know that." He said to his older brother.

Elon and Blaine kneel in front of Kirby. "Listen Kirby, I don't want you to cry even though the adventure is ending. You should be happy, you're about to go home to your dad who's probably worried sick about you. It was a great journey but you'll always have the memories." Elon said.

"He's right. Your family is what's most important right now. It's going to be hard for us to say goodbye too. I don't know what it is about you and your brother, but you two bring the brightest out of all of us." Blaine said.

"He's right, you and your brother's optimism really has shown me that going against something bigger than yourself alone just won't cut it. Sometimes you need friends." Shiba said.

"But we still haven't found the people responsible for bringing those monsters here and kidnapping those kids." Kirby said, rubbing his eyes.

"You can leave that to us. I don't know if it was fate that brought us together. But now none of us are alone on this mission. You two brought us together and together will find who's controlling those monsters and kidnapping those kids." Azuro said.

"Count on it!" Galvan said.

Everyone begins to circle around Kirby to cheer him up.

"As long as you keep someone in your heart, no matter how far away they are, they will always be with you." Aziza told him.

"Ebondre are you okay?" Ivorious asks.

"It's nothing." Ebondre said rubbing his eyes, Ivorious notices Ebondre sniffling.

"Are you sure? Sounds like you're about to cry." Ivorious said.

"I said it's nothing."

"Are you still suspicious of them now?" Ivorious asks.

"No. Now shut up." Ebondre said.

Just as Kirby stops crying, Terri tells them to move because of an incoming red blast of energy. The camera pans to the man with the Blues mask, blue cloak from before along with Red mask.

"Geez. What are you trying to do to kill them? Remember to make them suffer, don't kill them." Blue said to the red mask. "How touching. I mean really you got me all misty eyed." Said Blue mask

"I thought it was a little sappy, but they are talking to a baby."
The red mask said.

"What the huh?" Terri said.

"I must admit, I thought it would take a little longer for you to
get here. But I guess it's a good time." Said Blue mask.

"Do any of you know this guy?" asks Rashida.

"Nope. Nah. Never met him." Everyone responded.

"You may not have met me, but I know you've heard of me."
Blue mask.

"The two from the mountain! Remember? Blue eyes and Red
eyes. Look at their masks." Shiba said.

Aziza gasps.

"No way." Said Chrome.

"Right here right now?" Pryce asks.

"So, you're the one who attacked Jabari and Kirby from the
very beginning?" Elon asks.

"Yep, you got it green bean." Blue mask said.

"And the one that's been attacking us every step of the way?" Blaine asks,

"You bet fire flicker."

"Those shadow beasts? The one that attacked my friend, why her village?" Azuro asks, glaring and balling his fist.

"One must have gone astray." Blue mask said casually.

"Astray!? Is that all you got!?" Azuro screamed.

"The kids, where are they?" Shiba asks.

"Those kids are unrelated to my plans. And well that's none of your business?" Blue mask said.

"Do you know how many parents are worried to death?" Aziza asks him.

"Don't know, don't care, and like I told you they are not part of my plan."

"Why are you doing this?" Cornelia asks.

"What's wrong? I can have a little fun." Blue eyes said.

"Why did you bring us here?" Jabari asks.

"I'm pretty sure I answered that." Blue eyes said.

"No, brought us here to Hue, to Palette, from earth?!" Jabari asks.

"Yeah, didn't you like your vacation? I made some friends, met a nice girl." Blue said, teasing him.

"Why appear now after all this time?" Jabari asks.

"It's it obvious? What's a better way to make an appearance right before you think you're going home."? Blue said.

"What's that supposed to mean?" Blaine asks.

"He means you aren't going anywhere. Fathead!" Red Mask answered.

"He's right. You and your friends aren't leaving just yet. Not till we send you back bruised, battered, and beaten." Blue said.

"Don't like the sound of that?" Pitou said, hiding behind the group.

Book One
Chapter Twenty-Seven
Deep Blue and Vast Red

Blue Eyes Begins to fire blue spheres of energy at the group but they leap out the way in the nick of time. The aftermath of the blast leaves a huge crater in the ground. The blast sends both Pitou and Terri flying over the dock.

When they reach the end, they fly through an invisible barrier. Pitou and Terri get up to look around and see golden roses across the field. They look forward and see two buildings. Pitou recognizes one of the buildings as Jabari's and Kirby's home.

"Oh, my god it's just like Kirby describing two buildings in a valley of golden roses surrounded by a forest." Pitou said.

"Hey, how did we get here? Where are we?" Terri asked.

"We're in Zanatar's Valley." Pitou told him.

"We are? But how?"

"I guess Kirby's vision was showing how close it was to the dock." Pitou said.

"But why the dock at all?"

"I don't know but we should look around."

"Shouldn't we go back through whatever and tell them?"

"Not while they are fighting those guys. They might come here and wreck the place. Let's go to the house, maybe we'll find something."

Meanwhile outside the barrier, the group is scattered because of the blast.

"What the hell? That could've killed us!" Aziza screamed.

"Well of course! He's been trying to do this the whole time!" Cornelia said.

"Kirby, where are you? You okay?" Jabari asked, looking around for him.

He responds to him from behind a crate. "I'm behind this crate and I'm fine." Kirby said.

"Everybody, are you all okay?" Jabari asked.

"We're all fine, could be better." Ebondre said.

"Hey, so what's the plan?" Elon asked.

"Simple, we kill him!" Azuro said.

Azuro runs towards Blue mask, ready to strike him down but he evades it with ease.

"What a nice saber you got there. Too bad you're too angry to know how to use it." Blue Mask said. The blue masked man grabs Azuro by his neck and lifts him.

"My, I see so much hate in your eyes. You must really want to kill me. But I don't remember doing anything to you personally." The blue mask said chuckling.

347

"One of those damn abominations of yours hurt my friend's village." Azuro told him.

"Aw am I to assume that this person is more than just a friend? Is she a lover? Or he? It's okay I don't judge." Blue mask said while chuckling.

Azuro kicks back at Blues mask and he loses his grip on his neck. Azuro then leaps back 12 feet to put distance between him and Blue. But then he appears behind Azuro.

"Well, aren't you quick on your feet!" Blue mask said startling Azuro.

"The hell?" Azuro said in disbelief that a person could be this fast.

Just then Elon comes from behind and tries to thrust his lance through Blue. He tells Azuro to move but he not only misses Azuro, but Blue is also able to avoid his fast strike. Both him and Azuro look at each other in confusion. Blue then pops up right next to them and says, "You're fast but I'm faster."

Blue unleashes a fury of punches, hitting them in their face and chest. You can even hear a rib crack and see them spitting up blood. He then knocked both back with little ease. They both go flying across the ground to their friend's feet.

"No! Azuro! Elon!" Kirby screamed.

348

"You son of a bitch!" Jabari said while lunging at Blue mask.

"Look at you finally doing something!" Blue said while clapping.

"He's not the only one!" Blaine said.

"You'll pay for that!" Galvan added.

Jabari leaps forward for an attack then Blaine and Galvan come from the sides. But Blue moves, then all three of their weapons clash with each other.

"Shit!" Jabari said.

"Where did he go?" Blaine asks. Then Galvan yells for them to look up!

Blue can be seen hovering over them on a transparent blue disc.

"So, I guess I pissed you off when I whooped your two little friends? So, sweet." Blue said.

Winn leaps upwards to strike him down, but he evades. Blue gets low, then Chrome and Brock try to trap him in walls made of steel and earth. After the fight seems to be over a blue makes a force field from within the walls causing it to shatter.
Ebondre and Ivorious both charge at him from the front. He tries to get ready but slips on the ice that Pryce put under him

and loses his balance. As he does both Ebondre and Ivorious use their pike and sword to form a scissor formation. Blue's neck is now pinned to the ground.

The others get on top of him and hold him down. But a shock to all, he can overpower them and knock them off.

"Did that just happen?" Aziza asks in disbelief.

"Really wish it didn't." Cornelia said.

"We need to help. Kirby gets Elon and Azuro out of here. We'll help them out. Until it's safe, stay hidden." Shiba told them.

"Come on." Aziza said.

Aziza summons a giant indigo colored X shaped beam; she fires it and lands a direct hit on him. Yet he is still unnerved. Cornelia creates a violet-colored sphere hex, then fires. But he deflects it.

"Girls, girls, girls calm down. There's enough of me to go around." Blue said.

"You're disgusting! How can you find this funny?! All of the things you've done, how is that funny?!" Aziza asks.

"Calm down sweetheart and lighten up." He spoke.

"Don't call her sweetheart. It's not a compliment from you." Cornelia says as she tries to blast him. But he avoids and gets in her face.

"Then can I call you darling?" Blue asks as he gets in her face.

"Call me a distraction." Cornelia said grinning.

"What?" Blue said looking confused.

Cornelia moves out of the way after a massive shadow looms over blue. It is Rashida throwing a ship, he tries to move but he is nailed down to the ground by a fury of arrows thanks to Shiba. The ship comes crashing down on him.

"Did we do it? Is he dead?" Shiba asks.

"I think so." Rashida said.

Blue walks up from behind Shiba and Rashida and speaks.

"I think not."

He grabs both and hurls Shiba at Cornelia and Rashida at Aziza. As Kirby hides behind a crate with an unconscious Elon and Azuro he is shocked. The combined effort of 13 people can't subdue this one person.

"Oh no, what are we going to do? That's right, you guys can't answer me, you're unconscious. Wait, where is Pitou and Terri?" Kirby said.

"Wherever they are, they're safer than you." Said the red masked boy.

"Oh snap."

Meanwhile, in Zanatar's Valley, Pitou and Terri walk to the front door of the house. They walk in and look around to investigate.

"It looks just like Jabari and Kirby's home but bigger. Okay, we're here but what in Kirby's vision made him think we can get home through here? There is literally nothing special about this house, except the fact it's surrounded by a barrier." Pitou said.

"Hey, look at this big door! Help me open it." Terri said.

"Why?" Pitou asks.

"To be nosey. And besides, I think I can hear people." Terri said.

"Let me listen." Pitou said, putting his ear to the door.

Pitou listens through the door and hears a familiar voice. It is the voice of Ishtarel.

"We need to get this door open!" Pitou said.

"Oh, so when I say it you look at me like I'm nosey." Terri said.

"One, you said to be nosey and two....opened the door! That voice, it's their dad!" Pitou said.

"Oh crap! Open your damn door!" Terri said, pulling.

Meanwhile back at the port Jabari and others are hard at work trying to defeat Blue. But even all of them combined is not strong enough. And what of the boy with the Red mask.

"What do you want? Why are you two doing this?" Kirby asks.

"I could tell you, but I would rather hurt you instead." Red told him.

A malicious red aura surrounds him, he channels it into a golden rod with an orb shaped end, with two wings.

"Take a guess at what I'm about to do with this." Red told Kirby.

"You're going to show me how to hit a home run?" Kirby asks.

"What? No. What is a "home run"? Never mind! I'm going to hit you with it!"

"Wait! Wait! Wait!" Said Kirby as he threw up his shield. When Red swings his rod and hits the shield, this knocks him back into a wall.

"Hey! Are you good?" Kirby asks, looking at an unmoving body but hears a groan.

"This is really exhausting!" Aziza said huffing and puffing.

"Not for him." Cornelia said.

"How in the hell is he taking on all of us and not even breaking a sweat?" Blaine asks.

"He's mocking us! He hasn't even taken his sword out yet. And that stupid grin on his face!" Galvan said.

"It's not going to be there for long, I'll wipe that smile off his face!" Ebondre said.

Blue toys with Ebondre by stepping up to him, getting in his face and saying. "I'm in your face so, do something!" Blue tells him, smiling.

"Hold him there!' Jabari told him.

"You wish." Blue said.

Blue then grabs Ebondre and throws him at Jabari. Jabari avoids him then with a quick strike with his sword he can land a hit on Blue right side. This blow breaks a piece of Blue's armor, even cutting him.

"Shit! Dammit!" Blue said, holding his side.

"Azure!" Red mask yells.

"So that's your name, Azure." Jabari said.

"You'll pay for that!" Azure said.

Azure takes his sword with his sheath still on and knocks Jabari back. The blow leaves a bruise across his chest.

"We need to think of a plan to help Cornelia." Aziza yelled.

"How? The only person who's been able to hit him is Jabari. And he barely got that hit in and made it out alive." Cornelia tells her.

"What does it say on that crate behind you?" Aziza asks.

"It says gunpowder and napalm." Cornelia said.

"I have an idea. Hey, Blaine, can you guys distract him long enough?" Aziza asks.

"I got you. I'll tell the others." Blaine said.

"Want to tell me the plan?" Cornelia asks.

"We'll spread that stuff around the port, when the time is right, we'll set it off. Kirby keeps Elon and Azuro at a safe distance." Aziza said.

"Okay." He spoke.

"Hey Jabari, Aziza says she has an idea, we need to keep him busy." Blaine tells him.

"I don't think that will be a problem, he seems pretty pissed." Jabari said.

"Need help?" Red asks Azure.

"No Ro! Stay out of my way!" Azure said.

"Fine. I'll go back to... hey where'd he run off to now?" Ro asks.

Kirby moved Elon and Azuro over to the pier where Pitou and Terri flew off.

"I hope that their plan works." Kirby said.

With Elon and Azuro unconscious and Aziza and Cornelia laying out their plan Jabari and the others try to handle Azure. Blaine, Galvan, Ebondre, Chrome, and Brock all charge from all different directions. Blue uses his sheath to block them, but he is slower now.

"Aw, what happened big guy? You're moving slower than usual." Blaine said.

"And you're not talking out your neck anymore." Galvan said.

"And I see that little smile of yours is gone too." Ebondre said.

"He knows after that last hit from Jabari he's not so invincible." Chrome said.

"I think this is the first time you've looked shocked." Brock said.

"And it only gets worst." Shiba said.

Shiba fires arrows at Azure from behind, the others move but Azure's feet are frozen from Pryce. The arrows strike him, and he seems irritated. Then he's pelted by rocks flying at high speed. It's Winn using the wind to form a tunnel, one end sucks up rocks and the other end shoots them out.

Azure is still unable to move because of the ice. Rashida goes in for some close combat and starts delivering blow after blow to Azure's face. Punch after punch, you can tell he is getting tired of them.

"Enough! I have had it with all of you. Who the hell do you think you are taunting me?!" Azure said, getting angry.

"Azure?" Ro said, calling out to his partner.

"Quiet!" Azure yells at him.

"But?"

"Quiet!"

"Okay. But..."

"What is it?!"

"Those girls."

Ro points towards Aziza who has set traps all over with napalm and gunpowder.

"What is this?" Azure asks.

"A trap! Everyone to the pier." Aziza said.

Everyone jumps to the pier where Kirby was hiding, and Aziza sets off the gun powder and napalm. This causes several explosions blowing away Azure and Ro, they then retreat.

"I tried to tell you." Ro said.

"Shut it." Azure said.

"It worked!" Aziza said.

"How much did you use?" Jabari asks.

"The whole thing." Cornelia answered.

"Are you insane?! That much gunpowder and napalm will cause a massive explosion that would destroy the whole port!" Shiba said.

Aziza and Cornelia look at each other and both say oops. Without hesitation, Kirby takes his shield and forms a force field around the whole group. The blast was strong enough to knock the force field through the barrier. With enough force from the blast they keep going, they fly through Zanatar's Valley.

"Uggh why won't this door open?" Pitou asked.

"Hey, do you hear something?" Terri asked.

The force field filled with our heroes' blast through the front door. Pitou and Terri grab on to it, the whole group burst open the closed door. The group travels through a tunnel of light with flashing colors and on the other side they pop out in front of Ishtarel and the others. Kirby looks up to see his father.

"Dad!" Both sons said the moment they saw him. "Jabari! Kirby!" Ishtarel said. They run to hug their father in relief.

"Boys?" Ishtarel said.

"Yeah, dad?" They both answered.

"Who the hell are these people?"

"Nice to meet you sir." Terri said.

"Where are we?" Elon asked waking up.

"What happened?" Azuro asked in confusion.

"We'll tell you later." Blaine said.

"These are our friends we made when we crossed over. Blaine, Elon, Galvan, Azuro, Ebondre, Ivorious, Chrome, Pryce, Brock, Winn, Aziza, Cornelia, Shiba, and Rashida." Jabari said.

They all decide to meet in the living room and catch Ishtarel up on what happened.

"Well, I'm glad you two are safe." Ishtarel said.

"Um, dad?" Jabari began to ask.

"What?" His father responded.

"Don't you think you need to explain a couple of things?" Jabari asks.

"Like what?" The father nervously asks.

"The door. The shield and sword." Kirby said.

"Why did a door, in a house, in a valley, hidden by a barrier, in another world, bring us home?" Jabari asked.

He looks at them then sighs. "I really thought I could avoid this but here it goes. First thing I should tell you is that we I mean I am not of this world, like you two are. You two were born here, your mother and I are from Palette, we crossed over twenty years ago so that we could be together. We decided to settle here in this place called Virginia." Ishtarel tells them.

"The seal was put on that gate because I didn't want to be bothered with the Palette anymore. I wanted to have a new life with my family. But this Azure, he must have weakened it to the point where he could drag people through." Ishtarel said.

"Dad, I have a question. In Palette people can manipulate elements. But I can only do one. I was able to use multiple. How?

"Okay um. How can I explain? I am not technically from Palette as much as I am from a realm above Palette. I am an Angel whose ability is to manipulate elements and other abilities, but you only asked about this one.

Jabari and the others look with confusion not knowing how to process this information.

"Wait so that means... I'm half..." Jabari said uncertainly.

"Yes, you and Kirby are half angels. Demi angels? If that is even a term. There has never been being like you before. I honestly didn't think you two would inherit any of my abilities but to be safe I put limiters on both of you." Ishtarel said.
"In case I had an origin?" Jabari asked.

"Yes. Wait who told you about that? Never mind, do you understand now? Any more questions?

"I have one. Can all of you get off my back." Ebondre asked.

"1 just realized something." Kirby said.

"What?" Winn asks.

"We didn't say "Hey" to my Uncles and Aunts. Hi everyone!" Kirby said.

"Hey, Kirby." They all replied.

"Wait a minute if these are our uncles and aunts from your side of the family. Does that mean there are angles too?" Jabari asked.

"You got it, sweetie. Such a smart boy" Yuriel said.

"Why didn't you tell us?" Jabari asks his dad.

"I was trying to leave it behind for both me and your mother."

"Look you're back and from what you've told us we have bigger problems." Tazama said.

"True. Whoever took you, knew of this gate. And I have no idea who could've opened it or why." Ishtarel said.

"And this Azure sent these shadow beasts after you." Una said.

"Do you guys know him?" Kirby asks.

"Never heard of him." Asharo said.

"None of us have but we'll look into it." Jushura told them.

"But until then how about y'all get cleaned up, because y'all stink and I'll get dinner ready." Ishtarel said.

They all go upstairs and take turns using the bathroom.

"So, it's called a shampoo." Ebondre said.

"Yep." Jabari replied.

"Which is soap for your head?" Ebondre asks.

"Uh-hu."

"'Repairs damage, dry, flakey heads.' Why do people in this world buy things that insult them?" Ebondre asks.

Others are fascinated with the things earth has to offer. Kirby tries to introduce them to tv.

"I don't get it." Azuro said.

"Nobody does but that's "Keeping up with the Kardashian" for you. But there is "How to get away with murder" and "Scandal"!"

"They teach people how to get away with murder in this world with these boxes?" Ivorious asks.

"Yep. I know how to dispose of bodies." Kirby said cheerfully.

"Amazing." Ivorious said.

"I've grown potatoes my whole life. Never have I ever thought they could be this good." Galvan said while eating French fries.

"Is he eating French fries?" Pitou asks Kirby.

"Yeah, I left those here when we got pulled in." Kirby said.

"That was weeks ago! And those are the ones from that place with the clown." Pitou asks.

"It's ok, their French fries never go bad, everyone knows that Pitou." Kirby told him.

"I'm astonished by your collection of books Kirby. Did not know they could have pictures like this. What were they called?" Pryce asks.

"The ones with color are called comic books. The black and white ones are called manga." Kirby told him.

"I never read a book until now. I like Wonder Woman, Black Panther, and Deadpool." Winn said.

"I like this thing you guys call Rap!" Chrome said while blasting Jabari's music through the headphones.

"Who is he listening to?" Pitou asks.

"Something called a playlist. Who are these people? Kendrick Lamar? J. Cole? Childish Gambino?" Brock said while reading Jabari's playlist.

"Hey, Aziza came outside." Cornelia tells her.

"What is it? Why did we have to come outside?" Aziza asks.

"So, how do you like it?"

"Like What?"

"Earth. Looks pretty nice."

"Yeah, but I don't think I could leave the Palette."

"Yeah, I figured."

Jabari steps out, thinking there is no one else out here.

"Hey." He said to both girls.

"Hey." They both replied.

"Didn't know you were out here." He spoke.

"It's okay I was getting ready to go back in, but Aziza wanted to talk to you." Cornelia said.

"Huh?" Aziza said.

"Bye. Kirby's going to show me this thing called "Steve Universe" So bye." Cornelia said leaving them both outside.

"Um hey." He said again.

"Hey. Your family seems really nice."

"Yeah, they are. My dad is setting up beds for you guys."

"Thank you, I'm grateful for your father's hospitality. I'm sorry for prying. I couldn't help but notice when your dad mentioned your mother. You had a pained look on your face."

"Yeah, she died when I was young."

let me ask you, are there any other survivors from the war here on earth?" Terri asks.

"I know that there are two in Los Angeles and two in Atlanta. That's all I know." Pitou tells him.

"Looks like I'm not the only one to flee here and to think I was being original."

Kirby comes around the corner. "Hey, guys my dad wants to have a talk with us."

"Clearly there are forces at work between our worlds. So, that is why Jabari and I have thought of a proposition for all of you." Ishtarel said.

"From what my dad has told me, I have a duty to have people who I trust by my side. So, I'm asking you guys to help find out who this Azure is and to put a stop to him. I need disciples to help fight this guy and I hope you guys will agree and join me." Jabari tells them.

One by one they agree. "Of course, we'll help you. This guy has caused us all major problems." Azuro said and everyone agreed to it.

"But dad, I have a couple of more questions about my powers. How am I able to manipulate multiple elements? And why did Kirby and I have those visions?" Jabari asked.

"Okay listen closely. Before I left the realm of angles twenty years ago. I was the head disciple of a high-ranking god known as Valatykashia. He was known as the elemental god who gave the gift of Quintessence to humans 7,000 years ago in the world of Palette." Ishtarel explains.

"What?" Everyone says in confusion.

"Yes. Magic had already existed in that world, but it was only so much and barely any could use it but when the between ten major countries broke out. They were all on the verge of wiping each other out. Until my master stepped in, when he entered the human realm, he released a powerful energy that was only known to Gods, Angels, Demons and Devils." Ishtarel said.

"Quintessence also known as life force energy. His very presence of coming into the world of the living gave humans the ability to absorb it and use it to perform magnificent feats ranging from magic to elemental manipulation. He gave each of the ten countries the ability to manipulate one element, not only that but other countries gave the ability to use magic. This exposure created something in people called "Magical and Elemental pools" where they could absorb and store the quintessence. That's also why anyone who can manipulate elements has some origins back to the ten countries but that's not what you asked for." He continued.

"Before I left, he gave me a parting gift for my marriage with your mother. He bestowed upon me the ability to manipulate the elements. So, you inherited this ability from me. I didn't think it would manifest but you unlocked these powers at a young age even with the Angel Seal I put on you. The seal on your back which limited your Angel side."

"Why did you have to limit it?' Kirby asked.

"You need to understand the very presence of Gods and Angels to mere humans is dangerous. We exert a powerful force called "Pressure" and exposing humans to that pressure will cause seizures, panic attacks, heart problems, physical, mental, and emotional trauma even death if we get too close to people or stay too close to them. When you emit pressure, it basically shows off the level of Quintessence your body can absorb, contain, and then release. You both have a seal for that reason. Your Uncles and Aunts and I have seals too. The point is it is too dangerous for us to be around regular people" He told his son and his friends.

"But wait, if our presence could do all that, how did your master enter the world of humans and not kill everyone?" Jabari asked.

"Before he broke through the barriers that divide our realms, he slowly poured Quintessence into the atmosphere of the human world. So, the humans will develop a little bit of an immunity to his pressure so he wouldn't accidentally kill anyone but not enough to where he could have been there long. He was there long enough to give it to teach them how to use it and that was it."

"Now to answer your second question is going to be more difficult. Angels have an unconscious ability to attract people to them. Some good, some bad but in the end, they attracted people to them who are going to affect their lives. That's how I met your Uncles and Aunts. Angels have visions about how these people can affect their lives by showing them mostly vague visions. That can explain yours, but Kirby's might be a little different. See, your brother inherited many of your mother's facial features and personality but he also inherited some of her abilities." The father said and he picked his youngest son up and placed him on his lap.

"Sweethearts tell when touched the shield you said you had a vision of the port and where to go?" Ishtarel asked.

"Yes sir." His son replied, shaking his head vigorously.

"And the same thing happened with the man in the hospital, right?" he asked his son and the son replied yes again.

"See this was your mother's ability called "Seer into the Heart" a power that let one see into the hearts of other people. Your mother used it to tell if people were lying or to see anything that had affected them emotionally. Kind of like mind reading but with the heart instead. This let her know who she could trust and what intentions they had. And you can use that ability to avoid bad people sweetie." Ishtarel explained. They proceeded to ask them if they had any more questions.

"Are our Uncles and Aunts related by blood?" Kirby asks.

"No, they are just really close friends who became family. But that doesn't change the way you feel about them does it?" He asks.

"No. Of course not!" he said with conviction.

Just then Kirby yells for everyone to come into the living room. But then his attention is darted to the T.V. he gets up and runs in the living room. "You guys get in here!"

"Kirby what is it?" Ishtarel asks.

"Look at the commercial!" Kirby said.

"This isn't the time to talk about water." Jabari told him.

"No, look!" Kirby pauses the T.V. and points to the man on the screen.

"This is the same guy whose water was being advertised during the Tournament. That's Giovanni Waters. The slogan is the same "Water so good the Gods approve" And look what happens when I rewind it. The girls are right there drinking the water. They're advertising clothes, the same clothes from the shops in Wawa city. " Kirby said.

"Those are the girls from my village! I recognize them." Shiba said.

"Why are they on a commercial for water?" Terri asks.

"Why is that guy selling water in both our worlds?" Elon asks.

"Do you know what this means?" Tazama asks.

"What does this mean?" Kirby asks.

"It means that whoever this Azure is, he has ties and allies on this side of the gate." Ishtarel said.

"I thought the door in the guest house was the only one." Jabari said.

"Whoever took you to Palette, must be working with this Giovanni to abduct children." Ishtarel said.

"But why? What for? To sell water?" Pitou said so confused.

"Also, clothing." Terri adds.

"Jabari, you and your friends get some rest, because tomorrow we train." Ishtarel said.

Meanwhile back in Palette at the Rangi port.

"I tried to tell you. Now they're gone. So, what now?" Ro asks.

"Don't worry, they'll be back, I told our friend on the other side to get their attention. They won't have a choice but to come back. And we'll be waiting." Azure said as a wicked smile can be seen on his face. The screen then fades to black.

To Be Continued.

# ABOUT THE AUTHOR

I grew up watching Saturday morning cartoons and late-night anime. I've always had a big imagination and daydreamed all throughout high school. Sitting in class I would go off in my mind and I could be anywhere but there. To me, an imagination is a horrible thing to waste and not having time to yourself to think and imagine sounds terrible. I think taking time to imagine is a great gift to give yourself.

www.ingramcontent.com/pod-product-compliance
Lightning Source LLC
Chambersburg PA
CBHW050909250626
47155CB00001B/157